It Takes A Village

An Optimistic Anthology Speculating about the Meaning of Care

Edited by Eric Klein

PURPLE TOGA PUBLICATIONS

Copyright © Purple Toga Publications, Inc., 2024

https://purpletoga.com

Individual stories, foreword, and introductions are the copyright © of their respective authors.

In the inspiration for the story Off We Go, lines from the song Rocket Man Rocket Man: By Elton John and Bernie Taupin, Copyright © Universal — Songs of Polygram International Inc. are referenced under fair use. Also, the song at the start of the story was modified from the original Army Air Corp song "Wild Blue Yonder". Made public domain by the United States Air Force.

All rights reserved. No part of this publication may be reproduced, stored in a retrieval system, or transmitted, in any form or by any means, electronic or mechanic, by photocopying, recording, or otherwise, without the prior permission of both the copyright owner and the publisher of this book.

The stories in this anthology are works of fiction. Names and characters are the product of the authors' imagination and any resemblance to actual persons, living or dead, is entirely coincidental.

Any links in this eBook to a specific product, process, website, or service do not constitute or imply an endorsement of same, or its producer or provider. The views and opinions contained at any links do not necessarily express or reflect those of Eric Klein or Purple Toga Publications.

Cover art features:
girl-father-portrait-family-1641215 by ddimitrova / Pixabay
lake-moon-landscape-sky-nature-4257206 by John_Nature_Photos/ Pixabay

Published by Purple Toga Publications, Tasmania, Australia.

ISBN 978-0-9944493-8-2

1st printing

Dedication

The publisher and editor would like to dedicate this anthology to all those who care for someone special in their lives.

You deserve recognition for your altruism.

CONTENTS

Foreword   1
By Allison Maynard-Gibson, K.C.

Introduction   7
By Hila Fogel-Yaari, PhD

Editor Notes   13
By Eric Klein

The Bureau of Society Betterment   17
By Anaïs Chartschenko

The Trial of the Typist   33
By Meir Michael Fogel

Off We Go   39
By Eric Klein

The Quiet Revolution   55
By Jane Jago

Mountain View   67
By Assaph Mehr

The Trial of the Typist — End   93
By Meir Michael Fogel

Balance   95
By Cindy Tomamichel

What? Today?   117
By Joyce C Mandrake

Addie   121
By Douglas Lumsden

Counting   153
By Joyce C Mandrake

Swords to Plowshares   155
By Eric Klein

On Her Majesty's Mission 177
By Ulff Lehmann

Quantum Monkeys 189
By Assaph Mehr

The Trial of the Typist — Alternative Ending 197
By Meir Michael Fogel

Her Final Wish 199
By Kody Boye

Caring Credits 233
by Marie-Hélène Lebeault

Suggested Reading 257
Fiction

Non-Fiction

Stories and related materials are written in the author's native version of English. This includes American, UK, and Australian spelling.

This is not a mistake, and was done intentionally.

It Takes A Village

FOREWORD

By Allison Maynard-Gibson, K.C.
President (2009–11), International Women's Forum

The timing of this anthology is impeccable.

Every country in the world and most people are impacted by Artificial Intelligence ("AI"), technology, mechanization, especially the use of robots who, it is said, "think" faster and are more intelligent than human beings. Decisions are made and problems solved at lightning speed. It has been said that today problems are defined and solved before we know that we have a problem. Concurrent with these "advances" are significant increases in loneliness, suicide, isolationism, otherizing and polarization. The manifestations of anger and hate pervade the media and other spaces, including our homes. They are inescapable.

Someone from Jupiter might consider this immensely strange, especially knowing, as we do, that humans were created to live in communion with other humans, in harmony with nature and connected to our source of life. Psalm 8 says, *"what is mankind that you are mindful of them, human beings that you care for them? You have made them a little lower than the angels ... You made them rulers over the works of your hands; you put everything under their feet"*. The 5th Commandment exhorts us to honour our father and mother so that our days may be long. Although these references are to Judeo-Christian texts, holy texts of other religions advocate and support the same principles.

The spiritual messages are clear. For a wholesome and better world, recognize that humankind is "a little lower than the angels", live in harmony with each other, maintain responsible dominion over creation, honour your father and mother (the elderly).

The foundation for successful living in harmony with each other, and others, starts in the home, where there is the plan for intergenerational living. It is a safe space where children first understand their place in the world, where parents compromise and adapt so that they may live in alignment with self, each other, and others, and where grandparents and great grandparents transition to different phases in their lives and maintain relationships with others. It is in the home where intergenerational exchange of ideas happens, and where knowledge and wisdom develop, and are exchanged. It is in the home where everyone sees every day the full circle of life. In this circle of life, exists the safety and security that help shape personality, character, attitude, and values – all important to every aspect of life. School and the workplace are subsequent societal circles around the home. From the home also, children are taught the essentials, as described by Eric Klein, in "*Swords to Ploughshares*" – "How to find food, shelter, water, and everything you need to survive was emphasized to us." The home is foundational.

Over the long arc of history, we have seen immense progress and development in all areas of life. Many of them have improved tremendously the human condition and appear to have comported with the aforementioned spiritual messages. This anthology presents possibilities of moves away from anger and hate towards societies, a world, where wholeness is restored.

These are not pipe dreams.

The COVID-19 Pandemic taught us all that we can pivot to meet the challenges of any circumstance.

It Takes A Village

Let us envisage a society where child rearing and elder care are the most valued activities, where they are seen to be the responsibility of all adults and where in homes, workplaces, schools, places of worship and in the media, they are promoted, and people recognized for their contributions in these arenas. Let us envisage the kind of society that allocates resources to and promotes the spiritual values. Let us reclaim and recreate a society where the home is foundational.

This kind of society promotes community, not individualism. We will develop people who see themselves as belonging to and connected with a community at all stages of their lives. Everyone will teach children, and others, how to find and develop everything needed to survive and thrive. In this society, loneliness, suicide, isolationism, otherizing and polarization will dramatically decrease. The same principle applies in all societies, whether it is society torn apart by war or western societies torn apart by poverty and homes torn apart by violence. The fact is that when I am teaching someone how to develop what they need to survive and thrive, that person, and I, recognize that we need the same things to survive and thrive. We recognize that we need each other and that we are more alike than different.

We can develop societies where Gross National Product ("GNP") and Gross National Happiness ("GNH") are both important indices of the health and sustainability of society. We can find balance between the spiritual concepts measuring GNH on the one hand and the speed of technology combined with AI measuring GNP on the other hand.

These concepts are embodied in the United Nations' Sustainable Development Goals – accepted by UN member nations.

I hope that this timely anthology is translated into all of the world's key languages and is made easily available to everyone, especially decision and policy makers. In so doing people will be moved to readily accept the exhortation of Jane Jago in "*The Quiet Revolution*", "…you have before you a

It Takes A Village

stark choice. You can live your lives dictated to by anger and hate. Or you can join hands together in the hope of a better world."

Allyson Maynard-Gibson, K.C.

April, 2024

It Takes A Village

About Allison Maynard-Gibson, K.C.

Allyson Maynard-Gibson KC is a barrister, politician, and community rights advocate, particularly with regard to laws affecting women and children and access to justice. She has served twice as Attorney-General and Minister for Legal Affairs of The Bahamas (from 2006-2007 and 2012 to 2017). During the second term, she was the leader of government business in the Senate of the Bahamas. From 2002 to 2007, she was the member of parliament for the Pinewood constituency and from 2002-2006 the first ever Minister of Financial Services and Investment.

Her work has included significant legal reforms. In the financial services arena these include the Bahamas becoming the first jurisdiction to provide for common law foundations. Reforms affecting women and children include: statutory maternity leave with guaranteed employment upon return to the workplace after confinement; protecting the identities of rape victims; and, domestic violence and sexual harassment laws. In the international legal arena she was a member of the First People's Tribunal on Economic Crime, Johannesburg, South Africa — February to November 2018; Member of the Executive Committee of the Caribbean Council of Legal Education 2012 to 2017 and Chair of Caribbean Financial Action Task Force 2013–2014.

In 2011, Maynard-Gibson was honored by the All-China Women's Federation for "Outstanding Contributions to Women's Leadership". In 2013 she featured on a list celebrating the top 100 women of influence from diverse backgrounds working in fields ranging from government to philanthropy across the major international financial centers (IFCs). The following year she was named again on a similar list, "The 2014 IFC Power Women Top 200", which focuses on influencers and professionals, and "recognizes women of achievement who are opinion-formers, helping to promote business excellence in their home jurisdiction and consolidating the reputations of the financial services industry globally." In 2013 she was inducted as an honorary member Alpha Kappa Alpha Sorority, Inc. In January 2015, she became the first woman to be appointed a Queen's Counsel in the Bahamas. On 19 February 2015, she was honored with Barry University's Distinguished Alumni Award, recognizing "distinguished professional achievements and contributions to society through service". She is currently a member of the board of trustees of Barry University and the youngest person to have graduated from Barry University at age 18. In December 2017, Celebrating Women International, award her as a Woman of Distinction — Global Leadership in the Legal Profession.

It Takes A Village

INTRODUCTION

Mitigating Gender Bias by "Adulting/Nurturing Weekday Afternoons" Being Indicators of Leadership Ability: An Anthology

By Hila Fogel-Yaari, PhD

While we have been working hard to create a more equal society, gender bias is still prevalent. Women still earn less than men and perform more of the less-appreciated individual-facing organizational citizenship behavior, i.e., they are more likely to take on the small tasks that no-one else wants to, like mentoring new employees and organizing events, which take away time from promotion-worthy tasks or leads to faster burn-out. When I present my work on gender inequality, I am almost always asked: why should we care? And more importantly, does the gender differentiation really indicate a bias? For example, are women inherently better at jobs that bring less value to organizations and their lower pay accurately reflects their smaller contribution to the bottom line?

Do women inherently prefer performing less-valuable tasks? No. Drs. Linda Babcock, Maria P. Recalde, Lise Vesterlund, and Laurie Weingart conducted an experiment (published in the American Economic Review in

2017[1]) and showed that women do not inherently prefer the less desirable tasks. Their experiment also showed that women are more likely to be asked than men to perform the less desirable tasks and more likely to agree to do them. An on-the-job example includes supermarket employees. If women are assigned to the cashier more frequently than men, they have fewer opportunities to learn the aspects of the job that warrant a promotion, and they burn-out faster for more intensive customer interactions. The differences that result in women agreeing to less valued tasks also result in women dominating professions that have lower compensation and higher burn-out rates, like education and healthcare.

Why should we care? Inside an organization, employers should care because gender biases may result less efficient resource allocation. Employers are interested in choosing the best person for a job, but biases detract from an optimal allocation. As a society, female-dominant professions tend to be associated with lower pay. Unfortunately, these are the same professions that take care of the weaker individuals in society and shape future generations. These are the professions that provide public goods that we all benefit from but wouldn't pay for individually.

Efforts to increase gender equality, such as granting long maternity leave, often backfire because the source of the bias is in our internalized and automatically activated stereotypes. The stereotypes attribute competence only to men and prosocial skills only to women. If most of us grow up

---

[1] BABCOCK, L., RECALDE, M.P., VESTERLUND, L. & WEINGART, L. (2017). Gender differences in accepting and receiving requests for tasks with low promotability. American Economic Review, 107(3), 714-47.

learning that women are supposed to take care of the kids and men are supposed to work long hours to provide for the family, we in turn apply these expectations in conforming to what is expected of our gender and in evaluating others based on their gender[1]. The "leaky pipeline", maternity leaves, and career-focused women delaying having children, all contribute to the next generation of children growing up with the stereotypes that hinder gender equality.

To achieve equality, and change the stereotypes, women need to be able to both contribute professionally and to have a family. Today, women either choose between the two or take on two demanding jobs (professional or caretaker[2]). For us to improve women's opportunities, we should first do so for men. Men should be allowed and encouraged to be actively engaged in their children's upbringing, including afterschool care, without either giving up their own careers or needing to first be divorced then be able to blame shared custody for spending time with their kids. To allow everyone time to focus on their jobs and still have time to be a part of their family's life, we all need to contribute.

A great way to reduce the stereotype would be for us to expect employees to take off one weekday afternoon a week to take care of another

---

[1] See further discussion in:
BOL, J., & FOGEL-YAARI, H. (2023). "Death by a Thousand Cuts: The Impact of Gender Bias on Career Progression" in Why Diversity, Equity, and Inclusion Matter: Challenges and Solutions (Chapter 4). Singapore: World Scientific Publishing Co. Pte. Ltd. Edited By: Bin Srinidhi.
[2] Even women who employ external help for their caretaking obligations still carry the mental load, which can detract from focusing on their professional performance or lead to burn-out. There are many academic papers on this, but for the non-academics out there, I recommend watching "Diary of a Prosecutor" episode 8 (available on Netflix).

human being (a grandchild, a niece or nephew, your own children, an elderly family member or neighbor, etc.). This would have to be very visible and interpreted as them building their human capital. This Adulting or Nurturing weekday afternoon would be interpreted by everyone around them as indications of being a better leader: being better at managing other employees, being better at dealing with difficult situations, being a more responsible person who we can count on. In this way, we would add nurturing to the male stereotype, freeing mothers to spend more time at work so they can actually be rewarded for the time they do spend with their kids, improve social connections, and contribute to everyone's wellbeing.

Us all coming together to take care of other people is not only beneficial to employees' career progression, but it's also beneficial to us humans as social creatures.

About Hila Fogel-Yaari, PhD

Dr. Fogel-Yaari teaches accounting at University of Texas at Arlington. Her research focuses on gender issues and work balance between the household and workplace.

After earning her Ph.D. in accounting from the University of Toronto, she has since worked at Tulane University and is now at the University of Texas at Arlington. Her research focuses on audit quality, corporate disclosure quality, and innovation. Her work has been published in peer-reviewed academic journals, including Auditing: Journal of Practice and Theory, the Journal of Accounting, Auditing, and Finance, and the Journal of Accounting and Public Policy.

It Takes A Village

EDITOR NOTES

By Eric Klein

When Hila approached me about this topic I was intrigued. Modern society makes a number of assumptions and requirements about what are promotable skills and what are things that hold people back. We still have presumptions that a woman can't advance because she will be the primary caregiver for children and parents, and thus won't be able to concentrate on the business. In fact, many young women have resorted to freezing their eggs so that they can have healthy children later in life.

I grew up on more enlightened fiction starting with Star Trek, so I never understood the stereotypes or rules. Growing up, there were many books and shows that depicted a different view. Ones where there was a single parent or different gender roles.

- Who's the Boss (1984 -92): is probably the best example of this category. Here, a retired baseball player becomes the housekeeper to help his daughter have a chance at a better life. He goes from out of work former athlete to housekeeper and caregiver to respected teacher. All while raising his and his boss' children.

Others include:
- Mr. Mom (1983): where a man is laid off from his job at the automobile factory, and when his wife finds a job, he takes over caring for their home and kids.

- ➢ Mrs. Doubtfire (1993): where an out of work actor pretends to be an older woman so he can be the nanny for his kids when his ex-wife is at work.
- ➢ The Daddy Day Care 2003 (and later a film series), where two men can't find jobs and start a start a day care service to help fund their families.

There are others, but you should see my point.

But my first serious look at this was in The Left Hand of Darkness by Ursula K. Le Guin. Here a human man is tossed into the political intrigue on a planet where there were no genders. They are normally asexual, and only at breeding time do they "chose" which gender they will be. Thus, a lot of prejudice in our own society was exposed by contrast with his experiences. This was just the first of Ursula's stories that look at roles and assumptions in a society.

Watching a woman I worked with brag that they gave birth on a Friday and were back in the office on Monday, just so they would still be taken seriously as part of management, made me realize that there are inherent flaws in our system. Later I heard stories from academia from my wife. There were many where a promising PhD student was told that she wouldn't get a recommendation from her advisor for a post-doc because "why waste the slot on you, when you will just get married and have kids before leaving academia?" There were multiple variations, but this was very much the presumption of many of the male advisors. And for this still to be the case in the twenty-first century really bothers me.

So, when Hila approached me about this topic and how hard it is to do clinical research (privacy rules, etc.) I suggested we do this anthology. While I can only hope these stories will help change the world, I realize that it will be a slow process. But if we want the Utopian life of Star Trek we need to start somewhere.

It Takes A Village

As the stories came in we expanded the theme a little bit, to include stories that showed people working to better society as a whole. This enables us to include all sorts of options from fantasy, science fiction, and even a few dystopian selections. Culminating, as I feel, in a great collection of people making things better for everyone even under the worst of conditions.

I hope you enjoy the stories.

Eric Klein
April, 2024

It Takes A Village

It Takes A Village

THE BUREAU OF SOCIETY BETTERMENT

By Anaïs Chartschenko

When asked what inspired this story, Anaïs responded:

> In futuristic science fiction, the environment becomes a character. The Bureau of Society Betterment was inspired by architecture concept art depicting alternative ways to build cities as well as the way the color white can be used as a torture method within a space.
>
> From there, I imagined how a utopian ideal of community care of children and seniors could fail. There are always a minority that gets left behind.
>
> How would two people who had lived outside the norm form a family with one another? People are messy so I tried to make it an imperfect new family unit, yet they have hope. The hope is what brings them together, and will tie them back to this society's utopian ideal — even if in other ways darkness remains.

It Takes A Village

THE BUREAU OF SOCIETY BETTERMENT — Anaïs Chartschenko

The apartment was spacious. Richly carpeted with pale blue, each room was trimmed with golden paint. It was pre-furnished with crafted bedroom, living room, and dining room sets. In addition to those, there was a special shelf with scrolls which promised knowledge she'd been unable to access before.

Picture windows faced outward toward the greenery beyond. When she allowed herself to dream, she wondered what it must be like to walk among the tall hedges and gardens on The Out. From here, she could see where the Elites lived in their elegant multi-pod homes.

Once in awhile, she'd heard, one might be able to watch a few of them amble by. Even rarer than that, they'd put on a parade for the monolith to thank them for providing the energy, goods, and materials used in daily life. The most talented of the Elites put on a show rarest of all, with acrobats, dancing, and singing. When that happened, the monolith artisans received extra CAVES.

The Elites would lift their premier pets so that all could marvel at the beauty of their fur. And then, Celeste's favorite part. The leader of the Elites addressed the monolith directly. If one worked hard enough, they might be able to move directly from the lowest caste directly to live on The Out with the Elites! While she couldn't recall anyone who'd achieved such a feat, she didn't doubt that it happened. She'd been so taken by the idea that she'd maneuvered her way up the levels through social engineering.

She hummed with excitement as she finally viewed The Out. It was more vibrant than she'd gathered from seeing it onscreen. More green. The sky! Such an intense bright blue she had to squint in order to take it in. She ran her fingers against the cool glass of the window. Nothing could be more beautiful.

It Takes A Village

"I'll take it," she said. She was careful. It was lowlith to sound too eager.

Mr. Holger's well-groomed mustache twitched. He placed his hand close to the rim of his glasses. "Ah," he said. And a moment later, sadly, "Ahh…"

"What?" Celeste placed her hands to her hips.

"Seems the SCAVO reports that you don't have the required CAVES. Would you like to follow me? There's a cozy apartment thirty-eight floors down that would meet your needs fine." He eyed her, "Just fine."

"Check again!" She hadn't spent the last years watching kids for fun.

And that didn't account for the CAVES hopeful men transferred her in their pursuit. She should finally have the CAVES required to move up the monolith. She'd done the math every night as she fell asleep and again to pass the days for years. She knew down to the Cav how her finances were.

"No, no mistake. Come this way," Mr. Holger was genuinely sad.

A girl like Celeste didn't come around often, and when they did, they were already attached to some rugged man drowning in CAVES. Celeste was most definitely unattached, and if one could get past her unpleasant demeanor- which he was sure he could- she'd make a most attractive mate.

Too bad there were too many CAVES between them. His mother would simply not allow the match.

"But, Mr. Holger!" she said.

"Come along," He said, with regret.

"There has been a mistake!" She no longer cared how she sounded.

"I suggest contacting the Bureau of Society Betterment."

She reluctantly tore her gaze from the window one last time. When would she next see a slice of sky?

No doubt the "cozy" apartment he'd show her was the size of the closet she'd toured. That meant shared latrines for all the residents on the floor. They were always dirty from the sheer mass of people using them daily. That paired with the communal kitchen where you'd wait in an endless line for slop which echoed the rank smell of the latrines.

The lucky ones lived on the ends of halls, furthest from both utilities and closest to the adjoining escalators which brought people directly to their work pods. Their pods featured slabs facing the escalators. They'd set up their chairs and watch commuters go up and down.

She followed Mr. Holger through the finely wallpapered hall. They boarded the downward escalators. They rode in silence. She was determined not to lose her composure the deeper they went.

But when Mr. Holger finally ushered her to her newly assigned pod, she turned to him in desperation.

"Mr. Holger!" she cried, flinging herself into his arms.

He held her for a moment, and then set her aside. His eyes no longer held the warmth they once did.

"Get ahold of yourself," he said. He spun on his heel and left her.

She stood motionless in the door of her new windowless pod, located next to the latrine.

~*~

The Bureau of Society Betterment was housed inside a boring white pod. White walls, white floor, and a shameless white ceiling. The Monolith Motto ran in an automated bright, white-lit display around the top of the room over and over. It was enough to drive Celeste mad. Her eyes roved around, starved for color. Besides a discreet potted plant next to the glass booth, there was no relief in sight.

She tapped her foot. The receptionist glared. She crossed her arms. The receptionist rolled their eyes. She sighed, her bangs puffing upward. The receptionist swiveled around in their chair, and left Celeste without anyone at all to express her displeasure to.

She glanced up towards the ceiling again and then looked away. The familiar clash of emotions happened every time she was subjected to the MM. Everyone else she knew recited it with such speed she knew it didn't trouble them. It was another saying out of many sayings that reflected the morals and expectations of society. Celeste believed in the Monolith Motto — to a degree. She understood the value of everyone giving their hard-learned lessons to children, and, again, the value of elder care.

Where she stumbled was her heart aching every time she had to watch a family close ranks around her when it mattered; when it was their family's holiday event, when she had to listen for hour after hour to their happy chatter afterwards.

No one cared much about the plight of orphans because everyone was consumed by their certainty they were living the Monolith Motto themselves. Celeste was around, sure.

After her parents died when she was a child, other parents tacked her life onto their work pursuits. Then they dropped it off as she reached maturity, preferring to focus on their own children and the children of their extended families.

The elders talked on and on about their children and grandchildren when Celeste sat with them during her after-work time. She didn't blame them, but she got tired. Exhausted, even.

When the men started noticing her, they weren't serious about choosing her as a wife as she didn't come from a good lith family. They pursued her only as a desirable novelty. That didn't stop the women from hating her, finding opportunities to make her look the fool. They'd brag about their parents, husbands, and children, knowing Celeste was without.

It became hard to feel bad when men transferred CAVES behind their mothers' or wives' backs, because it was the only way she'd ever earn a bonus or a raise.

And then she stopped feeling bad about tuning people out. She'd smile and nod and count CAVES in her mind. Move up the lith, to learn a whole new set of peoples' family names and fortunes. She'd wait out the time before returning to her empty apartment in the singles pod sector.

Time passed. She stopped fidgeting, and instead let her eyes un-focus themselves as she stared at the white floor. She blinked, let her eyes un-focus, and then blinked again. Tiny lights danced in her vision.

"Ms. Bradford?" a male voice said.

She looked up, vision blurry, at a dark shape looming above her. Her vision focused and then dark shadow settled into a tall, handsome man wearing a deep blue suit. The copper detailing in his tie brought out his eyes, framed by the latest design in SCAVO glasses.

She preened as he cast his eyes over her, smiling in appreciation at what he found. She could work with this!

"Yes," She said.

She stood, making sure she positioned herself closer to him than strictly necessary for their handshake.

He made up the difference, and they practically stood in an embrace.

"I'm Mr. Evans." He said. He kept her hand in his.

"Heard you're having a problem? Terrible! Must be a system error. I'm a second liner; I can manually fix anything." He dipped his head closer. He licked his lips.

Celeste lifted her face towards his. Bold if he kissed her now, but it wouldn't be the first time that had happened. Powerful men were like that. And this man — well. Not as good as a first liner, or even a pre-eminent… Not to mention an eminent, but as far as it went, a girl could do worse.

"Would you be free to join me — "

"This one's for me." A dour woman stood at the door.

Her SCAVO was fashioned into a broach, which emitted a dull white light. Her hair, pulled into a stern low bun, white. Her pantsuit was white on white. Her low pumps were the same. The effect was her face, at first glance, appeared to be floating against the white wall.

Celeste shivered.

Mr. Evans stepped back from Celeste, dropping her hand. He pulled himself to his full height.

"Are you sure?" Mr. Evans asked.

"Mr. Evans." She said.

He crumbled. It was clear he'd overstepped by asking. She was sure. Always sure.

Celeste felt the windows with a view slipping away. The way the other woman fixed steely eyes on her, perhaps windows at all. Forever.

She'd be assigned a room even closer to the middle of the monolith, deep in the layered pod design. No doubt in close proximity to the dreadful Bureau of Society Betterment, which long held as the location of the very center, or — as they boasted — the heart of the monolith. The older woman motioned Celeste follow, and she went.

"How do you not lose your mind here?" Celeste asked, trying a tack she'd used before to good effect.

"What do you mean?" The older woman asked.

"All the white. It's — " She picked up a white pencil holder.

The older woman snatched it back. "Eggshell. And the desk is ecru, the chairs oldlace, the walls whitesmoke. The floors — the floors are my special joy — seashell, though I haven't the distinction of having seen a fossil of that caliber before. I've heard they are quite lovely. Nothing white, as you can plainly see. If you'd pay attention. Which brings us to our inevitable meeting today."

"What color do you wear then, is it linen? No... uh, ivory!" Celeste said.

"Ms. Bradford."

"That's me! And what did you say I could call you?"

"I did not." The older woman steepled her fingers.

"Oh."

"Mmm. Not used to my kind, are you?"

"Your kind?"

"The astute."

Celeste didn't answer.

"Let's go over your many infractions." The older woman didn't press her SCAVO. She merely waved a hand and an image appeared. Celeste straightened in her oldlace chair. Only the Elite had access to this sort of display. "Tell me, what is the Monolith Motto?" the older woman asked.

"If we're not learning, we're teaching, and if we teach we learn," Celeste recited.

"So you do know it." the older woman said drily.

Celeste nodded.

"I'd like you to watch this, and when it's over, do explain to me how you have lived by the MM." The older woman performed a quick series of motions and the image shifted.

Celeste sat forward as the image changed to show Celeste herself, as a child.

"I'll return after you've finished." The older woman stood.

"Ms. Bradford?"

"Yes?"

"You may call me Ms. White."

It Takes A Village

~*~

Ms. White opened the door. She walked slowly to her desk and sat. She ran her hand over her chair's worn armrests. Celeste watched her, puzzled by how the other woman caressed her chair. It took all kinds. Another Motto.

Ms. White didn't speak. She raised a finger, and Mr. Evans entered, carrying a pot of tea. He carefully poured two cups and then left, without looking up.

"It's always good to remind a man like that he is not a god, I find. That's good advice. Though you might already know that. Hmph." Ms. White said. She twisted her mouth, thinking. She handed Celeste a cup of tea before taking up her thoughts once more.

"I assume you've watched it all. I have too. And I can see a dreadful work history. You have worked all over the lith, and not once were you elevated as the leader of your group. Even so, the top performers stay where they are, while you have moved up the lith consistently." Ms. White said. She sipped her tea. "Go on, take a drink, Ms. Bradford."

Celeste picked up the fine teacup. It felt so thin, she was afraid she'd crush it. She sipped and despite her rapidly beating heart to be at such a dismal point in her life, she closed her eyes to savor. It was unlike anything she'd ever had in her life. She couldn't fully unravel the flavor, but it tasted of rose and honey.

"Thank you," she said sincerely, but Ms. White waved Celeste's gratitude away.

"Did you watch it all?"

"Yes."

"Well?"

Celeste stammered.

It Takes A Village

"Those weren't words, golden tongue."

"I did my assigned work and completed more After Work Care than anyone I know."

"Children learn nothing from you. You offer no nursemaid care to our elders. It's a marvel." Ms. White said.

"I didn't know everyone hated me. Thanks."

Ms. White laughed, and the sound so surprised Celeste that she jumped.

"That's just it! Impossibly, you fell under the radar so long because everyone likes you! In fact, I'd say you were thriving."

"And yet my CAVES were removed by the Bureau?" Celeste paused, understanding. "By you!"

"Well, it would be difficult to approach you the way I wanted if I left you in that hellhole apartment on the seventeenth floor. And as I said, children learn nothing, elders and so forth..."

Hell hole? Celeste blinked, the gorgeous picture windows filling her mind.

"You are good at finding the thing people think they want, and then changing their desires to align with whatever you want. They have no idea they're being managed until you're long gone — with a tidy stack of CAVES, no less. And still, those same people remember you fondly. Notwithstanding the scorned wives. I am giving you a pass on that because I hold the men accountable for their own situation."

Celeste flushed.

"I'm not admonishing you, girl, look at me." Ms. White said. She tapped her pencil against the desk. "As you can see, I'm getting on in years. The position as Elite of the Bureau of Society Betterment is being opened."

Celeste blood turned cold. She'd be set back to zero under a whole new Elite — and this, after she'd only found out an Elite was actually inside the monolith! She'd lost it all, and it took so long to build! Her bitterness tasted of latrine slop.

~*~

Ms. White poured Celeste another cup of tea.

Celeste forced a smile and sipped. Tea burned her tongue. She didn't wince. Instead, she gazed down into the cup noticing how tea leaves and petals clung to the edges despite having been strained through the pot. There were always cracks for mistakes to slip through.

Ms. White had rehearsed how she would present to Ms. Bradford and cursed herself. There was no accounting for emotions getting one off track, and here she was mucking the whole thing up before she'd secured Celeste to her scheme. She tried again.

"One important facet of what I do is match people as best I can with suitable placement, should the need arise. I excavate data, try to pair those individuals with what brings out missed strengths. The result should show that previously un-contributing members become a vital part of our community." Ms. White paused.

"Generally, this position is passed down from parent to child. But I never found the time to marry, much less raise a child. I find myself in a bind. I interviewed candidates. The people on The Out are spoiled." Ms. White said. She sipped her tea and shook her head. "They lack discipline. They've forgotten why we have the monolith to begin with!"

Celeste's brow furrowed. She wasn't sure either.

Ms. White took a breath.

"I've chosen you to be presented as my daughter, my heir." Ms. White said.

Celeste gasped. "I don't know what to say!"

"You don't have to say anything, I've taken care of it."

"I —"

"It's a role I feel would bring out your strengths."

"I —"

"This has been my most thought-out, most important project."

"I —"

"If I didn't think you were just right for this, I wouldn't have taken extreme steps to ensure its success."

Celeste made a strangled noise.

"You don't have to thank me, please don't. Think of it as another placement in your long series of placements — but you won't be leaving to another job. It's a lifetime position."

"I —"

"Does that bother you? I'm sorry, I've wrestled with it, and you'll come to see what I did. It makes sense."

"I —"

"Oh! I'm nervous! I haven't been nervous since… Ms. Bradford. Say something!" Ms. White said. She leaned forward, jostling her cup with the precious tea in it. Some of the hot liquid sloshed out and landed on Ms. White's hand but she didn't notice.

"Are you certain you want me? As you've pointed out, I've done poorly in many aspects." Celeste said.

She wanted to kick herself. When offered a higher position, the only thing to do was say you are perfect for it, even when you had doubts. This time, she had many doubts.

"I don't need you to be good at folding laundry or secretary work. For our station in life, politics is everything."

"Our?"

"Yes. Ours." Ms. White said firmly.

It Takes A Village

They stared at one another for a moment, as if each was daring the other to say it could not be so.

"Elite?" Celeste breathed.

"Elite."

"Will I meet others who were chosen to leave the monolith? Or…" A terrible thought chilled Celeste. "Am I to stay in lith forever then? To run the Bureau?" She set her teacup down with shaking hands.

"There is no one else to meet. You'll be the only one who makes the move, and no one but us is to know."

"Ms. White?"

"That was a campaign to bring hope. I believe it was a great success, it gave the people something to strive for. Production was up forty percent when we launched it."

"Production."

"Production is the top priority. Hope is a wonderful thing! All profit, since we didn't spend a cent."

Celeste was very still, the enormity of what she'd been told settling on her.

"You may not see it now, but we have many similarities. The differences I found are fascinating! You have so much to learn. I suppose I do, too. I'll find out when I teach you." Ms. White said. She studied Celeste. "I have been told I have a knack for teaching. You needn't look worried."

"What do you want me to do?" Celeste asked. She thought about the window, the green and the impossible blue of the sky. It faded into a blur.

"Taking this position does require you to work, but it uses skills you've honed yourself as the foundation. You are responsible for keeping the monolith functioning smoothly, for enforcing the Monolith Motto. It is essential to follow it, so its people are productive, healthy, and happy communities. Productive is of the upmost importance because all the world depends on the monolith for its exports. It can be thankless, but when you pull it off, a thrill! Adding your own touch..."

Celeste wanted to ask what 'world' meant but it didn't seem to be the right time.

"This is my last day here, inside the monolith. Oh — I suppose I could ask you if you refuse the offer, but I made that choice rather..." Ms. White managed to look like a mischievous child, "Smelly... I would apologize except I'm not sorry about it."

"Is this a choice?" Celeste said.

Ms. White was flustered. "I want it to be."

Celeste nodded.

"I want it to be very much." Ms. White repeated, suddenly looking very small at her big white desk. "You'll be my daughter."

"How can I be when I am Ms. Bradford? Won't people question it?"

"You'll be the next Ms. White. With training and a new style no one will even recall a Ms. Bradford. You've no family left, no close friends in the lith... I made work my life, and have no one." Ms. White said quietly. Ms. White paused, and the words no one seemed to echo throughout the room. "No one questions small incongruities when you declare it was always thus with authority. You'll see."

It seemed impossible, but Elites were the ones who decided what was possible. Celeste didn't think she'd miss being Ms. Bradford. She burned with wanting to make things possible, the way Ms. White could do. The idea was a terrible new hope, a hope that poorly hid the other, more dangerous hope.

"You are the daughter I never told anyone about, come from overseas!" Ms. White brightened.

"We'll walk the gardens together, perhaps, take my dog for a stroll after dinner. Maybe you'll get a dog? You'll like that! Clear air."

It Takes A Village

Celeste trembled with emotion. Maybe one day, she'd find out what all these new words Ms. White used meant. Dog? Overseas?

It almost didn't matter if she was a daughter with a — She couldn't think it yet. With a Ms. White.

She knew she was influenced by the idea of becoming Elite, and she wasn't sure if it was a choice or a command, but she didn't care.

"Yes, this is my last day here..." Ms. White was lost in her memory now, as some older people tended to do.

They sat together, in comfortable silence, as Ms. White savored long years with the Bureau, and then the precious years training with her father for the role. She found herself flush with joy at the thought of spending her golden years with her new daughter. Perhaps one day the younger new Ms. White would choose to have a family. No one would fault her for dreaming of grandchildren. She blinked back the tears, startled by the idea taking root.

It had never been for her before, yet now, anything was possible. She wanted to cry with the joy of it, the shock of a long buried hurt healed, if only they could be happy together.

And Ms. White knew she could, so she would make sure her new daughter was as well. At least she would make the effort. But all that crying and blubbering was for later.

"Thank you. You're quite good."

"Ms. White?"

"You let me have my moment," the older woman said simply.

She straightened, and then rose gracefully from her chair.

"Come," Ms. White said.

Celeste went.

It Takes A Village

About Anaïs Chartschenko

Anaïs Chartschenko hails from the Canadian wilderness. She has come to enjoy such modern things as electric tea kettles.

As an author, her published works include The Weightless One and Sailing Toward Us. She illustrated Biron the Bee Who Couldn't (written by Gregg McBride).

You can find Anaïs' books at:
amazon.com/author/anaischartschenko

THE TRIAL OF THE TYPIST

By Meir Michael Fogel

When asked what inspired this story, Meir responded:

> I wrote about the flip side of what I assumed would be the other stories in this book because I thought that they were all about a perfect utopia, and by the time I found out otherwise the story had grown on me.

It Takes A Village

THE TRIAL OF THE TYPIST — Meir Michael Fogel

"Order, order, I call this court to order," said the judge.

This was the trial of The Typist (he had his name legally changed), a programmer, and an alleged criminal. According to the accusers, in exchange for money, The Typist would use medical simulators, pictures of people, and editing software to make pictures of his clients spending time with their children, when they were not. Given that such pictures are used to claim paid time off work for the care of others, The Typist was charged with defamation, fraud, conspiracy, wire fraud, assisted robbery (as his clients made extra money illicitly), and fraudulent reporting on government documents (some of his clients worked for various governmental organizations).

"Let's do this quickly", said the judge, "the prosecutor will go first".

The prosecutor cleared her throat. "I now call the first witness to the stand," she said, "Presenting Y X."

As Y X stood up to the witness stand, The Typist gasped.

"You!" The Typist exclaimed angrily, "You —" (the next few words said by The Typist were censored due to their vulgar nature).

"Sit down," boomed the judge.

After The Typist was seated, the trial continued.

"He is guilty," said Y X. "I saw it with my own two eyes. Well, I did not see it, but I know he did it, because I was one of those who paid him to do it."

The whole courtroom gasped, and then swelled with mumbles and whispers as the audience talked among themselves about it. The jury spoke excitedly to each other.

"Silence!" the judge boomed once again. Speaking in a quieter tone (which no longer caused hearing loss), the judge asked the prosecutor if she was finished to which she replied with affirmation.

It Takes A Village

The defense attorney stated that he would like to cross examine the witness.

The attorney and The Typist whispered to each other for a while. Then the attorney asked Y X, "Is it true you are facing criminal charges? And remember, you are under oath."

"Yes."

"Is it part of your plea bargain to testify against all the people who helped you illegally?"

"Yes."

The attorney smiled a huge grin and asked: "So, are you only saying these things about my client because you took a plea bargain before this trial?" Before the witness could respond, they continued, "You don't have to answer that."

The jury and the audience whispered among each other about the most recent development.

Turning towards the jury, "What, none of you knew", said the attorney with a horrified tone and a small smile. "After all, my client was only arrested because Y X was caught embezzling, and when they checked further back, they realized all his other crimes. Y X agreed to a bargain that lets him get off free, so long as he told the court about all his associates. Y X falsely accused my client to make this list seem longer."

The judge dismissed Y X.

"Do you have additional evidence to present?" The judge asked the prosecutor.

"Yes, as a matter of fact, I do", replied the prosecutor. "Here are the police pictures of the accused's house," the prosecutor said as she lifted a file filled with pictures.

It Takes A Village

"As you see, here are the pictures of the room where he took the initial pictures, here is the computer where he changed the background of the photos and made the medical simulators appear as if they were real people."

"Additionally, I would like to enter exhibit B," the prosecutor said while taking some important looking files from her briefcase. "Here are his bank transactions, and if you look at the highlighted times when suddenly large sums of money were deposited, it coincides perfectly with when several rich people posted pictures of themselves doing stuff with their families that there are no other witnesses or security footage, or any other corroborating evidence other than the pictures that show them doing it."

The jury whispered to each other after she had finished.

"Do you have any other evidence?" asks the judge.

"No," replies the prosecutor, "the prosecution rests its case".

"Then the defense can make its case now", says the judge to the defense attorney.

The attorney cleared their throat and said, "As you have seen, the prosecution only showed photographs and one witness, who is already facing criminal charges and is only testifying as part of a plea bargain. Also, the deposited money can easily be explained by tracing contract payments accrued during The Typist's job as a project manager. In fact, if you look at these documents you will find that the money matches the dates that he finished his contracts flawlessly," said the attorney, while pulling out papers from their briefcase. "The medical simulators were bought at a garage sale and if you look at the pictures you will realize that they are all wearing the defendant's own clothes in natural positions. It is his way of avoiding clothes hangers, simply an innocent hobby conducted in his garage. This trial was triggered by the complaint of Mrs. X, the neighborhood's busybody, who is known to find trolls under every bush. The defense rests," said the attorney.

It Takes A Village

The jury went to their room, and soon loud shouting erupted, loud enough to be heard through the door, and words like stereotypes and stereotypical behavior could be distinguished. What started as whether The Typist was innocent rapidly degraded down to swearing and name calling, about the morality of both Y X and The Typist. When it got to the point of a massive brawl, the judge sent the court bailiff to restore order.

Fifteen minutes later, the jury emerged from their room, all looking angry, frustrated, and beat up to some degree, muttering among themselves.

"Enough," the judge said. "Has the jury reached a verdict?".

The jury all quieted down, still looking annoyed, though now they looked annoyed not just at each other but at the judge as well.

The prosecutor nibbled her lower lip nervously, the attorney was already packing their things in their suitcase with a smile on their face.

The speaker clears their throat and says, "We declare this man…"

About Meir Michael Fogel

Meir Michael Fogel lives in Texas with his dog and his family. From the very first time a book was placed in his hands, he has loved books, to the point of teachers complaining of his preference for books above all else. Once his verbal ability developed, he has not stopped telling stories.

Meir is 13 years old at the time of publication. This is his debut.

It Takes A Village

OFF WE GO

By Eric Klein

When asked what inspired this story, Eric responded:

> While working to organize this anthology I was listening to the radio. On came a cover of Elton John's Rocket Man as sung by Kate Bush. When she sings the line
>
> > I'm not the man they think I am at home
> > Oh, no, no, no
> > I'm a rocket man
>
> This really got me thinking. Until now space has mostly been the exclusive area of men. For example, as of March 2023, seventy two women have flown in space, while more than six hundred men have flown into space. So, it is easy to expect that your crew or pilot would be a man.
>
> And thus, this story was born.

It Takes A Village

OFF WE GO — Eric Klein

Off we go into the wild blue yonder,
Climbing high into the sun;
Here we go zooming on a roar of thunder,
At 'em now, past the sun! past the sun!
Down we dive, spouting our flame from under,
Down with one helluva roar!
— Anthem of the US Army Air Corp (later Air Force)

Two more hours and I can offload this batch of tourists. Usually, I don't mind herding this bucket of bolts on the back and forth to Mars. Most trips are filled with scientists or colonists, either group is usually so caught up in what they will be doing once they get to Mars that they are no trouble. Even those returning to Earth space are usually absorbed in reviewing data or writing reports. Either way, they keep to themselves and don't get in the way of the operation of the ship.

That was before the colonies went independent. I know that we aren't supposed to think of them that way anymore, there was very limited travel between Earth or Ceres and them, but now there are tourists on each of these passenger runs. While tourists are bad, students are worse. They want to be entertained all the time. They will barge in while you are in the head if you don't double lock it, and everyone wants to "see the bridge." Then, they get two major disappointments. First is that the bridge doesn't look like what they have seen in their favorite holoprograms. "Where are the windows, I mean, view ports?" As if a modern spaceship needs view ports! We do everything based on video feeds to our screens and holoprojectors. Most pilots, let alone captains, wouldn't know what to do with a direct view of the stars. Then they take a look at me, they are expecting to see Captain Spiff, embodied by a blend of frontier grit and interplanetary savoir-faire, his grizzled Van Dyke beard a testament to voyages across the solar system. But what they see is me, a petite woman who is a mother's essence embodied. They look at me as if they are expecting me to pull out a tray of fresh baked cookies. Where would I cook cookies on the bridge? That is what the galley is for.

Today's trip was even worse than usual. Two of them decided to join the "Beyond Orbit Club," forgetting that we are not in zero-G for more than a few minutes when I do the skew flip in the middle of the trip.

After hearing the announcement that we would be in freefall for a short time, two of them rushed to one of the airlocks to try, while a third went to record it on their wristpad for social media. I barely got there in time to prevent them from spacing themselves when the inner door was latched open. And you can guess what the Admiralty thinks of losing a whole ship of high-school students.

To make it worse, the recording went live on social media with me yelling "What are you trying to do, space us all?! Gravity will hit in a few seconds, and you are using the airlock override to hold yourself up. Are you nuts?! Back to your rooms right now!"

"You're not my Space Mom."

"No, for you it's worse! If anything, I am Captain Space Mom. Your mother can only send you to your room. I can have you locked up for the rest of the trip, and then you will be arrested when we get back to Clarke Station for reckless endangerment. So, are you going to your room on your own?"

"Yes, ma'am."

Walking back to the bridge, I heard that conversation multiple times from different open doors. I took a quick look, and it has over a million views on 3 planets and who knows how many colonies.

It Takes A Village

The ribbing started as soon as I got within real-time radio range of station Clarke One. It started with greetings of "go to your room," and by the time I was done docking, I was known as Captain Space Mom.

As I turned in the flight report with traffic control, I heard my name on the station wide: "Captain Shackleton, please report to the Port Admiral Kinnison's office immediately." Damn, who was that passenger and how much trouble am I in because of them?

Outside of the Port Admiral's office there are two MPs on either side of the door. This is not looking good. The higher ranking one looks up at me as I approach, "Captain Shackleton, please go right in. The Port Admiral is expecting you," and he opens the door for me. Damn, the admiral is expecting me.

As I enter, the Port Admiral looks up. "I see that everyone is now here." I look around and see that there are fifteen or twenty others seated in the room. There is one empty seat at the front, and the Port Admiral points to it. "Please sit-down, captain."

Standing, he starts: "I am not sure that all of you have heard the latest development." I take a deep breath; the Port Admiral has a nasty temper, so I am expecting to get blasted. "Captain Shackleton," oh no, here it comes, "has reported back that TRAPPIST-1e is perfect for colonization." Wait, this is not about what happened to me? "As you know, there have been 6 missions looking for habitable planets. After all these failures, the world had begun to think that human-habitable worlds were even rarer than expected, as each one visited was reported back as 'too hot,' 'too cold,' 'dangerous chemicals in the atmosphere,' 'unstable star,' and so on. Each world that was checked was more disappointing than the previous. If this last one had come back without a positive result, The United System Congress on Cyrus was planning to discuss canceling the program." He pauses. "Then an hour ago, word came back to Earth via Captain Patrick Shackleton's messenger drone that his team had found that

It Takes A Village

TRAPPIST-1e was a habitable planet. One that we could reach and put a colony on with only a six-month flight using Heinlein anomalies. We appear to be alone, but now have room to grow."

Another officer stands. "For those of you who don't know me, I am Admiral Zim. We are preparing a colony ship for TRAPPIST-1e, which will be ready in under a year. One of you, or Captain Shackleton, will be in command of the first human extrasolar colonization ship. Now, we have all of your records and piloting logs to review. We want to make sure that this historic trip is captained by the best possible person, so all of you will have the opportunity to apply and be tested. As most of you are civilians, I can't order you to take the tests, but I strongly encourage you to do so. With so many candidates, and the fact that we can't pull all of you off of your existing responsibilities, these will take several weeks. That should be enough time for Captain Shackleton to return and take them himself. Signup forms are in the captain's lounge and at traffic control, for those who would like to accept this challenge. Testing will start in 2 weeks. We hope to have choose a captain in under four months, this will give them time to pick and train their crew. You will be paid for your time being tested at your normal flight rate. You are all dismissed to consider your options."

As we leave, the Port Admiral calls out over the noise, "Captain Shakleton, please remain." Damn, I had hoped he had forgotten about me. I sit back down and wait for the room to clear. Best to take control and find out how much trouble I am in.

After the room had cleared, and it was only the Port Admiral Kinnison and Admiral Zim left, we start talking at the same time "Now, Captain Shakleton…"

"Port Admiral Kinnison, I can explain."

"We have something to discuss that I didn't want to say in front of everyone. What? Explain what?"

It Takes A Village

"Don't you have a complaint about me and the millions of social media views?"

He looks down at his desk. "Yes. There was a complaint that you threatened a passenger and didn't respect personal rights by confining him to quarters. When haven't I backed my captains? Separately, I had a report from the legal team saying that you were perfectly within the law in this, and there is no justification for the complaint. To be honest, I looked at the recording. And, Captain Space Mom, I would not have shown your restraint. I would have closed the inner lock and let them space themselves." Standing, he continues, "but that isn't why I held you back. While you were on your way back from Mars, there was a tunnel collapse. Some colonists were trapped, and a rescue is in progress. We would like you to do an immediate turn around to bring emergency equipment and specialists to help. This would be a high-boost mission: One G for a day and a half and then a two G deceleration for the last half day to get you there in just over two days. I cannot order you to do this, as you don't have the minimum rest required between trips, but I ask for your help — my son is one of those trapped."

"At one G we would get there in just over eighty-nine hours, delaying the flip and decelerating at two G would shave more than a third of that. So, yes, that would be just over two days. But could your team handle more? If we do it at two G, we could get there is about thirty hours."

"We can check if they can do this. Mostly they can be lying down, but I didn't know if you would be willing to take it, let alone at the higher speed. They are loading your ship now and will be done in half an hour. How soon can you be ready to go?"

"We can launch in thirty-five minutes. That will give me time to take a shower and kit up."

"The passengers will be aboard in thirty so you can do your preflight. Thank you."

It Takes A Village

Walking toward my cabin, I hear my name called out, "Captain Shakleton, please wait." One of the students from the airlock is rushing up to me. "I want to say that I am sorry; it was all my fault."

"You were one of the two girls about to have sex. Why? And why in the airlock?"

"I am not very popular, and in an old movie someone once said 'Well, if you really wanna be popular, consider two little words: sex tape.' So, I thought I would try it with Mike. But Jade pushed him aside, so he just stuck around to record it. And if I wanted it to go viral, I needed to show we were not just on an airplane. The airlock is the only place with a window, so that was the best place to take it. I'm really sorry. We had no idea it wasn't safe."

"First, never let someone pressure you into anything. Your first time could have been your last. If I hadn't stopped things, the airlock would have opened when gravity came back. In this case, I suspect an almost sex tape will prove to make you more popular than the real thing would have. That video had over a billion views on 3 planets before we docked, google knows how many people have seen it since."

"Oh google." She asked her wristpad, "Buffy, how many views does the video of me in the airlock have?"

"The video of you and Jade has over one hundred-billion views and a billion shares."

She fainted. So much for my long relaxing shower. I get her to sickbay and rush to get a quick rinse and grab my gear before heading to the docking bay.

The trip to Mars was exhausting. Twenty-nine hours at two G really takes it out of you. I had a few days' rest on Mars and then a nice slow trip back to Clarke Station with those needing more advanced medical care.

~*~

It Takes A Village

Eventually my cousin Edward, the other Captain Shakleton, made it back to Clarke Sation. Oh, didn't I mention that he was my cousin? That was what threw me off when they called us all in for the briefing. There was a week-long celebration on all the colonies for him and his discovery of a planet around a star that shares the name with an ancient order of French monks that followed a strict rule of silence. The irony was not lost on the media. He was in his element, out making speeches, being interviewed, showing off. Somehow, he always left the audience feeling that he has a heart that beats with the love of exploration. The call of the unknown stirred his soul, and the uncharted territories of the universe were his playground. He would always end by turning to the camera with a gleam in his eye that seemed to say that he had seen marvels that would leave poets speechless and encountered enigmas that would perplex philosophers for eons.

~*~

The next two months fall into a new routine. Trip out to Mars, and then testing when I get back. I realize that, not only is this a historic trip, but it is also a daunting task. They say that they are looking for the captain of a colony ship that possess not only the skills to navigate through the vastness of space, but also the wisdom and fortitude to lead their fellow travelers through the trials and tribulations of a long and perilous journey.

Rumor has it they also want someone that looks the part. This has caused a number of those who didn't feel photogenic enough, or those who have more visible replacement parts, to quietly drop out of the competition. I would drop out, after all a petite woman does not look like a Viking captain, but the extra pay will help pay off my daughter's graduate school, and to be honest, it beats just hanging around Clarke Station with nothing to do between runs. So, I decide to test for both Captain and Pilot.

It Takes A Village

During this time, all ships were called to Cyrus for crew evaluations. Even my engineer was hoping to win any posting just to get to be part of history.

Once all of the prospective crew and captains had arrived, we were all called to a briefing.

Port Admiral Kinnison called us to order. "Before you are tested and designated for the crew of this historic colony, Captain Shakleton will give you all an update about TRAPPIST-1e so you know where you will be going and what the colonist can expect. We anticipate that the ship will need to stay in orbit for a few months while things are ferried down and the colony established. So, your insights and assistance will be vital for their success. Captain Shakleton, the podium is yours."

Edward steps up to the podium and squares his shoulders; knowing him as I do, I know he is just loving the spotlight. "TRAPPIST-1e orbits an ultracool dwarf star known as TRAPPIST-1. This star is located just under forty-one light-years from Earth, and from here it is in the constellation of Aquarius. TRAPPIST-1e has a similar mass to Earth's and its radius, density, gravity, and temperature ranges are slightly lower than on the Earth, so the average is less like the tropics and more like northern Europe — around twenty degrees with a constant slight breeze from light side to the dark. More on that in a minute. The gravity on the surface of TRAPIST-1e is about eighty percent that of the earth. This is much closer to Earth normal than any of the colonies in the Solar System.

"Our findings show that in spite of TRAPPIST-1 being a red dwarf the stellar flux is about sixty percent of that on Earth, but more than on the surface of Mars, and I have been told that they have adapted solar power to respond to the stellar output in terms of wavelengths and quantity.

"One year on TRAPPIST 1e is just over six Earth days, about one hundred and forty six hours. Like Luna, TRAPIST-1e is tidally locked so one hemisphere permanently faces the star. The recommendation was to put the colony on the termination lines to take advantage of both the light and dark sides. This will affect how people live as there will be full time light or dark, with the colony in a band of constant twilight. One possibility is that the colony will actually be mostly between the twilight and darker side with mirrors to reflect sunlight at the appropriate location or times. This would also have the benefit of reducing the risks of high UV or x-ray bursts from the sun. I am told that the initial colonies will be underground to better maintain the Earth's level of light and sleep cycles with the intention of extending farming into the constant light zone (shades can be used for plants that can't handle continual light), and industry into the constant dark zone where solar power can be provided while keeping the temperature constant.

"We found that there were a variety of climates ranging from warm temperate along the termination lines to frozen on the dark side. These temperature differences can also be used for power generation.

"As a habitable planet, it is not surprising that we found life. The samples that we brought back are being tested on Ceres for compatibility with Earth life, but while there we found the water was refreshing and a few plants that registered as safe to eat. While to our eyes the star light was white, while we were outdoors the plants were mostly red, reflecting the red wavelengths of the solar light. Inside, under white light, they were much darker, almost a mud brown in color. Some the plants were dark gray both inside and outside." He points to someone in the back of the room, "do you have a question?"

"Yes, do you know if they are looking at using mirrors to light up or warm the dark side?"

"I understand that it is being considered around the edges, but I don't know if it is being considered for further into the dark. That is an interesting idea."

It Takes A Village

Admiral Kinnison steps forward. "Thank you, Captain Shakleton, for your report. We all eagerly await the results from the lab tests on the samples that you and your crew brought back with you. Once these tests are finalized, they will be defining the optimal genetics for the colonists. To answer astrographer Hermann, space-based mirrors can be used to increase the amount of stelar energy that reaches a specific point of the TRAPIST-1e. They have been theorized as a method of warming the dark side enough to enable growing or living there. Right now, it is unclear whether this will work, but the colony will be sent with the necessary satellites to enable it. Part of the colony ship's mission will be to put those satellites into a stable geocentric orbit to enable this. After that it will be up to the colonists to see how it works. Given the type of light and UV levels, air pressure, etc. we will be better able to identify people that might thrive there rather suffer. So, just as we found those from high altitudes do best with Mars' low atmospheric pressure, we will be able to define the same for TRAPIST-1e."

~*~

The crew tests are rigorous, designed to push the pilots to their limits and reveal any flaws in their abilities. Candidates must navigate through unknown space, execute emergency maneuvers, and demonstrate their command of the ship's systems. But it is not just their technical skills that are being evaluated — they must also prove themselves to be a leader, able to make difficult decisions under pressure and inspire confidence in those under their command.

The tests are worse than when I went for my pilot's license. Just to name a few of them with their official descriptions:
- ➢ Navigation Test: The candidate must demonstrate the ability to navigate through asteroid fields, using complex mathematical calculations and advanced technology to avoid collisions.

It Takes A Village

- Emergency Maneuvers Test: The candidate must show the ability to respond quickly to unexpected emergencies, such as sudden changes in course or unexpected obstacles.
- Leadership Test: The candidate will be put in charge of a team of crew members and must demonstrate the ability to lead and inspire them, even under extreme pressure.
- Decision-Making Test: The candidate will be presented with difficult decisions and must demonstrate the ability to make sound, rational choices in a timely manner.
- Systems Test: The candidate must demonstrate proficiency in operating the ship's systems, including navigation, life support, communication, and propulsion.
- Psychological Test: The candidate's mental and emotional stability will be evaluated under high-stress situations, such as simulated emergencies and prolonged isolation.
- Medical Test: The candidate must undergo a thorough medical examination to ensure that they are physically and mentally fit for the journey.
- Training Test: The candidate must complete a rigorous training program, including simulations of various scenarios that they may encounter during the journey.
- Communications Test: The candidate must demonstrate their ability to communicate effectively with other crew members, as well as with mission control on Earth.
- Interpersonal Test: The candidate's ability to work well with others will be evaluated, as they will be leading a team of diverse individuals on a long and challenging journey.
- Wilderness Survival Test: The candidate's ability to survive under unexpected circumstances will be tested as if something goes wrong and the crew may need to quickly adapt and improvise to the survive in the TRAPIST-1e environment.

It Takes A Village

Of these, only two are worth mentioning. First was the Medical Test: they wanted to see our medical results at both zero-G and at two-G to make sure we would be able to properly perform in any conceivable condition. Several people couldn't handle prolonged high-G, and were dropped from consideration. It seems that they had all the telemetry and results from my Mars run, so they waived my high-G test.

The second was not described, but they locked us in a simulated ship for what turned out to be a week, the clocks all ran fast so we thought it was longer. One part of this test was two kids, twins, who kept coming up to the pilot at random times and asking, "are we there yet?" Each time they would show up I would point to the counter of ship's days and ask them to read it and then tell me if was close to one hundred and eighty five. Each time, they would sheepishly say no and go away. Not everyone did so well. One of cargo the pilots cracked after the tenth time and went all Anakin on them. They sedated him and took him away to recover. The admiralty was understanding. He was allowed to leave the testing process to go back to his solo runs.

Over time, there were both betting pools and unofficial ranking boards. No one was surprised to see Shakleton consistently listed at the top. My cousin is basking in the praise.

As the weeks pass, the competition intensifies. The candidates are all highly skilled and determined, each one pushing themselves to their limits in an effort to stand out from the rest.

The Earth-based admiralty watches closely, analyzing each candidate's performance with a critical eye.

~*~

And so, at last, the decision was made. They call together all the crews to Clarke Station for one of the largest broadcast announcements. Port

It Takes A Village

Admiral Kinnison takes the stage. "After a rigorous search and many difficult tests, one person has proven themselves worthy of being the captain of this historical first colony ship. But first, we would like to announce the name of this historical ship. Many names were suggested, and all were considered. Names like the Cressy, Friendship, Har Zion, Hōkūle'a, Kusari, la Santa Clara, Mariposa, Mayflower, Sirius, and Zheng He were considered. In keeping with Captain Shackleton's historic discovery, the USES Endurance that he used to visit this potential colony will be preserved as a historical site. This first colony ship will use a new designation USCS, United Solar Colony Ship. In this case, it will be the USCS Kon-Tiki, and the ship's AI will be known as Tiki, after the first man created in Māori mythology.

"There has been much speculation about the kind of captain that we were looking for. Obviously, we want someone that has experience as a captain and can handle the majority of the ships systems should it be necessary. But in the end, there was only one captain that consistently impressed the review board.

"Would captain Shackleton please come up onto the stage?" No surprise that he won, he checked out the planet and was always on top of the ranking. "Captain Cecily Shackleton please join us on the stage." As I hear my name called out, I am floored.

As I step onto the stage, the admiral continues, "The admiralty thought long and hard about the key criteria for the captain of this historic trip. For exploration, we need someone that can deal with the unexpected and work in a small team. Obviously, for a colony ship we are looking for something different — someone who can not only navigate through the dangers of space, but also someone who can resolve interpersonal differences as well as technical challenges, inspire people as well as manipulate computer systems, build a community as well as a base. Captain Cecily Shackleton — or can I call you

'Captain Space Mom' — your record and experience show you as the perfect candidate." The audience erupts into applause.

After a minute of standing there bewildered, I realize that I need to say something. I have nothing prepared. My cousin, Captain Edward Shackleton comes out from behind the curtain. "Our family has a motto Fortitudinem Vincimus, which translates to 'Through endurance, we conquer.'" He smiles, "our umpteenth great-grandfather once said to one of his sisters: 'You cannot think what it is like to tread where no one has trodden before.' And he was right. It was amazing. But your passengers and crew will be doing it every day as they build this new colony." He gives me a hug and whispers, "enjoy this, and don't worry about me. I have other planets to find."

Then he reaches behind his back, "There is an old family tradition. Back in nineteen hundred and seven, Sir Ernest Shackleton brought twenty-five cases of Mackinlay's Rare Old Highland Malt Whisky on his trip to the Antarctic to keep his crew happy. Now it would be inappropriate to send that much with you." He hands me a bottle. "But we have to keep up the family tradition."

It Takes A Village

About Eric Klein

Eric is a lifelong science fiction and fantasy reader who has always enjoyed those stories that show how the science and technology can affect people's lives. By day he works in hi-tech, lecturing on telecom security (at the hardware level, not about the people who use phones to commit fraud).

As he has done quite a bit of travel for fun and business, he has included events in the story that are based on personal experiences. For example, several years ago he accompanied his wife to an International Scientific Congress in Montreal. That particular week had several major events going on in the city. Other than the congress, there was a weeklong comedy street fair (Think jugglers, mimes, other performers, shows, and street art like a tree made out of circuit boards), and the North American Gay and Lesbian Choir competition. As you can see it was a very mixed crowd. Some of those events have been recreated in the story.

He is experimenting with writing styles, and his debut book is written in the style of the Golden years of Science Fiction, giving more than a passing nod to some of greats Arthur C. Clarke, Isaac Asimov, and Robert A. Heinlein to name a few.

You can find Eric's works on Amazon:
amazon.com/author/ericlklein

THE QUIET REVOLUTION

By Jane Jago

When asked what inspired this story, Jane responded:

> The story was inspired by the idea that even a leviathan can be halted by a grain of sand. The model of a polarised society that was basically broken gave me a way to show that you don't have to be famous, or wealthy to change what needs changing, all you have to be is courageous.

It Takes A Village

THE QUIET REVOLUTION — Jane Jago

The teenagers sat in attentive silence as a bent old woman came and took her seat in the centre of the circle. She smiled at them and her very blue eyes shone brightly in the brown-seamed skin of her face. They settled to listen, expecting a fine story from such a venerable citizen. They weren't to be disappointed…

Her voice was quiet, but nobody missed a word as they listened to their history from the viewpoint of someone who had seen it with her own eyes.

When human beings came here to start a brand-new home, they called the place Utopia. Which was taking hubris to a whole new level, even if the intention was pure.

Things went smoothly enough when the first settlers set themselves to build Utopian cities or to cultivate the virgin land. Working from dawn to dusk on a newly terraformed planet doesn't leave too much time for factionalism and everyone was deemed to be of equal value. Maybe the spirit of sharing would even have lasted had not the final shipment of stevedores and manual labourers been drawn from Terran prison colonies where brutality was the norm. Sometime on their intergalactic journey, the convict labourers killed their jailers and when the transport landed their sole intention was to take the new planet for their own.

The beauty of Utopia was despoiled by greed and the lust for power, while running battles befouled the streets. Those who sought power fell into two camps: misogynistic men who called themselves 'alpha males' and considered women as no more than the vessels for their lusts; and misandristic women who saw no future unless men were subjugated and reduced to sperm providers or castrated as pets. Each camp boasted heavily armed militiamen and women whose sole function was to enforce the will of their leaders by whatever means they saw fit.

By the turn of the century, the two gender-based ideologies, who had more or less carved the planet up between them, became more and more entrenched in their beliefs and less and less likely to put aside their enmity for anything less than world domination.

It's not surprising, then, that those people who lived outside the militia-controlled cities started hiding their children away. Sure, some hid them to drive up the profit when they ripened, but most just wanted to keep their little ones safe from the marauding militias.

While men and women fought each other for every blade of grass and every drop of water, the Utopian beauty around them was going to hell in a handcart — until the quiet revolution happened and changed us all forever.

The change started unremarkably enough, somewhere out in the boondocks when a girl farmer fell into the hands of the misogynist militia. What she suffered was bad, but it would've been much worse except she was comely and soft spoken, and she caught the eye of their general who took her for his own. They say he wanted nothing more than to keep her, but she had other ideas and on one moonless night she disappeared.

She took something with her that night. The general's twin babies, warm and secure in her womb as she walked the secret pathways to her homeland. She came to her time in a partially ruined cabin of chinked logs where only a handful of half-tame dogs saw her travail. But she was as strong and placid as a plough ox and gave life to her babies with little trouble.

It was a worry to her to find that one was a boy, and a voice in her head bade her leave him for the wolves. She might even have done that if he hadn't cried and opened his milky blue eyes. When she was fit to travel, she carried the two children under her cloak as she made her way back to what the militia had left of her home. It wasn't much, but it was sufficient to shelter her and her young until they were strong enough to move higher into the forest where none but the country-bred would think to go.

Once they were safe, the children grew strong and tall in the good country air. By the time they reached adulthood the girl was as comely and gentle as her mother, and the boy was a young giant with his father's massy shoulders and huge hands. He was as red-bearded as his father too, but where he differed was in the gentleness of his soul and his innate respect for womenfolk in their every incarnation.

In the high mountains, people know that inbreeding isn't good for the livestock any more than it is good for the human race. This being the case, regular markets happen at the places where mountainous trails cross in hidden valleys. At one such market the general's son met the only child of a grower of crops who farmed in a valley far away from his own family. It was hard for him to say farewell to his mother and his sister, but the heart knows what the heart knows, and they married — setting up home in father's house.

Theirs was a happy union and they were blessed with twelve children, of whom I am the youngest child, and the eighth daughter. Us kids were as happy as piglets in mud, brought up in the old way in direct defiance of how the outside world sought to set man and woman at each other's throats.

We were simple folk, with little money and little formal education — except for first sister who was as clever as she could hold together and won a place at university in the city. For all her cleverness, the rest of us might have lived and died in obscurity had it not been for one single act of courage and affection that began a trickle of sand which, in turn, became a landslide.

I was six years old, and still learning my letters when it happened. It was autumn and the last of the crops had been gathered in when a runner came from the next valley with the unwelcome news that we had visitors. The misandrist militia was coming to pay us a visit. Father stretched his long bones and put a hand over Mother's fingers as they lay on the scrubbed wood of the kitchen table.

"If I go with them quietly, they'll probably leave you in peace."

Mother pulled her hand away and her eyes flashed fire.

"What if they do? There'll always be other families ripped apart by this senselessness. No. I'll not cut the heart out of my chest to feed their hatred."

Father took her face in his hands. "Would you have me run then? Or hide?"

"No. Not that neither. We'll stand together and defy them."

Father opened his mouth, but our oldest sister, the clever one who was home from her job in the big city for a holiday, hushed him with an upraised hand.

"If you two are brave enough, there could be a way. But nobody can guarantee your safety."

The look of trust that passed between Father and Mother gave us all a hope, and we sat quiet as mice while the grown-ups planned.

We littler ones didn't understand much of it, but what we did know was that every one of us had a part to play and we'd only have one chance to get it right.

Our brothers rounded up the livestock and headed high up the mountain's secret trails to where neither they nor the beasts could be found. The rest of us scurried around making sure there was no sign of boys nor beasts to be seen. We were only just ready in time because the last sweeping was being done when we heard the growl of a tracked vehicle heading up from the valley floor. Even though we knew it would have to stop in a clearing a good half mile from the house, the noise was such as to send fear into our hearts, but Mother and Father calmed us and we went to our assigned places.

I, being small and pretty, went with Mother to the front porch where she stood and waited. It took the uninvited ones a goodish while to climb the steep track but Mother and me waited in silence. I held on to her leg in its old khaki coveralls and I could just about be brave, although something in the way she stood made me understand that what we were doing was dangerous. I think I'd have given in to fear but the thought of them taking my tall, gentle father was enough to straighten my spine. I busied my mind by watching a drone buzz lazily overhead swooping and diving like an ungainly mechanical bird.

When our visitors breasted the rise at the end of the trail I counted a full thirteen militiawomen in their black uniforms. They were sweating some, and a couple seemed out of breath, but their leader stalked forward and glared at Mother.

"Madonna," she said harshly, "we come at the behest of the ruling council in the manner of you harbouring an entire male."

Mother looked at her coolly. "Entire male what? Dog? Horse? Sheep? Cow?"

"A male human."

"A man then."

The militiawoman spat on the floor between Mother's feet. "A rapist."

"A what?"

"A rapist. All human males are rapists."

Mother laughed, clear as a bell. "Not so."

"The law declares it so."

"Whose law is that, precisely?"

"The law of the ruling council of women."

"Who have no authority save what they take by force."

"What if that is so? It makes no difference. I and my company are here to take away your male creature and see it executed as is the order of the council."

It Takes A Village

I felt the tremor that ran through Mother's body, but she spoke calmly enough.

"Executed? On what grounds?"

The militiawoman softened her voice somewhat. "It must be killed, because it is too old for castration or the sperm bank to be options. Just stand aside and we will take it and go."

"What if I refuse to stand aside?"

"Then we will still take your creature, but we'll also burn you out and hunt down any male issue of your sick union."

She gestured towards a woman who carried a flamethrower across her chest.

Mother looked her in the face. "The answer is still no."

"On your head be it. Stand aside."

"I will not."

"Then I will shoot you where you stand. Would you make your daughters motherless, just for the sake of a rapist?"

"Would you make yourself a murderer, just for the sake of a lie?"

"It is not murder if I use my weapon in the carrying out of my duty."

She took the pistol out of her holster and levelled it at Mother.

It was my turn to speak now, and I found the courage from somewhere.

"Why are you pointing that there gun at Mother?"

"Because she puts the life of a man before you and your sisters' lives."

I pretended to be thinking for a few seconds before I shook my head. I was supposed to beg her not to shoot my Mother but that wasn't the words that came out of my mouth.

"She don't," I said. "She puts our family before folks what thinks it's okay to kill anyone what disagrees with them. And that ain't no manner of use coz vilence never solves nothing."

The militiawomen reared back as if I had slapped her.

It Takes A Village

"You little bitch," she hissed and turned the gun on me.

What happened next was so quick I didn't have chance to be frightened, Mother took half a step and put herself between me and the militiawoman at the same second as the woman herself made a queer groaning noise and dropped her gun before sinking to the ground. One of her own soldiers walked forward and looked down at her officer.

"We don't shoot little kids," she said. "Specially not ones who might even be speaking sense."

The silence was tense as her companions sorted out their feelings about what had just happened. It seemed as if most agreed with her. Only the one with the flamethrower was inclined to disagree. She turned the muzzle of her weapon on the hay barn where a year's fodder for the animals was stored.

"I'm not gonna kill anyone," she declared, "but there has to be a reckoning. We can't let these hayseeds disrespect us. Not ever."

As she spoke, Father and three of my sisters ran to stand between her and the barn.

Father said nothing, and neither did my sisters. The militiawoman's aim wobbled, but then she steadied.

"Move," she snapped, "unless you want to burn with whatever's in that store."

I heard the soft sound of a blowpipe and the flamethrower carrier clutched her neck.

Oldest sister stepped out of the trees. She had something strapped to her chest and she stood tall and proud.

"That was just a dart. The next one won't be so harmless. You aren't going to take my father and you aren't going to burn the fodder for the animals who will keep us alive through the winter. Face it. You lost."

Flamethrower woman hissed. "You'll have to kill us before we walk away without what we came for."

It Takes A Village

"Says who?"

"Says me." She turned to the rest of the group. "Best if we kill all of them. Say they were resisting and we had to shoot our way out. It's what we've always done. Who's to know?"

Sister pointed at the thing on her chest and at the lazy drone buzzing in the sky. "Just about everyone already knows. Every info screen on every street in every city is live streaming this."

The flamethrower turned towards my brave sister, but before it had chance to send its stream of obscene violence, its wielder fell to the ground alongside her companion.

Sister lifted a shoulder. "Sometimes violence is all we have when faced with extreme peril." She lifted her face to the drone in the sky. "Sisters and brothers, you have before you a stark choice. You can live your lives dictated to by anger and hate. Or you can join hands together in the hope of a better world."

The remaining militiawomen bowed their heads and my parents clung together like children.

I don't remember the days of quiet uprising in the fields and meadows, nor the horror of the battles that raged in the city streets, and it wasn't until I was full grown that I came to understand that The Quiet Revolution that brought about a society of true gender equality began on our family mountain where a tall man's gentle spirit inspired love that faced down the forces of prejudice.

But I suppose in the end all that really matters is that men and women work side by side now, nurturing the landscape and the children who are only born of love and consent.

My parents' bodies are buried in the Grove of Heroes at the Capitol and people make pilgrimages to lay flowers on their graves. I suspect they look down on their marble mausoleum in some horror, but it's okay, their hearts are

It Takes A Village

here on the farm where they lived their lives — buried side by side under the kindly shade of a great oak tree in the middle of the high pasture.

It Takes A Village

About Jane Jago

Jane Jago is an eccentric genre hopping pensioner, who writes for the sheer enjoyment of the craft and gets in terrible trouble because of her attitude. Her writing includes modern-day thrillers sitting side by side with sword and sorcery, wicked dragons, and short stories and verse.

In addition, she is proud to be the co-author of the *Dai and Julia Mysteries* with her good friend E.M. Swift-Hook.

Find out more about Jane at her blog: workingtitleblogspot.com
With her works available on Amazon via: author.to/janejago

It Takes A Village

MOUNTAIN VIEW

By Assaph Mehr

When asked what inspired this story, Assaph responded:

My mother passed away a couple of months before writing this story. Physically, at least. Mentally she hasn't been there for a few years, lost to Alzheimer's. My dad passed away nearly two years ago, and though he was mostly sound in mind, towards the end that cancer the has been eating at his body also started to affect his mind. I've seen my grandparents lost to dementia as their age tipped a critical point. Truth be told, the prospect of getting dementia scares the shit out of me.

I also miss their stories, their wit and humour, the passions that drove their lives throughout the tumultuous 20th century and the wisdom they gained. I wish I had more time to sit and listen to them. We don't do this enough, as a society.

It Takes A Village

MOUNTAIN VIEW — Assaph Mehr

Dawn came late at winter. The old man pushed his wheeled walker into the hall, turned the lights on, and began laboriously shuffling across the floor towards the other end, nudging the walker an inch after straggling inch.

"And here we have the main entertainment area," a prim woman in her late fifties said as she entered some time later. "It's where we hold bingo, sing-alongs, and families can visit their relatives. Well, those who have visitors; it's a rare occurrence these days. But this is the main day-area for those not bedridden, and where we try to herd them all the better to keep an eye on them."

The younger woman following her looked around the hall, trying to absorb everything with her large, dark-brown eyes. Her black frizzy hair was tied in a queue, and the nametag on her crisp new nurse's uniform read 'Cassandra Miller,' though she preferred everyone call her Cassie.

"And that, in a nutshell, is Mountain View Home for the Elderly. Any questions?"

"No, Ms. Mead. Will you introduce me to the residents?"

"Pfft. It's not like they'll remember you as soon as you walk out of the room. ISN'T IT RIGHT, MR. APOLLINARIS?" The older woman turned to the elderly man inching his walker across the hall.

Apollinaris didn't even turn his head, just stared ahead at the door at the other end. Wisps of white hair floated around his bald pate as he clenched his toothless gums in determination to continue step by stumbling step.

"See?" said Mead. "Mr. Apollinaris has this routine, where he turns the lights on in the morning, shuffles across the hall, and turns it off from the other end in the evening. Drives me batty, but at least he gets some exercise. Well, as much exercise as he can handle; he has to stop and sit on his walker to rest more often than not. They're all like that, minds lost to time. If you let them, they'll talk your ear off. Sometimes they can get quite difficult. We suffer the harmless quirks, but you'll do well to smile, wave, and ignore any of their outlandish requests."

"Don't worry, Ms. Mead." Cassandra ran her hands down her shirt to smooth her outfit. "I've had frisky gentlemen before and can handle them all quite gently but firmly."

"Oh, it's nothing like that. They're mostly senile and have no clue what they're talking about, and you can never be sure what's going to come out of their mouths next. It's their dementia speaking, and best to simply pay them no mind. Even the ones still ambulant, don't let them fool you. The other residents, those who won't leave their beds, are at least easier to manage. Anyway, stick to the schedule and get along with your tasks, and you'll do just fine. Now come along and I'll show you where the pool is. Some of our residents, Naphtali in particular, are enjoying aqua-aerobics classes."

Cassie cast a last look around the hall. Apollinaris put the brakes on his walker's wheels and sat down, wheezing but still staring ahead at the other side. A couple sat by a window, she knitting a small vest and he painting storm clouds in watercolours. Two men sat at a table playing checkers. A lone man tinkered with an old radio, its parts arranged on the table in front of him and a walking cane leaning against his chair. And a woman with vacant eyes slowly ate porridge, droplets of which dribbled on her chin.

"Ms. Miller!" came a cry from the corridor, and Cassie hurried out to follow Mead.

~*~

It Takes A Village

Cassie looked at the single line on the test stick in vague disappointment. She had almost given up, after so long. She chucked it in the bin, washed her hands, and went out of the bathroom.

Evan looked up as she entered the kitchen, and Cassie shook her head slightly. "Made you a sandwich," Evan said as he handed her a packed lunch box, "and I put in some of those special tea bags." He squeezed her shoulder, and Cassie wondered how long till he gave up on the whole idea of ever having children of their own. Gave up on her. They tried everything from IVF to herbal medicine, but nothing seemed to work.

Work, at least, had quickly settled into a busy routine. It kept Cassie moving and focusing on the residents, whose problems she could sometimes fix. "How are you doing this morning, Mr. Apollinaris?"

"Call me Saul," the old man said. "'Apollinaris' sounds so formal."

"How about we try something else today, Saul? Perhaps we could take a walk outside for a change, and enjoy the sunlight?"

"That's exactly what I'm doing in here, except I don't need to be reminded of the fucking swans." The old man poked a finger at his walker.

She patted the old man on his shoulder gently and moved on, having learnt when he's about to go off on a tangent. She helped Cheri with her porridge, cleaning up the spills and dribbles. The old woman was on a cereal-only diet, not for any medical reasons but simply refusing to eat anything else. She was physically fine, but Cassie wondered if her restricted diet contributed to her deteriorated mental faculties.

Joe and June sat in their usual place next to the window. "Why not try painting some flowers, or birds?" Cassie asked Joe, looking over his shoulder at yet another thunderstorm.

The old man kept at his watercolours, but his wife commented, "Let him have his lightning bolts, dear. His days of actual glory are long past."

It Takes A Village

"Hmph!" was Joe's only response. Cassie wondered how she and Evan would be as an old couple, if they'd even be together. Would they drift apart, or grow as comfortable as Joe and June seemed with each other — jibes aside.

Leonard was working on another mechanical puzzle, the old man fascinated by anything metallic. He rubbed his gimp leg absentmindedly, but otherwise seemed fine. Minnie was watching some talking head on the TV shouting about the stock market. Minnie was muttering under her breath as she was taking notes. She used to be a trader, Ms. Mead had told her, though by the looks of her she hadn't made a successful trade since the great depression. Cassie put her hand on the old woman's shoulder. "How are you doing today? Is the market going up?"

"My record's better at stocks than playing checkers against Martin today," Minnie said. "Would you be a dear and bring me a phone? I need to call my broker."

"Perhaps I can get you some more graph paper for your charts?" Cassie operated within Ms. Mead's guidelines; Minnie wasn't to call financiers or lawyers without Mead's supervision, as the administrator was concerned with diminishing mental capacity and squandering of funds. To Cassie's eyes Minnie seemed like she knew more than Ms. Mead and the TV pundits put together, but she didn't want to stand up to her boss about this.

"Graphs? I always trade on fundamentals, dear, on intrinsic value. Anyway, I want to listen to this next segment. The proposed legislation about AI will have dramatic impact on the venture capital landscape." She turned the volume up on the TV.

Cassie turned away and saw Martin wave her over. "Play a round of checkers with me?" he asked. "Marc went out on an errand, and it gets lonely playing against myself."

She looked around the room quickly, confirming all was well and Ms. Mead wasn't around, and sat down. "Why not?" She smiled at Martin. There

It Takes A Village

were always things that needed to be done, but as a geriatric nurse she saw her role as more than just caring for physical needs. Giving an old man's mind some exercise would improve his life no less than physiotherapy.

The game was quick, and by Martin's mischievous smile they both knew he had her five moves in. "Don't feel bad," he said, "Marc and I have been practicing this for ages. It'll be a good game to play with your child, teach them strategy."

Her smile was brittle as she reminded herself he didn't know her struggles and his comment was just good-natured. "I'm sure it will be, when the time comes," she said and stood up.

Martin put a warm hand on hers. "It will happen," he said looking deep into her eyes. "All you need is a sandwich."

"Wha…?"

"You've tried everything, didn't you?" Martin persisted. "Been to the medicine men and seen the wise women? And yet you still can't conceive. I'm telling you, there are other paths, and they start with a sandwich."

Cassie pulled her hand away and straightened her uniform. "I think it's time I checked on Virginia," she said as she fled the hall.

~*~

Cassie was fixing her makeup in front of the big mirror when Ms. Mead walked into the restroom. Cassie didn't know why the old man's words got to her so, and though she thought she had it under control her manager saw through her façade.

"What is it?" Ms. Mead asked in a surprisingly gentle tone.

"Oh, it's nothing. He didn't mean anything. Evan and I have been trying for a child for so long, and sometimes well-meaning comments hurt, you know? Even if they're good intentions. And then they all go off on a tangent, and telling me a sandwich can fix my problems…" Cassie let out a harsh laugh.

"Yes, well, you just ignore them, dear," said Ms. Mead. "When the elderly get dementia, they live in a world of their own, not one you want to sink into. Just smile and move on, and certainly don't give in to any silly requests about food outside their prescribed nutrition."

"Which reminds me," Cassie turned to face Mead, "should we perhaps alter Cheri's diet? She's only ever eating porridge, and I think perhaps some more protein might help with her deteriorating mental faculties."

"She gets agitated and fights it. Not worth the hassle, so the nutritionist devised her an adequate whole-grain diet. Just go with what the cook makes her, it's for everyone's best."

"And what about giving an iPad to Joe? He likes to paint and maybe that would help break his isolation."

"Most definitely no electronics! Please, just stick to the routine, and don't entertain any of their requests. They're fragile, in mind and body, and we know what's best for them regardless of their wild ideas." Ms. Mead was back to her usual prim self, and her eyes and her tone signalled she won't hear more of this, not if Cassie wanted to keep her new job.

~*~

A year passed, the seasons flashing by and only winter lingering, the earth frozen and plants dormant till it seemed the only natural state of things. Cassie and Evan hadn't officially stopped trying for children, even though the doctors ran out of ideas and tried to gently hint that perhaps it's time to move on. Cassie and Evan didn't talk about giving up, but felt they've exhausted all options. Exhausted themselves most of all. Cassie threw herself into the care of the residents at Mountain View.

It Takes A Village

"Does Joe still talk?" She asked June, who was knitting next to her husband as usual.

"Not much. I think he can, but he resents the world, resents being stuck here. That's why he paints the open skies."

If Joe heard and understood his wife's words he gave no sign, concentrating instead on the canvas in front of him.

"But why only storms?" Cassie persisted. She wanted to know her wards better, to give them warmth in the winter of their lives.

"He just loves the sky. Used to be up there every moment he could, you know."

"Was he an aviator? Is that why he's always drawing clouds and lightning storms?"

"Something like that."

"I thought perhaps a different medium might help. Look, I brought an iPad even though Ms. Mead said not to. I'm sure if we could get him to paint on it eventually the device might help him start communicating again."

Cassie started to draw a slim tablet from her cargo pants' side pocket, but the old woman laid a gentle hand on hers and pushed it back down. "Let's keep your electronics away, shall we? And let's leave Joe to his watercolour storms. Anyway, how are you doing?" June changed the subject. She held up her knitting — a baby's onesie suit — and said, "You strike me as the maternal type. Any expectation of pitter-patter of little feet?"

A sensitive subject, but Cassie felt only grandmotherly concern from the old lady. Her own parents, let alone grandparents, have passed away, and for a reason she couldn't quite fathom the words just bubbled up. "We've given up. We never talk about it anymore. We tried everything. The treatments just got expensive, and we tried the herbal remedies, and nothing helped. We just… stopped." She stared out the window lost in thought. "I know Evan loves me, but I fear we'll grow apart. I pray to all the gods we'll become stronger, not crumble into bitterness."

"Ah," said June. "Perhaps I can offer some advice? I've helped many women in your position, back in my day." Cassie turned towards her, and June said, "What you need is a strong foundation, a consecrated hearth. But seeing as Virginia is on her deathbed, you should speak with Martin. He's not the blustering macho people think. They forget who he was married to. Listen to him, follow his advice, and he'll help you with your problem."

Cassie scrunched her brow, but the old woman put her hand on hers, and something in the warm touch of the ancient skin dissolved the strangeness of the advice. Cassie glanced to where Martin was playing by himself, Marc gone on a trip again.

"Go," said the old woman.

Cassie went. "Ready for me to beat you this time?" She was getting better at checkers, though she was sure he was going easy on her.

Martin smiled, waved at the chair opposite, and reset the board. They played a furious couple of rounds, Cassie concentrating hard to try and beat the old man's strategy — and just not sure how to bring the subject up. What did June even mean? How could this elderly gentleman help her start a family?

She pushed the chair back to stand, but Martin smiled and asked, "Best out of three?" She leaned back in and helped reset the board.

That round was slower, thoughtful. "It's a game of strategy," Martin mused, "but people forget that 'strategy' isn't just about winning. It's just as much about your home, the prosperity of your fields, as it is about attacking."

Cassie stared at the board, calculating her next moves and letting him ramble on. It was a while before she realised he asked her a question and was expecting an answer. "Hm? What was that?"

"I asked whether you balance war and love in your life. You can't win one with the other, as I found out with my wife."

It Takes A Village

That brought up June's strange message and her own longing came flooding back. Was he doing it to distract her? She looked into Martin's eyes, and saw gentleness, homeliness. "We've been trying to conceive," she blurted before she realised she was speaking aloud, "but it seems like we're destined to be childless."

"Nonsense. People attribute to the fates much more than they should. You need a strong foundation with your husband. Why is no one teaching the old ways any more? Jumping straight to pills before addressing the real problem. Tell you what, you bring your husband here, and we'll have a chat, and you'll see some changes."

"I'm sure he's not — "

"Then skip him," Martin insisted, "but bring a sandwich and we'll sort things out. What have you got to lose, eh?"

"Sure," she said. "Maybe on Sunday."

She rose from her chair, and Martin grabbed her wrist. He was surprisingly strong for a man of his age. "This isn't to be trivialised. And not just any sandwich, but one from an Italian deli, and it must contain a slice each of ham, grilled lamb, and roast beef."

It was so oddly specific that it took Cassie by surprise. She knotted her eyebrows, but before she could respond Martin said, "The rest doesn't really matter, but the less garnishes the better. Just those three meats are important. Makes it easier to warm up and smell delicious."

Martin let go of her hand, but kept looking into her eyes. "Bless the foundation of married life, of hearth and field, and the fruits will follow."

Cassie stared into his eyes for a moment, and left without a word.

~*~

It Takes A Village

Another cycle with no conception, and Cassie felt as barren as the frozen winter earth. On the way to Mountain View she stopped at the shops to drop Evan's business shirts at the dry cleaners. Outside, she passed the early childhood centre as a gaggle of women emerged, chatting excitedly while cooing at prams or nestling bundled-up round-faced babies close to their hearts. She wiped a sudden tear from her eye before the wind froze it shut, only to see the women enter the warm embrace of Papa Romano's Continental Delicacies. The last woman to enter the deli held the door open as she looked behind her. She caught sight of Cassie and smiled at her. "Coming in?"

What the hell, thought Cassie, and walked in. The group of women settled in the corner, ordering cappuccinos and babyccinos from a teenager armed with an order pad. Cassie walked to the main counter, past an array of delicate cakes and savoury pastries, to a section dedicated to sandwiches.

The mustachioed man behind the counter smiled at her and asked, "What can I get you, bella?"

"Do you do fresh sandwiches?" she asked as she scanned the available selection.

"Of course! What would you like?"

"Um, it might sound a bit strange, but a bun with a slice each of ham, lamb, and beef. And minimal garnishes."

"Ah! You want the suovetaurilia. It's a classic, but these days people don't want it no more. They think it's bad for them, but they just don't know any better." The man started to putter around his station, slapping things together. "I'll do you the special, like it's supposed to be. Goes back to ancient Rome, you know, and you're lucky cause I have wholemeal spelt buns. So we put the ham-off-the-bone — the sus in Latin, the roast lamb — ovis, and the roast beef — il toro. And what we don't do, is put tomato. You think Italian is tomato, right? And often it is, but this goes back to before the new world, so I do it classico for you. Just a bit of pesto. Here you go!"

It Takes A Village

At the Mountain View parking lot Cassie picked the wrapped up cylinder from the passenger's seat, suddenly feeling foolish. What was she thinking? This was ridiculous, to say nothing about contravening the rules, which were for the benefit of the residents. The doctors and cooks knew what was best for the befuddled elderly. She would end up doing more harm with this dodgy sandwich, and all for what? For a silly idea just because she desperately longed for children of her own.

The sandwich reminded her of the mothers' group she saw at the shops. Babies and toddlers, smiling, crying, fussing, laughing. She thought about the children she would never have, would never see grow and become unique human beings. Would she and Evan see old age together, or were they destined to die alone? Like the Mountain residents, neglected by a society that had no room for the elderly, no time to visit them, relegating their care to professionals who dismissed everything they said as the rambling of dementia.

She stuffed the wrapped sandwich in her bag and hurried across the parking lot to start her afternoon shift.

~*~

As the sun sunk behind the mountain, old man Apollinaris reached the other end of the hall and turned the main lights off. The other residents took it as their cue to shuffle to the refectory and their evening meal. Cassie approached Martin as he was packing up the checkers set.

"This would probably taste much better than the boiled chicken and soggy carrots they're serving tonight." She smiled at Martin as she pulled the wrapped bundle from her equipment trolley.

Martin took the sandwich and unwrapped it with shaking hands. He bent over it, eyes closed, and breathed deeply the aromas of the three meats. There was a moment of stillness, of quiet peace. "I'll need you to say something," Martin said. "Repeat after me: Mars pater, eiusque rei ergo macte suovitaurilibus inmolandis esto."

"Err, what?"

The old man took her hand in his, his calloused skin warm and comforting. "There's so much that's different, but it's your intent of fertility that counts in the lustration."

"'Lustration?'"

"Purification. Now repeat! Mars pater…"

"Mars pater," Cassie repeated in a daze.

"Eiusque rei ergo…"

Cassie repeated the rest of the phrase after Martin, feeling like a schoolgirl learning some doggerel by rote. When they finished, he bent over the sandwich and breathed deeply again. He straightened with a smile as he looked at Cassie. Was he standing taller, his hair a shade darker?

"There was something about a father and this sandwich, but what did it all mean?" she asked.

"Think of it as a contract. You do something for me, this sacr… sandwich, and I do something for you. I took your intent at fertility as implied from our previous talks, and you have my blessing. Now all that remains is the fun part." Martin winked at her.

"Err, what?"

"Just go home to your husband." He put the partially unwrapped but otherwise untouched sandwich in her unresisting hands, and walked away. "I have to catch that exciting boiled chicken."

"What do I do with this?" Cassie lifted the sandwich.

"It's customary to share it with your household, but that's up to you," he said over his shoulder.

It was nearly midnight by the time she got home. Evan was watching a rerun of the Spartacus TV series. "Shall I make you a salad?" he asked her.

"Long story, but I have this leftover sandwich. Want some?" She unwrapped the sandwich, and though it was a few hours old the various roast meats still smelled appetising. She cut the sandwich in half and carried it on plates to the living room. They snuggled as they ate, watching the show which was more about prurient lasciviousness than historical facts.

They made love that night, and though she felt no different in the morning on her way to work a pair of swallows fluttered past her car.

~*~

Ms. Mead came limping down the hallway, cursing under her breath. "Are you alright?" Cassie asked her manager.

"It's that bloody awful Apollinaris! I swear he did it on purpose. Squishing my foot with his walker. You try to be nice, but they're all daft. I caught Joe trying to walk outside in his pyjamas during the rainstorm, and as I hustle him back inside and standing all wet Minnie shoved the Wall Street Journal in my face and prattled about business strategy. I try to go around her and Apollinaris runs over my foot. Now I'm wet, hurt, and cranky because they don't have the sense of roadkill." Mead took a deep breath to compose herself. She smoothed her dress, lifted her chin, and started to walk down the hallway. "It's no wonder their families don't come to visit them. Dementia is a horrible thing, and no one wants to hear jumbled stories born of an hallucinating mind."

Mead walked away, and Cassie hurried in the opposite direction. "I looked it up, you know, but it makes no sense," she told Martin when she cornered him at a quiet moment. "Suovetaurilia is some ancient ritual, it's not a sandwich."

"Things adapted over the centuries, often against our will," the old man answered.

It Takes A Village

"But you made me pray to Mars, the god of war and destruction. I just don't get it."

Martin sighed. "Sit down, you have a lot to learn."

They ended up in soft armchairs next to the bay windows, holding mugs of mint tea and looking at the blanket of snow outside. "Mars was a god of war, but also the god of fields. He was the protector. It's the Greek one, Ares, who was the brutal god of war, the reviled god of bloodlust and savagery. Conflating the two was natural, even though Joe grew to resent it. The relationship between humanity and its divinities is… complex. And fluid."

"That still doesn't explain anything," Cassie said.

"Humans think in symbols. And over time, the same symbol may acquire different meanings. So Father Mars, the protector of fields, was co-opted into Mars Ultor. And Quirinus was a different god of the people in peacetime, though you'll later find attestations of Mars Quirinus because they both wielded spears, quiris. And now no one remembers my br… him. And instead, when the Romans conquered the Greek, it's the educated Greek who wrote down their legends and suddenly Mars and Venus are in love in a big fat farce, though I was perfectly happy with my first wife, and now people think it's all the same mythology but with Latin names."

Cassie just stared at him, her tea forgotten. Martin drifted off, sipping his mint tea and staring out to the snow-covered trees. After a while, he took a deep breath and spoke again. "Look. A suovetaurilia is a sacrifice of a pig, a ram, and a bull by a man who petitions the protector of fields to save him and his from sickness, barrenness, destruction. To guarantee the fertility of fields and flourishing of harvests. While it wasn't held specifically in the month of March, the Matronalia was, the festival celebrated by women honouring Juno Lucina, she who brings children into the light. War, fields, fertility, motherhood all intertwined. You have been kind to us, and we wanted to help. There were perhaps those better suited to appeal to with your request, but most of the others have lost so much of their power, except my damn wife, who's still out in the world, but let's not talk about her. That sandwich was hardly a fresh sacrifice, but at least I'm still on people's lips and carry some weight in the world so I could act on your petition, different as it was. And now your womb is quickened, with our thanks for the kind ear you've lent us in the twilight of our existence."

Cassie's involuntarily laid her hand on her stomach. "Are you saying that by bringing you a sandwich you helped me get pregnant?"

"Well, yes. I thought you've picked up on who we are already," Martin replied. "You've got one of them thingies, right? You tried to give one to Joe. Just look up the origin of the name Martin."

The senile old man was playing some sick and twisted mind games on her, she thought. Cassie stood up, not trusting herself to speak. Ms. Mead is right, she thought as she walked out of the room. They were demented elderly patients, and she should focus on the chores of their care rather than listen to their fanciful hallucinations.

Four days later, her convictions about the Mountain View residents changed with the appearance of a plus sign on the home pregnancy test kit.

~*~

She googled the etymology of the name Martin. She googled a lot of other things, too. Cassie even went down a few internet rabbit holes of the occult, though she suspected most of those were no better than fantasy. She looked instead at the patient records, and when fact-checked they looked like as much fantasy as the wacko websites. Slowly, things began to make sense in a way that frightened her. But there was no denying her pregnancy, and though she hadn't told him yet there was no denying the sense of warmth and security about her and Evan's home either.

It Takes A Village

Cassie found June at a rare moment when she wasn't by Joe's side, and asked her to chat. Or was it the other way around? June was knitting yet another baby onesie, and eyeing Cassie's midsection with a sly smile.

"The others are your family, aren't they?" Cassie asked. And when the old woman nodded, she added "Would you tell me about how you all got here? I'd love to hear the truth, because everything I thought I knew seems wrong."

June gave her an appraising look. "Yes, you would. You're the first one to really listen in decades, you know, centuries even. We are a family, though who's the offspring or brother or husband of whom is a bit more complicated. We're old, and things get fuzzy over time, as you've seen. That's why we're here, in part." June looked at the confusion on Cassie's face, and said "Oh dear me, listen to me prattle. Let me start again."

The old woman's knitting needles kept clacking as she resumed speaking. "Symbols have a life of their own, never really dying. We are as much a part of nature as nature itself, as humanity and science are. No one perceives reality, no single mind can, and thinking is just an act of filtering to a manageable level of sense. Because imagination is more real than reality, the dedicated collective hallucinations of humans gave us consciousness and power. We live in the spaces between minds, the same as cultural identity. Later, humans remembered us but no longer needed us, and so we became… this. What you see before you. For many these memories weren't enough, and fading into obscurity meant fading in existence."

June let out a harsh chuckle. "I'm not sure who're the lucky ones, them or us. But let me tell you about those of us here. Take Martin for example. Fields and war were interlinked in early agrarian societies, needed to be defended and sometimes forcefully acquired. But then some politician values war for reasons of greed and personal glory and you get Mars Ultor, the avenger. Or they start to think Mars and Venus make a cute couple, imagining themselves in the gods' images — a circular logic if ever there was one! — till no one remembers Nerio, his first wife. And when people of different nations meet and get over the first instinct of trying to kill each other, they try and find commonality. So your Ares is our Mars, and we swap stories, and then confuse each other about who was a protector and who was a bastard. This is why Saul hates the name Apollinaris so."

"Saul?" Cassie was doing her best to keep up, but that last remark threw her.

"The sun is such an important aspect of life, so naturally people deified it as Sol Indiges. Saul used to ride his chariot of the sun across the sky, the same as Luna rode hers across the night. They loved their horses and chariots, those two, and the people worshipped them right at the Circus where all the races were held. But then Apollo took over from Helios in Greece and over Sol in Rome. And Apollo's chariot was drawn by swans, and Saul misses his beloved horses and hates the confusion."

Cassie took a moment to struggle and make sense of it. "And the others?"

"You haven't guessed?" June looked at her with a twinkle in her eyes. "Tell me what you see, not what you've been told to ignore."

Cassie thought of the residents at Mountain View, and the odd stories or phrases they let out occasionally which the other staff were quick to dismiss. "Joe is Jupiter? He keeps painting lightning storms."

"You would forever be on his good side if you called him Father Iovis. Jupiter is a mispronunciation of a slang concatenating his proper name, Iovis Pater. A presence of open spaces and vast skies, of storms and lightnings. That's why we keep him away from electronics, because he gets excited and tends to fry them. But other than that he isn't nearly as henpecked as his Greek equivalent." The old lady's lips closed in a tight prim line as she clicked her knitting needles.

"And you're June — Juno, his wife?"

"Good. Keep going."

"Marc would be Mercury, right? That's why he's always travelling on errands."

"Correct again. One of the few of us still roaming the world."

"There are others still amongst us?"

"Yes, indeed. That bi... ahem. Venus, still has worshippers aplenty. Love and desire have been constant basic elements of the human experience, and she never left people's lips. Especially these days, when she assumed the godly aspect of superficial vanity as well and lives on as the goddess of beauty-product influencers. But do go on."

"Naphtali is Neptune? Is that why he's doing aquatherapy daily? I thought he was just a creepy old man, perving on Jenny the instructor. She certainly said he tried to pinch her butt."

"The two aren't mutually exclusive, dear. He's the god of the seas and oceans, forced to spend his time in a tepid pool. He was never particularly squeamish about who he mated with, so he tries to get what he can."

Cassie made a mental note to speak with Jenny later, but kept at unravelling the puzzle. "Minnie is always reading the business papers, so she would be Minerva. But Cheri?"

"Ceres, goddess of crops," said Juno.

"Is that why she only eats porridge? She seems to suffer from real dementia."

"It's all the GMO and pesticides. They've killed her soul."

Cassie shuddered. She filed all the implications for later, to rethink her diet and buying habits. "Who's Virginia? She's on her death bed."

"Vesta, goddess of hearth and home."

"Is her state due to the decline of family values?"

"Pfft," June chuckled. "That, throughout human history, has been the same, a constant. Every generation bemoaning the decline of morals and crying for a return to family values they never adhered to in their youth. No. The poor dear hung on to the wrong things, and these days no virgin is hand-milling flour to bake salt cakes. But let's get back to our residents here. I'll save you the next one; Diana has all but faded away, but managed to escape. When people replaced the forests of trees with concrete jungles, when the hunt was lost to sniper rifles, and when the media became obsessed with some precious little princess, Diana was all but gone. But she found a home with the neopagans, and some of them take it just seriously enough that she managed to escape death here, fuelled every time some new-age Wiccan references 'the goddess.' She may lack her power of old, but still she lives."

Cassie did a mental count of the residents. "That just leaves Leonard, but I can't place that name with the other major deities that might have survived."

"Again, dear, what do you see?"

Cassie looked at the old man pulling apart a clock on the far side of the hall. His cane was by his side. "An old man, limps, tinkers with gadgets. I don't get it."

Juno sighed. "He's Vulcan, god of fire and blacksmiths, who made a neat transition to industrial technology but hasn't quite survived the information age."

"But why the name Leonard? Why not pick something like, I don't know, Valentin?"

"Because he has a quirky sense of humour, so he named himself here after the most famous Vulcan of the 20th century."

Cassie did a quick count. "And that makes twelve, for the twelve Olympians?"

"Again with the interpretatio graeca. We were different, uniquely Roman, and there were a heck of a lot more of us. But as people started to think of us as just Greek gods with Latin names, as even the Romans changed how they view and spoke of themselves, so many of us fell into obscurity." Juno's knitting needles clacked with an annoyed cadence. "Even the name of this place, Mountain View, is an allusion to a place we never occupied."

Two questions still nagged at Cassie. "But why was it Martin that helped me fall pregnant, out of all of you? And why help me at all, in the first place?"

"You might think that the female divinities, those who've looked after childbirth in ages past, would be more suited. And possibly we were, but your condition was beyond our current grasp as our powers waned. We chose Martin to help you because he still has some influence left. It gave him pleasure to return to his days of protector of fields and homes."

"Why help at all?" Cassie persisted.

"Because you listened, dear. Because you sat with us, not looked down upon us. Not for any expectation of reward, but simply because you cared, regardless of how society has relegated us. And fulfilling our contracts with humanity has always been the basis of religion."

"Does this make me your high priestess now?"

Juno laughed in good-natured surprise. "If you wish."

"I don't think I can quite manage sacrificing live animals, but there are so many like me out there, who would do anything to get your assistance."

"Oh no. I'm afraid those days are behind us. Grumbling aside, most of us have come to accept the reality of age and are content to just watch the world. Besides, there aren't enough people who truly believe in us for us to affect enough change in the world. It took a lot out of all of us to grant you this one gift."

"But I could tell them! People will come for small miracles, and the more you do the more people will believe. You could resume your glory days and help people. All we need is to get the word out."

It Takes A Village

Juno laid a warm hand on Cassie's and just stared silently smiling at her for a moment. "And what do you think would happen to you should you start talking like this in public? To the same people who've made up their minds and consigned us to obscurity? Besides, we've done our duty and we now want to enjoy our retirement. The last thing we want is hordes of academics coming to ask questions, trying to sort out the inherently messy history of humanity." Juno paused for a moment. "You want to be our high priestess? Here's our charge to you: go out and spread the message that the elderly have led interesting lives, and no matter how busy you think you are there is always benefit in slowing down and just listening. It'll do everyone some good."

Cassie turned it over in her mind. Ministering others was ingrained in her — it's why she chose nursing, after all. To her, nursing was more than addressing the immediate physical needs, it was about building human connections, about taking the time to care. And yet, she knew so many women in similar situations as she had been, who loved to care for others and deserved better.

"Tell me," Cassie asked the goddess, "are there other nursing homes like this one?"

"I believe so, yes." Juno looked puzzled. But as she looked at Cassie's twinkling eyes, smiles spread on both women's faces.

~*~

Bjørn followed Ms. Wulf as she was giving him the grand tour of Field Hall Nursing Home. He paid just enough attention to repeat what was said should Wulf ask, and pop up with the occasional observation or question. They already got over the male-nurse-raised-eyebrow obstacle, and at least with geriatrics it wasn't as pronounced as with early childhood. Bjørn knew how

It Takes A Village

homes for the elderly worked, and when it came down to it, after you mastered the quirks of the local janitorial procedures the rest was pretty much the same.

It's the residents that interested him. As Ms. Wulf was rattling off lists of abstract conditions, medications, and treatment plans, he was looking for the humans behind them. We are the sum of all our experiences, he knew, and reducing a person to a clinical laundry list was a gross injustice. Let the doctors address the medical issues, he saw his role as sitting with the person and giving them space to be their full selves in the time they had left. He wasn't the only one who thought this way; there were whole internet groups for nurses, and he and others were vocal about the meaning of care.

Bjørn liked doing that, and even liked the home and residents where he had worked until recently, but he also had a burning personal need that drove him to quit his old job and seek a new place of employment. Being around people at the end of their lives fuelled an insatiable desire within him to create more life, yet modern medicine gave him an unequivocal diagnosis of sterility. He was sorely disappointed with the tests and options, which he found too clinical, too mechanical.

And then a friend of a friend reached out to him through the nurses' social networks. That friend-of-a-friend, Cassie, loved what he was saying on social media, had twigged about his personal situation, and this might sound crazy, but she really wanted to meet with him for coffee and chat.

Cassie turned up with a pram and a cooing baby girl, and she was right — she did come off a bit out there in her ideas. But she convinced Bjørn that sometimes a change of circumstances, of environment, would kick off other changes. Bjørn told himself he was just desperate enough to listen to anything, but it wasn't like Cassie was getting anything from it.

So Bjørn quit his job and came to work at Field Hall. Cassie told him to keep doing what he believed in, and pay attention to the residents. They looked like every other group of old people, Bjørn thought. There was an old man with a white beard and eye-patch, napping in a comfortable armchair and wearing on old rock concert T-shirt with a drawing of ravens on it. A big man who must have been a weightlifter in his youth was losing at cards to a slim man with dark hair and twinkling eyes who, he barely caught the motion, was keeping cards up his sleeve. At the far corner, a brother and sister — the resemblance was just too much to be anything but twins — were sitting and chatting quietly with a stately matron. The old woman caught his eye and smiled briefly, making Bjørn feel quite warm and welcome. He wasn't sure why, but he felt he would enjoy spending time with the residents here and that the future held bright promises. Whether the Cassie-inspired hope for children of his own turned just a wild fantasy mattered less; he was here to care.

It Takes A Village

About Assaph Mehr

Assaph has been a bibliophile since he learnt to read at the age of five, and a Romanophile ever since he first got his hands on Asterix, way back in elementary school. This exacerbated when his parents took him on a trip to Rome and Italy — he whinged horribly when they dragged him to "yet another church with baby angels on the ceiling", yet was happy to skip all day around ancient ruins and museums for Etruscan art.

He has since been feeding his addiction for books with stories of mystery and fantasy of all kinds. A few years ago he randomly picked a copy of a Lindsay Davis' Marcus Didius Falco novel in a used book fair, and fell in love with Rome all over again, this time from the view-point of a cynical adult. His main influences in writing are Steven Saylor, Lindsey Davis, Barry Hughart and every single science fiction and fantasy book he has ever read.

Assaph now lives in Tasmania, Australia, with his wife, kids, two cats, one dog, and — this being Australia — assorted spiders. By day he is a software product manager, bridging the gap between developers and users, and by night he's writing — he seems to do his best writing after midnight.

You can find more of Assaph's novels and stories at egretia.com
And his newsletter on: egretia.substack.com

His novels are available on Amazon at:
amazon.com/author/assaphmehr

It Takes A Village

THE TRIAL OF THE TYPIST — END

By Meir Michael Fogel

"Guilty," finished the speaker.

The judge then said, "In that case I sentence you for a life in prison for all your various charges as an example."

The defense attorney turned to his client and said, "Pay up."

"What?" replied The Typist.

"Pay up."

"But you lost you—" (the five words were censored)

"It doesn't matter, we agreed that if I represent you in this court then you would pay me in full, double if we won, but we didn't win so I will just take my fee and go."

Meanwhile, the prosecutor was congratulating herself under her breath. The judge was already almost outside the courtroom, as he was late for his wedding anniversary date and didn't want to get slowed down by reporters. The crowd and jury disappeared while reporters rushed in to ask the jury questions about which side of the argument were they on, and The Typist got hauled off to prison still arguing with the attorney.

It Takes A Village

BALANCE

By Cindy Tomamichel

When asked what inspired this story, Cindy responded:

This story was a result of a random prompt from my local writing group – that AI was going to take over the world. Would that necessarily be a bad thing? Are the conspiracy theories right about AI? Was the future really going to be as dark as most post apocalypse scenarios?

We debated and shared very different stories, and I remembered the village and caring theme for this anthology. Perhaps the future could take a different path. So while some of it is gritty, there was immediately a lot of family love which dominated the storyline.

So while it might take a village to create a future for humanity, it also took the group effort of my friends to develop the story. With their caring support the story blossomed and was finally completed. It seems fitting that it finds a place in an anthology about humans cooperating for the good of all.

It Takes A Village

BALANCE — Cindy Tomamichel

The domes glowed pearly white and pristine in the distance. From the wasteland outside the domes they looked like paradise. Inside, people lived clean, ate clean. For a price. I could hear my Grandpa saying. He had a lot to say about the domes and the people who lived in them. More than I wanted to hear. I squinted through the brown haze. It looked like they were building an extension. Swarms of bots roved the surface, placing globs of the solar energy plastic roof in a mosaic that set hard and protective.

I grubbed up another twisted carrot and checked on my little sister. She had rickets, so we let her be in the sun as long as we could, between the cyborg surveys, but the air brought on her asthma. I'd had a few years when we still had respirators, but the tech had broken down. I hacked and spat, noticing more blood this time.

"Come on, sweetheart." Ruthie raised her arms to be picked up, and I swung her onto my back. It was nearly noon and would take till dinnertime to get home. We walked through the sparse forest, the trees sick and dying. But there were still a few butterflies, so I made up a silly song to make her laugh. The path twisted in amongst the trees, in under a few wire arrangements that my grandfather thought protected us from surveillance. I didn't have the heart to tell him they probably knew where we were, they just didn't care.

I had been a baby when the internet started. It's hard to think about how much people used it. I grew up with a smart phone in my hand, always online, chatting with friends. Playing games… Lord, that seems a long time ago. I shifted Ruthie on my shoulders and gave her the carrot to gnaw on. Games. I'd heard someone say the phones had more computing power than the computers they used to send a rocket to the moon. We played games when we could have travelled the stars.

It Takes A Village

It was getting dark by the time I reached the shack, and Ruthie drooped on my shoulders. I put her down near the stream, and she squeaked when I put her dirty feet into the cold water. Not for drinking, but washing was probably ok still. I glanced up the hill. The shack blended into the hillside, the timbers built into the stone wall rotting with the damp.

"Watcha thinking about, Moses?" Ruthie asked.

"The before time, when I was your age."

"Bet it was better. I could have had a calculator instead of doing my sums with a stick in the dirt." She coughed and wiped a drop of blood off her lips.

I bent down, grabbing her hand. "You been bleeding when you cough?"

"Yeah. But maths keeps my mind off it." She gazed at me, her light blue eyes bright in a scrawny face. "I worked out the circumference of the earth today."

"Don't tell Dad."

"I know." She sighed a very grownup sigh for such a little girl, and I had to hide a smile. "But even Galileo knew the Earth was round."

"I'll have to raid another library."

"Yes, I've read all of the books you got me last time. I'll give you some topics to look for." She sniffed and glanced at her bowed legs. "I wish I could go with you."

I squatted down so she could climb up for a piggyback. I pretended to be a horse, neighing and galloped up the path until I heard her giggling. I'd be coughing tonight, but it was worth it to hear her happy for a few minutes.

At the shack, Grandpa was chopping wood, while Dad ate something gloopy from a bowl. I sniffed. Porridge again. Grandad and Dad had been preppers for a long time, and oats kept well. Too well. I'd eaten a lot of porridge over the years and would be doing so again tonight most likely. There was no game around here. The forest was dying, no animals lived in it. Ruthie had told me about ecosystems, and I reckon ours was broken.

"Where's Mum?"

"Gone hunting. She saw a stray dog down near the creek eating something and was going to scare it off."

Porridge suddenly sounded pretty tasty compared to a second-hand carcass.

I settled Ruthie into her chair with a notebook of equations. She scribbled happily, her tongue stuck out as she figured. I sat down with a weevilly bowl of porridge and thought of the domes. What was in them? I peered into my porridge suspiciously. How had we gotten to this? I flicked a weevil into the dirt and tried to remember.

We were leaving for a holiday, Dad said. But he'd packed the trailer and Mum told us to take everything we cared about. I packed my phone and charger, plus my textbooks, hoping to get ahead on homework. Grandma was already in the car, a big book of sudoku clutched in her hands.

I helped Mum into the car. She was eight months along with Ruthie, and we all looked forward to a baby in the family. I patted her and got her a drink for the trip. She looked tired and worried, glancing at Dad, who was watching the sky.

"They're coming," he muttered. He was wearing his faraday hat that he hawked on his website, designed to stop the internet controlling your brain. Mum shook her head slightly at me, and I got into the back seat and said nothing.

"We gotta get to the bunker. Be off grid. It's the only way, you understand, don't you?" Dad whispered to Mum.

Mum waved at the neighbours as we drove past. "No one else is going."

"No one else knows what I know," he replied.

It Takes A Village

What did he know? He never went out and earnt money from his website selling crazy stuff to other crazies, and a podcast about AI taking over the world. He had written books too, after he'd been thrown out of NASA. I settled down and pulled out my phone.

"Throw that away," Dad screamed, screeching the car off the road and filling the car with dust. He ripped open the door and grabbed my phone and charger and threw them on the road. I tried to stop him, but he stomped them until the lights went out.

"I paid for them – that was my holiday money," I yelled.

"You'll thank me later," he snarled. "Get back in the car."

I was going to keep arguing, but Mum was rocking to herself and weeping silently. I contented myself with glaring out of the window.

Domes dotted the suburbs. They were cleaning the air and soil, one dome at a time. Robots and computers managed it all, and people paid lots of money to move into them.

Mum put the radio on. It crackled into a news hour, full of people arguing about climate change and the domes. Protests about artificial intelligence taking peoples jobs. Marketing jingles written by bots that trawled the internet for content faster than any human could.

"See!" Dad screamed. "I told you. AI is going to take over everything." Mum leaned forward and switched the channel to music.

The car sped for hours through the brown air. We left the city and the riots behind. The suburbs with their dead gardens and their don't-drink-the-water signs, and headed far into the hills. But they were not much better. The hotter weather, bushfires, floods, hurricanes. One of these and nature could recover, but not all of them.

Grandpa had a bomb shelter, and we lived in that for the first year. I don't know if bombs ever even fell, we were cut off when Dad ripped out all the electric cables. Ruthie was born, and Mum survived. I helped with the birth. Dad and Grandpa opened a bottle of whiskey to celebrate and had passed out by the time Ruthie yelled for the first time.

Grandma lost her mind. I think we envied her. I felt like I was too, listening to Dad and Grandpa rant about the AI and being controlled by robots, the apocalypse, and the state of the world we could not see. Their bile and malice, it tainted everything. We would have still been in the bunker if Mum hadn't opened the door the day Ruthie stood up and fell on her bowed legs.

I took a breath outside the bunker and coughed. The air seemed worse than when we went in, although I was glad to not be smelling the bunker mix of sweat, the poorly functioning compost toilet, and beans. Always beans.

We walked as far as we could, which was about how far we could drag Grandma and Ruthie in the cart. I wanted to stay closer to the city, arguing we could find food for some time. They wouldn't have taken food into the Domes.

"You don't get it, do you? They are going to build cyborgs that will hunt us down, drag us into the Domes to be slave labour."

"Why would robots use human slaves? That makes no sense. Nothing you say makes sense." That got me a backhand.

We finally stopped at an old shack in the dead forest. Mum and I worked to try and turn the dump into a home, while Grandpa set up a still and Dad raved about hunting squirrels. It was a full day to walk to a town, but I often made the trip. I walked the dead streets, wishing things were different. I did manage to find a working radio, although it only played music, crackly and faint. Mum would swing Ruthie around, laughing and dancing while Ruthie babbled happily. Dad found it and threw it down the hill. From the porch we watched it splinter and fragment, wires sparkling in the pallid sunshine.

Humans had invented AI. How bad could it be? AI could reinvent itself, create a new world. One I dreamed of, where Ruthie could run and learn maths. And me? Maybe a girl and a family, a garden where things grew properly, instead of twisted and wrong in the toxic soils. I remembered my phone and my friends. Maybe play a game once in a while, instead of this endless scraping existence.

~*~

I'd just finished at the library, toting a heavy bag which contained all the remaining physics and maths section for Ruthie, and a book on paediatrics for me. I'd also grabbed Mum's biochemistry textbook she had written back in the day. I figured she'd like to see it on the shelf we grandly called the mantlepiece. I'd even found a few comics for Grandma. I was gnawing happily on an old protein bar when I stopped.

A scream, just ahead.

I ran, glancing in the side alleys as I did. The old city was close to the Domes, and they were taking over, block by block. But lots of things lurked in the old cities now humans had gone. My backpack thudded on my shoulders as I skidded to a halt.

A girl.

She must have fallen from the roof. I squinted up and threw an old garbage bin lid like a frisbee towards the dogs that must have chased her up there. There was a yip and they scattered. I kneeled to examine her. She was unconscious, bleeding from a head graze and her arm was bent at an angle. Gritting my teeth, I pulled her arm straight and used a clean rag to wipe the blood.

She moaned and her eyes flicked open. A deep violet, with a silvery tinge I'd never even imagined before. I smoothed her hair, and her skin rippled.

I reckon my mouth dropped open as I watched the graze repair itself and her arm reformed, muscles bunching under the skin. The wound glowed faintly, and I thumbed blood off her unblemished skin.

It Takes A Village

My fingers started glowing too. Her blood seeped into the rough skin and small cuts I always had. As she woke, I sat staring as my hands also fixed themselves. Dizzy, I laid down beside her, the tall buildings tilting at crazy angles. I shut my eyes, my body feeling twitchy, like ants marched under my skin. Darkness.

"Hey, wake up." A voice, soft and gentle.

"Mum?"

"No, it's me, silly. Ladybug."

I opened my eyes to her violet ones. Something lurched inside me, and I was in love. She was the first girl I'd seen in years, and suddenly she was enough. My head was resting in her lap, and it was the best moment of my life.

"Ladybug. Pleased to meet you. I'm Moses."

"Thank you for rescuing me. It was my first solo assignment on the outside." She flexed her arm. "Nearly my last. It's more dangerous than they said. I didn't expect those dogs."

"I live here, I'll protect you. Show you around." I sat up. expecting to cough, but my lungs felt fine. In fact, I felt better than I had felt in like forever. What had been in her blood?

I chewed a lip as I thought, watching Ladybug as she got to her feet. She was graceful, her movements like a dance, and her clothes were clean. I sniffed, and over the rank smell of my own body, I could smell her. A mix of flowers, of sunshine on grass on a hot day. I stepped back, hoping she wasn't offended by the sweat and dirt that clung to me.

She glanced at the Dome in the distance. The extension had taken over another block just this afternoon. I glanced at the sun. It was nearly porridge time again.

"I must go." She turned, then glanced back. "You don't live out here, do you?" She waved an arm at the surroundings, and I saw them through fresh eyes. Abandoned buildings, the grey concrete blistered with iron stains, the windows shattered in the ancient riots. A few rats, and the scream of a seagull.

"I do. I must get back to my family."

She nodded. "I will see you tomorrow, then? I need to finish my survey mission."

"Yes. I'll be here." Nothing would stop me.

She ran towards the dome, light footed and skipped around the car hulks. A final wave and she was inside the Dome, the white plastic obscuring her. Could she see me? I waved and turned towards home. Survey? Mission? Was she controlled by AI like Dad said? Flexing my fingers, I pondered as I hiked back into the dead forest. Collecting firewood as I climbed, I could not help but see my hands. Healed.

My lungs. The air rushed in and out. No coughing. What had happened to me? But mostly I just thought about her. Ladybug. What a funny name, but it suited her somehow.

Ruthie greeted me with a squeal of delight, lurching off the porch into my arms, and demanding to know if I got the books. I left her with a pile of texts, bemused as always as she scanned pages faster than her stubby little fingers could turn them. Her crippled legs caught the last bit of sun, and I fished in my pocket for the vitamins I'd found. Out of date, but I hoped of some value still.

Mum was butchering a small carcass, a squirrel I hoped, a rat most likely. She smiled and nodded to the bowl near Grandma. I stashed my backpack away and picked up the bowl of porridge, sprinkling it with a vitamin tablet and stirring. She gummed up a mouthful and I wiped a bit of drool off with my finger.

Grandma stared at me, her blue eyes with the dark yellow webbing for once both focused on the same thing. She smiled, stroking my face and murmuring. "Soft," I caught. I touched my own face. Yes. She nodded again.

It Takes A Village

"Changed." A few champs of her gums and she managed another mouthful of porridge.

"I got you some comics. You can sit in the sun tomorrow and read them."

"Good boy." She dozed off, smiling and I pushed her closer to the fire, tucking her blankets out of the way.

"She was a good midwife in her day. You take after her, Moses."

I smiled and dug around in my bag for her textbook. "I got you a present."

She sighed, running a fingertip over her name embossed on the cover. "Not that long ago, but so much has changed." Her lip trembled a little as she stroked my hair. "I don't know how we would manage without you."

"We should move to the Domes." I whispered.

"Your father would never hear of it."

"Who cares? Ruthie needs more than this." I grabbed her hand. "We all deserve better than this."

The porch creaked. Mum threw the book to Ruthie who caught it and hid it in her blankets before pretending to be asleep.

"Better than what?" Dad walked in, snarling. I could smell the moonshine on him from across the room.

"Nothing, dear." She passed him a bowl of porridge.

He glared at it in disgust and threw it at the wall. "I'm tired of this shit too, but I'll die before I let the AI take my brain." He kicked a piece of broken crockery and wiped porridge off his face. "And don't think I'll go down alone." He slammed the door on the way out, and a line of dirt crumbled out of the back wall, trickling down to join more mud on the floor.

I cleaned up the porridge, watching Mum joint the rat for a stew, her face wiped of emotion. She moved like Grandma did, slow and bent over. I suddenly wondered how old she was. Not as old as she looked.

It Takes A Village

"Dad can keep this dump," I whispered, giving her a kiss as I went out.

Ladybug pressed her palm against the Dome and stepped quickly inside as the door lens opened. The horrid air outside was replaced by clean smells, the scent of jasmine as it climbed over the trellised gardens. The gardens disguised the disinfection process, and she barely felt the small bots as they raced over her skin like transparent leaves, skittering and collecting data and bugs in equal measure. They flew out behind her and tickled her neck as they cleaned her hair, leaving it flowing in the purified breeze from the ducts.

Moses. What a strange name. He had been strange too, but maybe living outside made you a bit strange. She frowned. Outside. It had been her first trip alone.

She walked along the gravel path to the main village centre. So many had died in the riots and climate changes of the last century that humans now lived in villages, their genetics carefully controlled by the AI. She had learnt that in school and never questioned it. One day, she would be selected and a compatible stranger would be her mate. She smoothed down her tunic over her stomach, thinking of the future. Babies. She could have as many as she wanted. With so few humans left, all children were cherished. But there weren't that many.

She slowed as she walked, and soft music played in the background. She waved at her parents, both half asleep in the sun, a drink in their chubby hands. A servo bot handed them food.

"Weren't you going to visit the neighbours this afternoon?"

"No, dear, too much effort." Her mother slumped into sleep, and a servo bot covered her with a blanket.

"Why would we go somewhere? We have all we could want right here. I don't have to work for the rest of my life. You don't know what it was like on the outside in the old days." Her Dad finished his drink and laid back down, tilting his hat over his face. "Paradise," he muttered before snoring.

It Takes A Village

The outside was a lesson none of the old movies could have taught her. The bad times, when society functioned to make profit. When profits came from making others' lives a misery from what she could figure out. Working and working to produce more stuff. The oldsters had been neglected, and children too. She had been horrified when her mother told her childcare had been one of the poorest rewarded occupations, and mostly done by women. The environment had nearly been destroyed, and humanity had nearly gone, too. AI had saved them. Humans didn't need to be slaves to a profit anymore.

Self-replicating, always learning. Performing its design of cleaning up the planet so humans could live safe inside the Domes. It was too dangerous outside. She had grown up knowing death waited outside.

She stumbled, catching herself. But there were people outside.

No one had told her that.

What else hadn't they told her?

~*~

"I reckon we need to move." Grandpa spat a gob of mucus over the rail. It landed near my face where I listened under the porch. It quivered in front of me, and an ant ran to investigate then backed away, its antennae twitching.

"Where?" Dad grunted. The rattle of foil again as he wrapped a fresh layer around the tattered baseball cap. We had gone to see a game and he bought that hat for himself. I'd got a hotdog. Hot and salty, full of fat and gristle. Saliva filled my mouth as I remembered it.

"There's an old military base up further. A few days hike. They built good bunkers those days, and I bet there's food there, all the MRE's we can eat."

"Yeah. Maybe a ham radio too. I could broadcast, see if we can find others out here."

It Takes A Village

"Community, that's what we need. Build a new future for humans. Free from AI."

"Yeah. AI caused all this. The politicians all had it in for the masses, wiped us out practically, 'cept the ones they probably keep as slaves. Only us still free. Bet the politicians and billionaires aren't eating porridge with fucking bugs in it."

"Course not. Sitting pretty in their doomsday bunkers, watching porn and eating vat-grown meat."

"Course, it would be too hard a trip for the women." Dad rasped, guzzling moonshine.

Grandpa grunted. "Lots of pretty girls out there of breeding age, I reckon."

They stopped as Mum came out and sat the stew between them and walked back inside. I scooted away with the distraction, biting my lip to stop me making a sound. The taste of blood was welcome. Anything to distract me from listening to monsters.

~*~

I'd always known Dad was not really my father. He had made me call him that when he moved in with us. I didn't know what Mum saw in him, she often seemed scared more than anything. She had been a scientist at the institute, but that all changed one day, the day Dad came to live with us. The only good thing was Mum was having a baby. I'd always wanted to be a nurse, and I looked forward to the birth. In the meantime, I looked after Grandma who lived with us, did my homework, and kept out of Dad's way.

They were my family. Dad and his father, Grandpa, were not. I took a deep breath in relief, I guess. I wasn't related to these people, I owed them nothing.

It Takes A Village

I inched my way out from the porch and stepped quietly past Dad and Grandpa. They were snoring, the empty bottle of moonshine broken in the dirt yard. We could have done with the potato peels they used, but it did buy us all some peace from the ranting about AI and the apocalypse.

Mum was tucking Grandma into bed and brushing the thin yellowish white hair off her face. She looked exhausted, and I suddenly thought of how well I felt. Energy I hadn't felt for years while the apathy of malnutrition and despair had seeped into me. I sat down beside her and hugged her. She felt frail, and I made a decision.

"We have to go." I jerked my head towards the porch. "They are planning to murder us and move up into the hills."

Mum's face was pale, but she nodded. "How are we going to do it?" She got up, moving to the back wall of the shack.

Ruthie opened her eyes and sat up, throwing the blankets back and attempting to get out of her chair. "I'm coming with you, even if I have to crawl."

I nodded and glanced at Mum. "We can get to the city tonight, then make our way to the Dome in the morning."

I looked around and winked at Ruthie. "We won't be able to take your books."

Ruthie smiled. "I've read them all, they are all up here." She tapped her temple.

I picked up a blanket and gently shook Grandma awake. She grumped a bit at me, but settled on my back and Mum tied the blanket under her. Good. I took a breath, delighting in the sensation of not coughing, as well as the realisation I'd never smell this dank hole again.

Mum pulled aside a board in the wall and pulled out a plastic file. She brushed off the dirt and pushed it into Ruthie's shirt. "Keep this hidden,

It Takes A Village

whatever happens." Ruthie nodded, her eyes shining silver in the light from the dying fire.

Mum paused on the porch, eyeing Dad and Grandpa in disgust. "He told me this morning." She rubbed her bruised cheek. "He forgot I used to be a chemist."

The empty stew bowls took on new meaning and I gazed at her. "How long?"

"Morning at least." She shrugged her shoulders. "Maybe forever, I didn't bother measuring the dose." She picked up Ruthie and started down the hill, following the worn trail through the dead forest.

It was a long walk, but we made it to the town an hour or so before dawn and I settled them down in an old office while I scrounged for food. There wasn't much left, but I did find a few tins of tuna in drawers and a locked storeroom that had packet soups, water bottles and porridge sachets. I left the porridge, but the rest was a feast. A few plastic bowls, cups and spoons and I felt like a hero bringing food back to my family. We sat quietly, drinking cold soup and eating tuna from the cans.

"I read the file, Mum." Ruthie announced.

Mum jumped. "I should have known better than to leave you with something unread." She smiled and stroked Ruthie's dirty hair. "I should have told you years ago."

She heaved a sigh and glanced out of the window. Dawn was slowly lighting up the sky, but the feral dogs were still fighting in the streets.

"I was young once, and a scientist," Mum started, her fingers twisted together. "It was amazing to be a part of such a project, even more when they selected me. I wasn't just a chemist; I was a genetic analyst on a project that still haunts me." She held Ruthie's hand. "But I would not change my mind."

"What?" I wanted to get going, get everyone safe.

"Show him the file."

It Takes A Village

Ruthie pulled out the file and showed me the cover.

PROJECT RUTH. CLASSIFIED TOP SECRET.

The file was yellowed and full of printouts, diagrams, old photos that were faded to grey. Embryos, DNA strands and the computer webs of AI language and more I didn't know. Maths, lots of equations. Photos of a foetus. The top page was notes and I recognised Mum's handwriting. The birth. Ruthie's development.

"When I lost your father, I felt like my world crumbled around me. All I had was the Project, and that kept me going. It was his idea. The world was going downhill so fast – climate change, profit-making businesses destroying the environment and filling the world with microplastics. The melting polar caps shifted the earth's axis. Drinking water was scarce, and what was left was polluted. We had made such a mess of Earth, and it was killing us. Humans needed help."

"AI."

Mum nodded.

I jumped up as we heard yelling in the distance. "They've found us."

~*~

Ladybug walked past the houses, thinking hard. People were lying in the sun, bots buzzed around bringing food, drinks, cleaning them, everything. She rubbed at her arm, broken yesterday and healed by the nanobots that lived inside her. She was healthy and strong because of AI.

But humans were not going well. Screens flickered with old movies, nothing new was being made. AI wrote stories, regurgitating old stories with new names. They could learn and build on the past. But not improvise, not create.

It Takes A Village

In the distance Ladybug watched the Dome expand. Bots rippled through the soil, cleaning it of contaminants. Old buildings fell into dust and then rippled into soil. A mist spread out, soaking the new soil, and a green haze of plants sprouted. More and more space inside. She ran towards the forest that grew near the barriers. It had been houses but the need had shrunk and they biodegraded back into the soil, while trees grew from implanted seeds.

She got to the barrier, her heart racing. Outside. She had been there with Moses. The day before she had woken excited, determined to accomplish what no one had done before. To succeed where all others had failed. She was a searcher, looking for the one the AI had told her to find. Her target was nothing but a name.

RUTH.

~*~

A pack of dogs growled down the street, snarling over a bundle of familiar rags on the ground.

"I hope they eat him," Mum whispered, hugging Ruthie to her chest.

"They would choke," Ruthie whispered back, giggling softly.

I hitched Grandma tighter, and she dug her bony old heels into my stomach and smacked me on the shoulder. "Go get 'em!"

The Dome was close, glowing bright and clean in the rising sun. A slender figure waved at us.

Ladybug.

Dad left Grandpa to the dogs and ran towards her, shouting filth and incoherent threats about AI and bots. He carried a shovel.

"Hang on tight, Grandma," I yelled. Grandma and I belted down the road, dodging around potholes, and I leapt over a snarling dog. Grandma squealed in excitement and yelled back encouragement to Mum and Ruthie.

Dad spun around. "Where are you going, eh? I'm not letting you inside the Dome, I'll see you dead before AI takes you over. You're free out here." His voice had a whine to it, as if he could make me despise him more.

He swung the shovel he carried, and I jumped back.

"Get lost, loser. You were never good enough for my daughter!" Grandma screeched.

"Can you get to the Dome?" I eased her down and she started a determined crawl. I kept between Dad and my family, watching out of the corner of my eye as they got to the Dome. Ladybug grabbed Ruthie while Mum helped Grandma totter inside.

"Well, it's just you and me then, son."

"I'm not your son, and you were a shit father."

He flushed red, and I ducked the shovel. He turned and ran towards the Dome, the shovel over his head. I tackled him to the ground, and he grabbed me, twisting my arm behind me until the bone cracked.

"Stop now," Ruthie yelled. "Don't you hurt him, or I will hurt you." Her eyes glowed silver and she held her hand near the Dome surface.

"You little freak! I should have left you and your mother to rot in that lab." Dad screamed, kicking me out of the way.

"You kidnapped us and threatened to kill Grandma!"

"I protected you from the AI." He stepped forward and raised the shovel like a spear.

"I am the AI." Ruthie gently placed her hand on the Dome and closed her eyes. A swarm of small silver bots sped towards Dad, enveloping him.

Consuming him.

The shovel clanged to the ground next to a small pile of dust. Bots flew up, a green mist sprayed on it, and a white web of fungal spores grew, blossoming into a mound of mushrooms.

"Come inside," Ladybug said. "We need you."

It Takes A Village

Ruthie smiled and reached out her arms to me. We walked into the Dome without a backward glance.

~*~

It's funny now to look back. We all spent days getting repaired. I was in pretty good shape, already had the nanobots from Ladybug, as I'd begun to suspect. My family got them too, lining up happily as if all the years of listening to the dangers of AI and the bots was nothing but a bad dream.

Grandma got some new teeth and declared she was never going to eat porridge again. She galvanised all the older humans. She had read a paper on the Grandmother Hypothesis when she was a nurse, and all the oldsters were suddenly goosed into action, shamed and encouraged by her energy. They became teachers of all the things they had done over their lifetimes. The new areas of the Dome sprang into action with woodwork classes, baseball, nature walks and baby nurseries. She runs the village now, if not the whole world. I don't pay much attention to politics, but it wouldn't surprise me.

This trickled down to Mum's generation. She led tours outside, sparking interest in the world again. They found quite a few stray groups of humans. Mum works hard to not let them integrate too much. For their independence was what was needed. On the inside humans grew too soft, giving up what made them human for a life of sloth and bot-dominated ease. Somewhere in the middle is the path forward.

And babies! So many babies born that year, and in all the years after. Ladybug and I are grandparents ourselves now. I've spent a lifetime burping, feeding, and being pooped on, and I couldn't wish for anything more. Ladybug continued her research on the past, and we teach the bots to recognise where things went wrong.

It Takes A Village

And Ruthie? With her legs fixed, she never walks but skips or dances. With her are a cloud of bots, all devoted to keeping her healthy. I queried the system one day, curious. The answer? Ruth is the one we needed. The master program is her heritage. The AI knew it needed something greater than itself, an insight that humans were unable to apply to themselves.

I worry she spends too long hooked into the system, but the bots love her, for that has been her legacy. Love. Tough love as it turned out. The AI had been programmed to help Humans, and it almost helped us into extinction. It would have been a clean planet but barren of sentient life. While that might be good from some perspectives, I am a bit biased being a human myself for the most part except for the teaspoon of bots inside.

The Domes that protected and rescued us turned into a trap. Humans are outside now, working alongside bots to clean up the pollution, adjust the climate, even bring back extinct creatures. The old ways didn't work and neither did the new ways.

A balance. AI could have no concept of the balance of a human – that all of us are a mix of darkness and light, of hope and despair, of creativity and sloth. Ruthie gave them that knowledge. She gave them herself, the essence of being human.

It Takes A Village

About Cindy Tomamichel

Cindy Tomamichel is a multi-genre writer. Escape the everyday with time travel action adventure novels, scifi and fantasy stories or tranquil scenes for relaxation.

Every book is a portal to a new world. Worlds where the heroines don't wait to be rescued, and the heroes earn that title the hard way.

Her great grandfather crossed the world seeking new adventures in Australia. Cindy has carried on that tradition, working as a geologist in remote areas where she was the first woman to work underground. Later, she continued working as an environmental scientist, focusing on cleaning up pollution. She has traveled around Australia, living in four different states before she celebrated her second wedding anniversary. She has also explored the South Pacific, the USA and South America.

Despite celebrating a recent birthday by jumping out of a plane, Cindy is happiest when writing, accompanied by the sound of cat purring.

You can find Cindy's writing on cindytomamichel.com
And her newsletter on: tinyurl.com/AdventureNews

Her novels are available on Amazon at:
amazon.com/stores/Cindy-Tomamichel/author/B07148BH5Y

It Takes A Village

WHAT? TODAY?

By Joyce C Mandrake

When asked what inspired this story, Joyce responded:

> I could say it was after reading the information regarding the anthology.
>
> My mind started working during the night, the words came, not in order but in snatches.
>
> In the morning it all started to fall into place with memories of family not seen and hope for the world.

It Takes A Village

WHAT? TODAY? — Joyce C Mandrake

What? Are you here today? Shuttled again for the third time? OH, I see the family is together today, all day. Of course, we can shuttle you to a position, say for two units? Excellent, we will send you the details and credit your time. You are greatly appreciated and thank you.

Mar leaned back from the screens and quickly noted the changes through eye movements, the left eye was twitching so the interface took twice as long. It was merely a nanosecond longer and it was bothersome. One more unit of time and Mar would be shuttled to the next assignment utilizing many other skills. Today was an archive assignment teaching and assisting young ones to read and find materials without the interface or any form of tech. There had been too many shutdowns, power grays and a decision had been made to relearn the old methods on hand, the basics of reading, math, and simple cooking. Of course, nurturing the ground, planting and harvesting were done daily as well without any automatics. Another bell chimed softly causing attention to be bought back to screens with another request, this time for a shuttler to be sent for four units. It might be hard to fill so quickly, but looking closely the requirements fit Mar's own aptitude quite nicely and it would be easy to adapt Mar's current shuttle schedule with all the rest of the assignments still being filled.

Mar left home with a smile, four extra units would be nice but it was the opportunities of learning, doing things and teaching which gave the most joy. Pulling up the portable screen one more time before gray down, Mar checked the address for the four-unit shuttle. The afternoon had passed quickly with the young ones, and, not surprisingly, Mar had learned much alongside the young ones.

It Takes A Village

Ah, the four-unit shuttle address was straight ahead nestled between several other structures with hanging down greenery, power panels on areas where the sun rays lingered. Small fruit trees grew in pots on walkway. Being late in the day, a shuttler was busy watering, making use of the shade to conserve water as the trees were out of the direct sun. Depending on where you live, depending on your shuttle assignments, this individual probably lived close by. It was all about freeing up time, using time, and, hopefully, managing time happily.

Mar tapped on the door, pulled on the bell chain and waited. Surprise overtook Mar's face as the door opened and Mar's parents were there. Behind them sat several grand ancestors smiling with candles lit as the gray shutdown came. It seemed a forgotten birthday was being celebrated. Mar's special day in fact. This was worth four units of time. The request had been after all, a request for a stand-in for a family member out of the area.

It Takes A Village

About Joyce C Mandrake

Joyce C Mandrake lives on the Central Oregon Coast with her husband. She works on writing as well enjoying walking, reading, and cooking. Joyce has been published in several anthologies under the name of Joyce Carletta Mandrake for her short stories and poetry: Children of the Dragonfly, Nothing but the Truth, Stories Migrating Home, and Traces in Blood, Bones & Stone. She says, "Life is an adventure and I wonder at my willingness to keep jumping in." She is a member of the Minnesota Chippewa (Ojibwe/Anishinaabe).

Find more about Joyce's work at shortnotesinmind.blogspot.com
Her work on Amazon are at:
amazon.com/stores/Joyce-Mandrake/author/B0D14DNXKQ

It Takes A Village

ADDIE

By Douglas Lumsden

When asked what inspired this story, Douglas responded:

My wife, Rita, and I have been running on our local rec trail three to five days a week for more than fifteen years. On every run, we pass by dozens of unsheltered people camped along this trail. They come and go, and the faces change over time. Most of them ignore us, some cheer us on, and we became acquainted with a few of the chattier folks, Scotty and Barney in particular, before they moved on. My conversations with Barney were enlightening, in no small part because he had no desire whatsoever to spend any part of his life enclosed by walls and a roof. He liked the solidity of the earth beneath his feet, the bite of the cold wind on his face, and the smells transported to his nostrils by wide-ranging and unrestrained air. Rita and I have engaged in numerous discussions, especially during the cold and wet months, about various proposals for local homeless shelters, which sound lovely in principle, but which come with as many cons as pros. It always strikes me that they might work for some, but certainly not for all. Certainly not for people like Barney. Government authorities and well-meaning special-interest groups tend to like one-size-fits-all solutions for people outside the mainstream, but the plain truth is that misfits come in all sizes.

It Takes A Village

ADDIE — Douglas Lumsden

The mystery to Noelle was why the crazy bag lady would choose to live outdoors instead of in one of the cozy shelters provided by the city. Correction, Noelle reminded herself: Mr. Farley at the Bureau of Domestic Service had told her not to refer to her new charge as "crazy," even though the ratty-toothed bitch had once cracked another homeless bum's skull with a two-by-four in order to steal his half-empty can of beer. She wasn't supposed to say "bag lady," either — or "bum," for that matter — and the raggedy tramp wasn't homeless, she was "unsheltered."

Words. The agents at the BDS could refer to her new charge as a IUFRA ("YOO-fra": Indigent Unsheltered Female Requiring Assistance) all they wanted, Noelle thought, but that didn't make the idea of caring for the old lush any more appealing.

According to Mr. Farley, the bag lady's name was Adelina Silva, and Noelle had suppressed a snort when the BDS agent told her that Ms. Silva preferred to be called "Addie." Noelle knew about "addies": she'd popped Adderall tablets by the handful while cramming for her final exams. Thank God for those magical brain pills, Noelle thought. Without them, she doubted she would have survived six years of college, much less walked out of there with an MBA. Once she'd been hired by Furman Bioenergy, she'd assumed her sleepless nights of white wine and pills were behind her, but now it looked like she had one more "Addie" to overcome.

Noelle hadn't met Addie yet, not face to face, but she'd read her file and studied the mug shot of a dirt-streaked, brown weatherworn face with a broad, crooked nose, a broken-toothed scowl, a pair of ruthless dark eyes, and a tangled mess of greasy hair that sat on the woman's head like a wasp's nest. The photo made Noelle's flesh crawl. This wasn't the face of a polite, civilized woman; it was the face of an animal, trapped, but fearless. Noelle could only imagine what this bestial woman must smell like. A cross between three-day-old roadkill and burning kerosene, she speculated. And alcohol. The files were clear about that. Addie had already shown herself to be the type of woman who would accept a drink if she had to beat the offer out of you with a stick.

Noelle parked her car up the street from the Sacramento River commercial port, turned off the engine, and sighed. The day had come for her to meet Addie in person, and Noelle couldn't imagine what the two of them could possibly have to say to each other. Mr. Farley hadn't been helpful. His only advice had been to be friendly, use her best judgment, and be ready to leave in a hurry if the tramp — check that, the IUFRA — became violent. Her mission was clear, though: it was Noelle's job to convince the outcast to move into a shelter, preferably in the next four weeks before the temperatures dropped to near freezing during the long late-autumn nights.

The BDS had first become aware of Addie nearly two years earlier, when the woman had staked out a spot for herself a few hundred yards up the river from the port. Local authorities had encouraged her to move into one of the nearby free shelters, simple structures to be sure, but each one offering four walls and a roof, plus a cot, a storage closet, a sink with cold and warmish running water, an indoor toilet, two barred windows, and a door with a lock and key. Addie had stubbornly rejected all inducements, declaring that she couldn't stand to be enclosed by walls.

She'd been trouble from the start, and the file was filled with incidents, both minor and more serious. Most of them seemed to be self-defense, or at least defense of the patch of riverfront she regarded as her personal territory. Noelle thought it hypocritical that someone who turned her nose up at indoor housing because it was too confining would also be overly possessive of unconfined open space, but Mr. Farley told her that it was a common theme among the unsheltered.

She'd been arrested after the incident with the two-by-four, which had sent her victim to the emergency room, and that's when the police discovered Ms. Silva's name and some of her history. According to the files, Addie was only thirty-two years old (much to Noelle's surprise) and unmarried with no children. The files made no mention of parents or siblings. Noelle was stunned to discover that Addie had once owned her own business, an art gallery in a trendy resort town on the coast. She'd sold the business five years ago and vanished. And now, here she was, living in the open air amid a grove of trees near the river.

Noelle suppressed a shudder. She'd thought she'd had it made after signing her employment contract with Furman. What could be a better sign of instant success than a six-figure income right out of school? Even her stepfather had been impressed. With the money, anyway. Not so much with the company that had hired her.

"Sock it away while you can," he'd advised her. "These alternative energy companies never last long. Once they go through their startup money, they find out that all that 'green' hokum is nothing but hippy-dippy bullshit. You can't compete against oil and natural gas by wiring up algae, and you can't run cars on corn syrup, or hope. Like I keep telling you: 'you go woke, you go broke.' At least you'll get some solid practical work experience out of it before they go under. It'll help when you're looking for your next job."

Noelle was looking forward to that practical experience, not to mention the money it would bring in. But, for reasons that eluded her, the "hippy-dippy" company insisted she devote two hours of each day to auxiliary work for the Bureau of Domestic Service. Much of Furman Biotech's startup money came from the government, and, as a condition of their grant, the firm agreed to make its employees available for community service work under the supervision of the BDS. It was all part of a federal government initiative to help the disadvantaged.

It Takes A Village

Noelle had no problem with the initiative in principle. One of the things she'd learned in her MBA program was that a country's overall economy improved after it stopped neglecting and began empowering its marginalized citizens. At the ballot box and in conversation, she supported progressive measures that benefited the people existing on society's fringes. She was firm in her belief that such things as universal health care, social security, small-business loans, racial and gender equality, and low-cost housing contributed to a strong economy and a healthy state. It's just that she personally wasn't well suited for direct community outreach. She didn't have the stomach for it. She was no introvert — lord knows she'd done her share of socializing in college — but poor people made her uncomfortable. It wasn't her fault, that's just the way she was. Other people were more naturally skilled when it came to working directly with people in need. They're the ones who should be helping the disadvantaged, she told herself, not her. She wasn't a social worker or a nurse, she was a financial officer. Or, at least, she was training to be one. But that meant she needed to be in an office at a desk in front of a computer, processing data and juggling numbers in between formal marketing meetings and informal ideating sessions. Not outside slogging through the woods in her brand new three-hundred-dollar boots on a gloomy afternoon.

But here she was, a hundred yards from her parked car, carefully avoiding the muddy puddles on a makeshift trail that wound its way toward the sounds of the rolling river, searching for the notorious Addie, as if she were bigfoot or something. They weren't exactly easing her into community service work. They admitted that her first charge was very likely going to be a hard nut to crack, especially for a rookie, but explained that their veteran workers were all otherwise engaged. Mr. Farley described it as a "discovery experience," a chance to learn about the wider world that existed just yards from the one she was used to, and an opportunity to acquire leadership experience. He shook her hand, wished her luck, and told her to do her best.

It Takes A Village

It wasn't fair. None of this was fair.

Following the trail, Noelle at last emerged from the thick grove of trees into a small beach area at the river's edge. She stopped and stared at the strange sight that greeted her. A thin ring of colorful pebbles, carefully laid in place to form a circle about six feet in diameter, surrounded the blackened remains of a narrow tree trunk that had either been toppled by a heavy wind or blasted by a bolt of lightning. The stub rose about five feet above the ring of pebbles, but the rest of the tree was nowhere to be seen.

Curious, Noelle stepped close enough to the tree stub to touch it. Someone had clearly meant to shape the damaged stub into a statue of sorts, but the attempt had been less than halfhearted. A crude pair of eyes, the outlines of a nose, and a crooked smile had been carved out of the darkened wood near the top of the stub, so that a black face seemed to be looking out over the river. Vertical lines had been scratched into the base of the stub above the roots in a pattern that suggested the tail of a large fish. A blue cloth — Noelle thought it might have been a tablecloth — hung from the jagged crown of the tree stub like a robe, and a knotted white cloth, probably an old sheet, served as a belt. To Noelle, it seemed that a child with a sharp instrument and limited aptitude had attempted to transform the broken tree into a mermaid.

"Leave it alone!"

Noelle nearly jumped out of her skin. With a gasp, she jerked her head around to gape at the figure coming out of the trees. She recognized Addie's rugged face from her mug shot, but Noelle wasn't prepared for how tiny the woman was. If she'd have been standing behind the tree stub when Noelle walked into the clearing, Addie would have been completely hidden from view. Noelle would have mistaken her new charge for a feral eleven-year-old girl if it hadn't been for the woman's prematurely aged skin and the fierce intensity in her eyes.

"Addie?" Noelle asked, caution in her voice, as if she were addressing a stray dog.

"Step away from the shrine," Addie commanded in a voice filled with warning. "Get clear of those rocks. And don't mess 'em up."

"Shrine?" Noelle frowned at the carved and clothed tree stub.

"That's right. And it's not there for you to paw at."

Noelle stepped carefully over the circle of rocks. "I was just getting a closer look."

Addie buried her fists in her waist. "And now you've fuckin' had your look. So get lost."

"Addie, I'm — "

"How do you know my name?" Addie lowered her arms and rolled her eyes. "Oh, shit. The fuckin' BDS sent you, didn't they. Those asshats never give up."

This wasn't going the way Noelle had expected, though, truth to tell, she had no idea what she should have been expecting. "They're just looking out for you," she said, and immediately wished she hadn't.

Addie snorted. "Well, who fuckin' asked them to?"

Noelle knew she needed to take control of the conversation. "Look, Addie. My name is Noelle, and I'm just here to see if there is anything you might need."

"I need you and all you other fuckin' do-gooders to fuck the fuck off. That's what I need. Now get the fuck away from my shrine before I have to fuckin' make you."

Noelle looked the foulmouthed Addie up and down and tried to reconcile the scrawny woman she saw with the fact that this gangly little creature had recently put someone in the emergency room.

Noelle attempted a do-over. "I owe you an apology, Addie. I think we got off on the wrong foot. I'm sorry I approached your... uh... your carving without your permission. I didn't touch anything, and I didn't mean any harm."

"Totem."

Noelle gave Addie a blank stare.

"It's a totem. It represents Yemoja."

"Yemmo Jaw?"

"Yemoja. The spirit of the water and mother of humankind."

Noelle slowly nodded. "Riiight, okay." She made a point of looking the totem up and down. "It's… very nice."

Addie lifted her fists back to her waist. "It's as nice as it needs to be. Not that you would know anything about that, you condescending piece of shit. Now get the hell out of here before I fuckin' lose it. You hear me?!"

Noelle knew she had utterly botched this first meeting with her new charge. Her shoulders slumped, and she let out a sigh. "Fucking Mr. Farley," she muttered. "They sure could have done a better job of preparing me for this bullshit. I've got a fucking MBA. I should be on a fast track to a CFO position, and I'm going to be stuck in the clerical pool for the rest of my fucking life because I can't talk a homeless chick into putting a roof over her head."

Addie's glare grew more intense. "What did you say?"

"Nothing, nothing." Noelle prepared to depart from the clearing the way she'd come in. "Don't worry, I'm leaving. I'll tell them you're a lost cause and that they should quit fucking with you." She lifted a hand and gave Addie a brief wave. "Nice to meet you, Addie. It's been… whatever." She turned to go.

She'd taken four steps when Addie called to her. "Hey! What'd you say your name was?"

Noelle stopped. "Noelle. It's Noelle. You know. Like Christmas."

Addie grunted. "Well, you're a real pussy, Noelle."

Noelle turned and leveled an openmouthed stare at Addie. "Excuse me?"

"You heard me. You're a pussy. You've got no fuckin' fight in you at all, do you. How do you expect to help anyone when you slink away the first time someone gets a little cross with you?"

Noelle's throat tightened. "What do you care? You told me to go, and I'm going."

"Just like that? Jesus Christ, lady. You got any smokes?"

The abrupt change in topic caught Noelle off guard. "What? Smokes? You mean cigarettes?"

"Of course I mean cigarettes, you dumb bitch. What do you think I mean? You got any?"

"No."

Addie let out a sour breath. "Well, bring some next time. Yemoja has a weakness for tobacco."

"Next time?"

"I'll see you here tomorrow afternoon. Don't forget the cigarettes. A six-pack of beer would be cool, too. Or better yet, a bottle of port. Douro if you can get it, but any old thing will do. I'm not as particular as I used to be." With that, Addie turned and disappeared into the trees.

~*~

Noelle told Mr. Farley that her first meeting with Addie had been a success. After all, she had a return invitation, and that wasn't nothing. Next step would be establishing a rapport with the caustic unsheltered Addie and persuade her to accept habitation in a shelter.

As she was making her way back down the trail to the river the next day, wearing cheaper shoes this time, she was startled by a croaking voice.

"You going to see Addie?"

Noelle couldn't quite suppress a yelp at the unexpected sound. She looked frantically back and forth before spotting a man sitting on a flattened boulder in front of a small pup tent that had been erected under the shade of an oak tree. He was munching on a sandwich packed in a cardboard box with a Salvation Army label, and an empty half-pint carton of apple juice lay crushed at his feet. If the man hadn't spoken, she would have walked right past him without even knowing he was there.

"Sorry?" Noelle managed to squeak.

The man loudly cleared his throat, turned his head, and spat into the dirt. "I heard you went to see her yesterday," he said in a voice that had lost some of its croak. "I'm surprised you came back."

"Yeah, well, I did. She asked me to."

"What for?"

"Uhh...." Noelle wasn't sure how to answer the question.

"You going to try to talk her into sleeping in a shelter?"

"Well... yes. I mean, I guess so."

The man laughed, coughed, and spat. "Yeah. Good luck with that. You won't be the first person that's tried. They try it with all of us, but most of us are fine right where we are."

Noelle caught sight of the scar partially hidden by the lank strands of sun-bleached hair hanging down the side of the man's head. "Are you the guy Addie attacked?"

The man reached up to touch the scar. "The bitch clocked me with a board. She's fuckin' psycho. You should turn around and go home. A nice girl like you don't want to be messin' with someone like her." He glanced down at the designer shopping bag hanging at her side. "You bringing her something?"

Noelle pulled the bag closer to her. "No," she lied.

It Takes A Village

Noelle didn't know where the knife had come from, or how it had come to be in the man's hand. He wasn't exactly threatening her with it, but in Noelle's eyes it appeared to be exceptionally long and sharp.

"Addie don't need it, whatever it is," the man said. "Why don't you give it to me, instead?"

Noelle clutched the bag's drawstrings with both fists.

The man gestured at the bag with his knife. "You got any cigarettes in there?"

"No. I don't smoke."

"My name's Butch."

"What?"

The man lowered his knife. "My name's Butch. What's yours?"

"Um… I'm Noelle." She hesitated a beat before adding, "It's nice to meet you."

"Hi, Noelle. You sure you don't have any cigarettes? Or some beer?"

"No, sorry. I need to find Addie." Noelle edged back a few steps, being careful not to trip over a half-buried tree root or a fallen branch.

"They call me Butch because I carry around this butcher knife." He raised the knife again, letting the sun gleam off the broad blade. "Don't worry, I'm not going to hurt you with it. I just make sure everyone around here knows I've got it. Fuckin' people out here steal whatever they can get their hands on. You can't be too careful. But nobody bothers me because they know I've got this butcher knife."

Noelle's knees weakened, and she struggled to stay upright. "That's… that's quite a knife."

Butch smiled at the blade. "I haven't actually had to use it on anyone. I just let the motherfuckers know I would if I had to."

Noelle wanted to continue down the trail, but her knees felt like jello, and she didn't want to let Butch think he was scaring her away. "I think I need to go now." The ground under her feet felt as if it had turned to quicksand.

Butch glanced at his knife before sliding it into a sheath that Noelle now noticed was clipped to his belt.

"Do you want to get out of the sun?"

Noelle blinked. "What?"

"The sun's bad for your skin. If you want to get out of it for a while, you can sit inside my tent with me."

Annoyed, Noelle let out a sigh. "No, Butch. I'm not going to sit in your tent with you." For some reason, the ground under her feet felt firmer now, and her knees had stopped shaking.

Butch tilted his head. "Why not? It's shady in there. I'll let you hold my knife."

Noelle didn't remember making a decision or turning away from the man, but the next thing she knew she was running headlong through the thick woods, Butch's croaking laughter following her down the makeshift path.

Ten minutes later, a breathless Noelle found Addie sitting cross-legged in the sand outside the ring of pebbles surrounding the totem. An empty lawn chair was unfolded next to her.

Addie indicated the chair. "I figured you weren't the kind of bitch to sit on the ground."

Wishing she'd brought along a clean beach towel, Noelle lowered herself carefully into the stained and ragged seat with a grimace, still panting from her run through the trees.

Addie's eyes lit up as she turned them on Noelle's tote bag. "You got smokes?"

Smiling, Noelle pulled a pack of cheap generic cigarettes, along with a book of matches, out of her bag and placed them in Addie's eager hands.

It Takes A Village

Within seconds, Addie was happily puffing away, eyes half closed and a dreamy expression on her face.

Noelle reached back into her bag. "I probably shouldn't have done it, but I got this for you, too." She held up a bottle of dark beer and an opener.

Addie's eyes widened. "Nice! That shit's not cheap. I was hoping for some Douro, but this'll do."

Noelle passed her the bottle. "It's my favorite brand. I got one for myself, too."

"Too bad you don't smoke," Addie said, taking another puff. "Maybe you'd have brought me a better brand of cigs. But beggars can't be choosers, right?" She raised the bottle and drained half the contents in three mighty gulps. "Yeah, baby!" she exclaimed with appreciation. "Now that's the fuckin' shit."

Noelle opened her own bottle and took a delicate sip. "Tell me about this totem."

Addie looked up from her bottle. "You like it?"

"It's um…. Did you carve it yourself?"

Addie snorted. "Of course not. It's hundreds of years old. It was originally planted on the banks of the Osun River by the Yoruba people to honor Yemoja, probably as early as the twelfth century. It was cut down and carried to Brazil on a slave ship. Then my great-great grandfather stole it from his slaves to give to my great grandmother. She passed it down to my grandmother, who passed it down to my mother, who tried to throw it in a fuckin' dumpster, but I rescued it. I put it in my art gallery, but I couldn't bear to sell it. When the gallery closed, I kept it and brought it here to live."

Noelle stared at the little weatherbeaten woman. "Wait… what? It was planted… where? By the who?"

"The Osun River. By the Yorubas. In Nigeria? West Africa?" Addie shook her head. "I'm guessing you never studied art or West African culture in whatever shithole university you went to."

Noelle narrowed her eyes at the carved tree stub. "You carried it here?"

"It was smaller then. I planted it by this riverbank because even though the Sacramento isn't the Osun, or even the Guandu, it's a nice little river, and it beats sitting in an art gallery. Yemoja liked it here right away and sent roots from the totem all the way to the river. That totem is twice as thick and twice as tall now as it was when it was on display in my gallery."

Noelle was skeptical, but she decided that humoring the crazy lady might be the best way to gain her trust. "That's a remarkable story. You say it's hundreds of years old? And it sprouted roots when you planted it here? I didn't think that was possible."

Addie let out a rasping laugh that ripped its way through her throat and left her coughing uncontrollably in its wake. When she'd regained her ability to speak, she said, "Girl, you don't have to fuckin' believe me. It don't matter anyways." She stood. "Bring your beer over here."

Noelle rose from her chair and followed Addie to the totem. After they'd stepped over the ring of pebbles, Addie poured some of her beer on the ground near the base of the carving.

Addie looked up at Noelle. "Go ahead. Give Yemoja a share."

After a moment's hesitation, Noelle tipped her bottle and spilled a bit of the liquid on a root growing from the tree. She waited while Addie stood silently, her head tilted toward her feet, her eyes shut.

After a few seconds, Addie opened her eyes and turned to Noelle with a smile. "Yemoja has accepted your offering. You're lucky. I thought she might hold out for a nice port, but I guess she couldn't resist a cute bitch with expensive taste in beer. Let's go sit down and we'll talk."

It Takes A Village

Once seated, Noelle asked, "Where do you sleep at night, Addie? Somewhere back in those trees?"

Addie sucked down the rest of her beer, keeping the bottle tilted and running her tongue around the opening until she was satisfied nothing was left. She turned to Noelle. "You wouldn't happen to have another one of these, would you?"

"I'm afraid not. I just brought one for each of us."

Addie glanced at Noelle's half-empty bottle with greedy eyes. "You gonna finish that?"

Noelle sighed, remembering the man with the scar on the side of his head, and passed the bottle. "Go ahead, but that's all I've got."

After a long sip, Addie gave Noelle an appreciative nod. "Thank you. Yeah, I've got a nice little set-up back there a little ways."

"Out in the open?"

"I've got a tent, but, yeah, pretty much."

"Do you have a change of clothes?"

Addie chugged some beer and wiped her mouth with a dirty sleeve. "Are you going to ask me if I've got any sanitary napkins? The fuckin' BDS is real concerned about my jam rags. Every time they send one of their do-gooders out to see me, that's the first thing they wanna ask me about. You ask me, it's some kind of weird-ass obsession."

Noelle reached into her bag. "Since you mentioned it…"

Addie pointed a finger at Noelle's chest. "Girl, if you pull a pad out of that bag I'll fuckin' brain you!"

Noelle froze. "I just thought…"

"I don't care what you thought. I'll take care of myself, thank you very much."

Noelle let the box of tampons she'd bought fall back into her bag. "Fine. Is there anything else I could get you?"

"Nope. I'm good."

"You've got everything you need? Okay, no problem. Do you have someplace to keep it? Somewhere safe? I hear that theft is a problem among… your community."

Addie let out another rasping laugh. "You mean among the bums out here? Yeah, they steal from one another all the time. Anything they can get their fuckin' hands on. The weak ones don't last long. But I'm not one of the weak ones. Nobody steals from me. They fuckin' know better."

"But wouldn't you feel more secure if you moved your belongings into one of the shelters? You could lock them away. Plus, you could sleep with a proper roof over your head behind locked doors, knowing that you were safe."

Addie rolled her eyes and pushed a fresh cigarette between her lips. "Here comes the pitch." She lit a match. "Look, girl. The last time I was locked away, it was in a cell. The thirty worst days of my life. No fuckin' way I'm going back."

"I'm not talking about jail. I'm talking about a shelter."

Addie blew smoke in the direction of the Yemoja totem. "What's the fuckin' difference?"

"The difference," Noelle began, straining to maintain her patience, "is that you can walk out of the shelter anytime you choose."

Addie shrugged. "I'm out now. I've made my choice."

"But you can also go inside if you want. For your own safety. Or to get out of the rain."

"I don't want to go inside. I'm already safe. And I like the rain."

A thought struck Noelle. "What about that man you hit across the side of the head with a board?"

Addie's eyes narrowed. "You mean, Butch? What about him?"

"I ran into him on the way over. He wanted to steal the cigarettes and beer from my bag."

It Takes A Village

A smile crinkled the corners of Addie's eyes. "Did he want the tampons, too?"

"I don't know. I ran away before he could look inside."

Addie shook her head. "What's your point?"

"He had a knife! A big one. Aren't you worried he might, you know… come after you?"

"Why would he do that?"

"You put him in the hospital. He might want to get back at you for that. Or steal your stuff."

"Ha! Let him try. I took care of that little bitch once. He's all bark and no balls."

"He's twice your size. And he's got a knife."

"And I put him in the fuckin' hospital."

"They put you in jail for it," Noelle reminded her. "Thirty days, you said. If something like that happens again, they'll put you in for twice as long. Maybe longer."

Addie blew more cigarette smoke at the totem. "So, I'm supposed to move into one cage to keep them from putting me into another?"

"It's not the same thing!" Noelle insisted.

"It is to me." Addie finished off the rest of the beer.

Noelle realized she was getting flustered and tried to regroup. "I'm trying to help you, Addie. You know that, right?"

"No you're not."

That stopped Noelle in her tracks. "What? If you don't think I'm trying to help you, then why do you think I'm here?"

"To help yourself. Look, girl. I wasn't born a bum. I was raised in a nice house. I went to college. I've got a degree in fuckin' art history. I had my own art gallery for three years. But it was all bullshit. And, to be honest, I drank my way out of that life. And there were some other things that I'm not gonna talk about. This is my life now, and I'm cool with it. But I haven't forgot my other life. I know what goes on. You're here to fulfill your community service to the Bureau of fuckin' Domestic. I know the drill. They send you out to help the 'disadvantaged' and the 'marginalized' so that you can 'broaden your perspectives' and 'develop leadership skills.' That's why you're here. For you. Not for me. To you, I'm just a 'charge.' That's the term they use, right? A fuckin' charge, like someone you're supposed to take charge of. But no one takes charge of me, and the sooner you know that, the quicker we'll start getting along." Addie crushed her cigarette butt into the sand and reached into the pack for another one.

Noelle sat in stunned silence, not knowing what to say. All she could manage after a while was a quiet "Wow."

Addie blew smoke in the air above Noelle's head. "Don't take it hard, girl. Like you said yesterday, they didn't fuckin' prepare you for me."

A soft chuckle escaped through Noelle's lips, which stretched into a rueful smile. "No, they didn't."

Addie flicked ash into the sand. "You really want to help me, girl?"

Noelle raised her eyes to meet Addie's. "It's Noelle. And, yes, if I can."

"Then quit trying, Noelle. You're not going to move me into one of those shelters. The shelters fuckin' suck. This riverbank is my home, and the only roof I need over my head is the sky."

Noelle nodded. "I guess that's what I'll have to tell the BDS. They won't like it, though."

"Fuck 'em. You aren't the first person they've sent to save my sorry ass." She held up her cigarette. "But you're only the second one to bring me smokes. And you're the first to bring me beer."

Noelle smiled. "I don't plan to tell them about the beer."

It Takes A Village

"Good move, girl." Addie laughed her rasping laugh and coughed a couple of wet coughs before taking another drag. She blew a cloud of smoke toward the totem.

Noelle noticed what Addie was doing. "I take it that Yemoja likes tobacco smoke?"

"Sure does. Alcohol, too. She's a bad bitch."

"You said she's a water spirit?"

A wide grin split Addie's face. "Not just *any* water spirit — *the* water spirit!"

"And you called her the mother of humanity?"

"Yep. Where do you think the first humans came from? From out of the water. Yemoja made them and sent them to live on the riverbank. She watches over those who honor her."

"People like you?"

Addie pointed at Noelle with her cigarette. "And you, too. You gave her beer, and she accepted it. Tell you what, girl. I'll teach you about Yemoja, and you promise to keep her memory alive. If you do that, and if you come back and give her more offerings, she'll extend her blessings to you. They could come in handy. She's a powerful spirit."

Noelle's jaw set, and she leveled her eyes at the other woman. "You're just trying to get me to bring you more cigarettes and beer."

"Bring wine next time. Douro port if you can get it. That's Yemoja's favorite."

"Yeah, I'll bet. That's a sweet con you got going there."

Addie smiled back at Noelle. "It's the best. But it'll be good for you, too. You'll see. Here's the thing, girl. I don't need you to save me by sticking me in a shelter, but I wouldn't mind your company from time to time. I get a little lonely out here sometimes. I know you're supposed to be on a service assignment launched by some government initiative, blah, blah, blah. Believe

It Takes A Village

it or not, I got the whole fuckin' pitch myself back before I left all that behind. But it's not really about helping people like me. The whole point of that service shit is to get something out of it for yourself. So, you tell those fuckers you've almost got me convinced to move into one of their bullshit shelters. You just need a little more time. You come back to see me, and I'll teach you about Yemoja. And that's what you'll get out of it. That's how you'll help yourself."

A movement from the direction of the trees behind the totem caught Noelle's attention. A man — Butch — stepped into the clearing. He held a solid piece of cut lumber, about a yard long, across his chest.

"Hey! Addie!" croaked the man. "Look what I've got. You should listen to that pretty girl. You never know who's going to come across your camp and take your shit when you're not around. But I don't need this little ol' piece of wood." He tossed the two-by-four back over his shoulder and pulled his knife out of its sheath. "Not when I've got this."

Addie rose to her feet, and Noelle lifted herself out of her chair.

Addie dropped her cigarette and crushed it out with her heel. "Hello, Butch," she said. "How's your head?"

"Fuck you, Addie. You're not holding no club now." He took a step toward the women and raised his knife to give them a good look at it.

Addie didn't flinch. "I fuckin' told you before to keep out of my things."

"You shouldn't leave them laying around. There's some bad people out in these woods."

"Yeah? And I'm looking at one of the worst of them right now. You get on out of here, Butch. You're not welcome."

Butch turned toward Noelle. "Why not? Am I interrupting your little girl talk? Maybe I've got a few things to say to her, too. Does your new girlfriend know you're a fuckin' witch?"

"She knows you're an ignorant motherfucker."

It Takes A Village

Butch sniffed the air. "I'm not so goddamned ignorant that I can't smell cigarettes. And beer, too. Tell you what. You give me some, and I'll find some other place to enjoy it."

Addie crossed her arms. "Beer's all gone. And you aren't gonna get any of my cigarettes. I don't like the way you asked for them. You're a rude motherfucker." Addie turned toward Noelle and whispered, "When I tell you to, you run to the water."

"What are you sayin' to her, bitch?" The man took another step toward Addie, pulling up even with the totem. "I ain't in the mood for askin' twice. Give me your cigarettes before I have to take 'em from you."

Addie bent down and lifted the pack of cigarettes from the ground where she'd left them. "You want some? Tell you what. You be nice and ask Yemoja."

Butch stopped in his tracks. "What?"

Addie nodded toward the totem. "Ask her for some smokes. But you gotta be polite about it. Get down on your knees and ask her nicely. If she says it's okay, I'll split the rest of the pack with you."

Butch turned toward the totem. He turned back to glare at Addie. "You're crazy, bitch! Here's what I think of this fuckin' piece of shit." He ripped the blue tablecloth off the top of the totem until it was hanging from the knotted white sheet. Brandishing the knife, he sliced and tore at the sheet until it fell away in pieces. The tablecloth fell to the ground, leaving the crudely carved tree stub exposed. Butch raised his knife and sliced through the carved face with the edge of the blade, leaving a deep diagonal scratch from one eye, across the nose, to the corner of the crudely carved smile. He surveyed his work for a moment before kicking at the pebbles surrounding the stub and scattering them in all directions.

Addie turned to Noelle. "Now, girl. Head for the water."

Noelle hesitated. "But…"

It Takes A Village

"Now! No questions. Go!"

Butch began advancing on the women, knife in hand. Noelle turned and ran.

As she approached the riverbank, a black cloud rose from the water, enclosing her in darkness. With a cry, she stumbled and fell into the river with a splash. As she struggled to regain her feet, she was pulled deeper into the icy waters by an irresistible current until the surface of the river was far over her head. Straining to hold her breath, she flailed her arms in a desperate attempt to fight the current and pull herself to safety.

It was no use. The frigid water chilled her to her bones, taking the fight out of her. With her heart pounding and her head spinning, Noelle knew there was nothing she could do. This was it: she was going to drown.

A calm descended over Noelle. The freezing cold numbed her body, which stopped struggling and went limp. Her heartbeat slowed, and her head cleared. Her lips parted, and cold water poured into her mouth and down her throat. To Noelle's surprise, she didn't choke. Instead, the water passed out of her throat and back into the river depths. She reached up and gently touched the slits that had somehow appeared on the sides of her neck. The slits closed as more of the river passed through her lips. A moment later, they reopened to let a stream of water back out again.

Breathing in with her mouth and exhaling through her newly formed gills, Noelle drifted through the pitch-black waters, numb to the freezing temperatures, floating like a feather in the wind, until her calm was disturbed by a heavy splash from above. As she strained to see through the darkness, she nearly leaped out of her skin when the outlines of a face appeared inches in front of her eyes. A muffled scream reached her ears as bubbles rose from the open mouth and floated toward the surface. Beneath the bulging eyes, the face was stretched and distorted almost beyond recognition, but Noelle knew that scar cutting through the patchy head of hair. As Noelle reached toward the face, it disappeared into the swirling darkness, as if pulled away by a sudden tug.

    The churning waters settled, leaving Noelle drifting in the peaceful flow. Dreamlike images formed in her mind, visions of flowing eddies and currents. These expanded until Noelle could sense the body of the river from within its depths. Reaching farther, she sensed more of the river until, at last, she could sense the entire course of the waterway, from the main body of the river known as the Sacramento, through the many scattered tributaries in its broad floodplain — all the way to its multitude of sources in the melting snows of the mountains of California and Southern Oregon.

    The vision didn't stop there. As Noelle drifted, both in body and mind, she saw how the river emptied into the mighty Pacific Ocean, and how the Pacific was really just one part of an even mightier world ocean, with uncounted numbers of rivers and streams flowing in and out of the massive body of water that covered more than seventy percent of the earth, dominating the surface of the planet, causing the land mass to appear small and insignificant in the eyes of Noelle's mind. She was filled with a sense of elation, of having been transformed into something beyond herself, something alien and powerful beyond measure.

    The feeling vanished.

    Confused — stunned — Noelle pushed her way upward through the water. As she drew near to the surface, an arm thrust itself through from above, hand extended and beckoning. Noelle reached for it and was pulled out of the river to the muddy bank, where she rested on her hands and knees and drew a breath of dry air deep into her lungs. When she reached to touch the side of her neck, she discovered only smooth skin. The gills had disappeared without a trace. Not even a scar had been left behind.

    Addie put a gentle hand on her shoulder. "Come. We need to talk."

Noelle followed Addie to the totem. "What happened to Butch?" she asked.

Addie stopped at the totem, waiting for Noelle to join her. She had replaced the blue tablecloth over the tree stub and tied it at the waist with the ripped sheet. Noelle noticed two additions to the carving. A deep scar now crossed the face, marring its crude features, and a sheathed knife now appeared at the side of the totem underneath the blue cloth. Noelle pulled the cloth aside and ran her fingers over the carving. It looked like the sheath that Butch had worn, but it was carved into the wood of the tree stub.

"How…?"

Addie turned to Noelle with a barely suppressed grin. "Yemoja is a spirit of celebration, of dancing and singing, eating and drinking. She's a real fun-loving party gal. She loves us humans, especially us women, but men, too. Good men. It takes a lot to make her mad. But she can get mad — real mad! And it can happen fast. My ancestors come from Portugal. They moved to Brazil after the great earthquake that destroyed the city of Lisbon. That was back in 1755. The earthquake produced a tsunami, a tidal wave, that might have killed up to fifty thousand people in Portugal, Spain, and Morocco. Maybe more. It changed history." Addie turned to the totem. "That's what Yemoja can do if you really piss her off. She was fuckin' fed up with the Portuguese using her waters to ship her people off to the New World in chains. The Portuguese government got the message and ended the slave trade a few years afterward. Officially, at least." She laughed. "The waves from that tsunami reached all the way across the Atlantic to South America! Hell, we're lucky that Butch just irritated her a little."

Noelle frowned. "She showed me something when I was under the water. I think she wanted me to get an idea of the extent of her…, I don't know… her reach, or her power."

Addie's smile grew. "She'll keep the scar as a reminder." She pointed to the carving of the sheathed knife. "And the knife, too. Not that she needs one, but I think she thinks its fuckin' cool."

"And Butch?"

"Forget about him. If you ask me, that asshole got off pretty fuckin' easy."

~*~

Two days later, Noelle stood in front of a small fiberglass and plastic hut, the color of bleached bone, one of twenty-five isolated structures arranged in a compact five-by-five grid, all perched atop a gray cement surface.

Addie stood at her side, a sneer on her upper lip.

After a time, Noelle let out a sigh. "I see what you mean. It's…"

"Dead," Addie finished. "Deadest thing I've ever seen. How can anyone live inside a thing like that?"

"It's got running water. And a toilet."

"I've got a river."

Noelle wrinkled her nose. "Ewww!"

Addie snorted. "Where do you think you're flushing all your shit to?"

"There's processing plants."

"Sure there are."

Noelle continued to stare at the hut. "Even I would rather be homele — um… unsheltered — than live in one of these things."

"So why don't you? You know, the folks down by the river are actually a pretty decent bunch. Daniel's a quiet guy, but friendly. He reads whatever book he can get his fuckin' hands on, and he makes these little dreamcatcher thingies. He sells them to the lookie-loos who come through, slumming, for whatever they're willing to give him. Charlie plays pretty tunes on his guitar, even though it only has four strings. Lili's got a real cute golden retriever named Gypsy, and she spends all day walking her up and down the bike trail and through the woods. She doesn't talk much — I think her mind is fried — but she's very sweet. Herbert sits next to the bike trail and gives all the bikers a big friendly wave. Some of them stop and chat with him, and he's full of stories. He lost an arm in Afghanistan and got screwed by the VA. It gives him trouble sometimes, but there's not much he can do about it."

Noelle continued staring at the sterile hut. "They don't sound like a bad bunch of people."

Addie grunted. "There's some real kooks running around, too, and you gotta be careful around them. Derrick runs through the woods screaming at the devils in his head. He needs medication, but it's too hard for him to get it. Marci hates Jews, and she thinks everyone she meets is a part of some secret global conspiracy that rules the world. She's annoying, but I don't think she's violent. She just yells abusive shit at people. But most of the folks are pretty chill. They pal around with each other and like to have a good time. Just don't try to have a political discussion with them. They'll spend hours bitching about stuff they don't know shit about. But, all-in-all, it's not a bad crowd. No worse than the people you work with, I'll bet."

Noelle chuckled. "You might have a point there."

Addie clapped Noelle on the back. "Stick with me, girl, and I'll make sure you're welcome here."

A shudder ran up Noelle's spine. "Ha! No thank you. I'll visit you, but I can't live like that. It might work for you, but I could never move out of my condo."

"Why not? It's just a bigger one of these." She gestured toward the drab little hut.

"Hmmph. Maybe. But somehow it's not the same."

It Takes A Village

Addie hunched her shoulders and extended her hands. "Hey, don't say I didn't try."

Noelle gave her head a vigorous shake, more to change the subject than anything else. "I sent in a report yesterday recommending that we stop trying to force you to move into a shelter. I said that you were fine with living outdoors, and that displacing you would cause you more harm than good. I told them that the best way to help you would be to leave you alone."

Addie shot her a quick glance. "Did you mention Yemoja?"

"I said that you maintained a shrine to an African goddess, and that moving you away from it would be a violation of your ethnic rights and religious freedoms."

Addie chuckled. "Nice one. It reminds them that I could sue their asses. Nothing scares those fuckin' stuffed shirts like the possibility of a lawsuit. I probably wouldn't win, but I doubt they would want to go to the trouble of finding out."

"I didn't mention that Yemoja gave me a set of gills that show up whenever I'm in the water, and that she showed me a vision of the world's waterways."

"Good move. You hit them with weird shit like that, and they'll stick you in a fuckin' ward and send some well-meaning do-gooder to take care of you for a couple of hours a day. And I doubt they'll be bringing you any of that beer you like."

Noelle lowered her eyes. "They're taking me off your case. I'm to be transferred to another charge, a woman in memory care who outlived her family. I'm told she likes to knit, and I crochet, so they figure that's close enough."

Addie let out a slow breath. "I suppose they'll be sending someone else to have a go at me."

"I'm not sure. They might give you up as a lost cause."

It Takes A Village

Addie snorted. "Well that would be a relief. Those fuckers at the BDS are clueless. They say they want to help us, but all they really want to do is put us behind walls so that no one has to look at us. If they really wanted to help, they'd make sure Daniel has enough books to read, and that Lili has plenty of food for her dog. Maybe they'd even find a way to make sure Herbert had access to a VA hospital whenever he needed medical attention, and that Derrick had a steady supply of meds. Instead of trying to impose a uniform set of values on us, they might take the time to try to find out what we actually fuckin' need." She reached over and gave Noelle's hand a quick squeeze. "You're the first person they sent out here who was willing to listen to me ramble."

Noelle smiled. "That may be true. But you have to admit you're not an easy person to talk to. First thing you tried to do when you saw me was run me off."

"Ha! What did you expect? You come out here with those fuckin' expensive shoes and your nose all stuck in the air."

"But then you invited me back. Actually, you kind of demanded that I come back."

"What can I say. I felt sorry for you. It was so fuckin' obvious that you were in over your head. And I decided maybe I shouldn't be so fuckin' judgmental myself. Besides, I think Yemoja saw something in you. Anyway, you showed interest in her, and you were willing to let me talk about her." Addie turned away from the shelter. "Come on, this place gives me the fuckin' creeps. Let's get out of here."

"Want me to drive you back to the river?"

Addie waved off the invitation. "Nah. I'll walk."

"Are you sure? That's five miles!"

"More like three if you're on foot. I know some shortcuts."

"If you say so."

It Takes A Village

When the two women reached Noelle's car, Addie stopped, a sheepish smile on her face. "So, I'm not your charge anymore, right? Does this mean I won't be seeing your scrawny ass again?"

"I still plan to come by and visit you, if that's okay. You and Yemoja. The river is pretty, and swimming underwater while breathing through my neck is pretty damned cool!"

Addie's smile broadened. "That's my girl!"

A thoughtful expression came over Noelle's face. "You know, you guys may have your problems and your challenges, but it seems to me that the one thing you've all learned to do is live in the natural world." She shot Addie a sidelong grin. "All us sheltered folk might be able to learn a thing or two from you guys if we stopped trying to impose our values on you and maybe took some time to understand your point of view, instead."

"Damn right," Addie agreed. "Yemoja should never have let humanity leave the river. We climbed out onto the riverbank, and the next thing you knew we were shutting ourselves up in buildings and cutting ourselves off from where we came from. But nature isn't going anywhere, and it's always going to be our home. What you have to realize is that Yemoja doesn't need me or anyone else to take care of her. She's way stronger than we are. You've seen that for yourself. She and other spirits like her just want us to remember and appreciate them, and to not piss them off so much. Because this world is still bigger than we are, and it always will be. And if we keep turning our backs on nature and disconnect ourselves from it, it's us motherfuckers that's gonna die, not spirits like Yemoja. The world will get along just fine without us."

"I can't disagree with you, Addie," Noelle said, "but I still don't want to live in the mud and the trees, or even in the river. I still want to buy nice shoes and live in a dry, comfortable place with secure locks on the doors. But I'll come see you whenever I can. And pay my respects to Yemoja, of course."

Addie gave her a warm smile. "You know, we'll be having a festival at the shrine at the end of the year. Maybe you can help out with that."

"A festival? What kind of festival?"

"A festival festival, you dumb shit. You know, dressing up, drinking, dancing, partying, drinking, singing, throwing offerings on the water.... Did I mention drinking?"

"Who comes to these things?"

"I've been holding the year-end festival for five or six years now. Ever since I first moved here with the totem. It's still small, but it gets a little bigger every year. They come down the river. Last year I think I had about three dozen people or so. Mostly women, but a few men, too. It got pretty wild. Not good for me to fuckin' drink like that, but, hey — it's just once a year, right?"

"I'll come and keep you in line."

"Ha! Fuck you!" Addie poked Noelle in the ribs with her elbow.

Noelle flinched. "Ouch! You're such a bitch! Sounds like fun. I'll be more than happy to help with the planning."

"Good. Don't tell the BDS, though. They sent you to save me from my degenerate lifestyle, not to enable me. If you tell them you're gonna help this hopeless little old vagrant throw a motherfuckin' shindig, they'll think you're a complete loser, and you'll never get those promotions you're dreaming of." Addie threw back her head and let out a braying laugh that echoed through the grounds of the shelter. "Poor girl. You'll be stuck in the clerical pool for the rest of your fuckin' life!"

It Takes A Village

About Douglas Lumsden

Douglas Lumsden's parents raised him right: any mistakes he made were his own. Hopefully, he learned from them.

Douglas earned a doctorate in medieval European history at the University of California Santa Barbara. Go Gauchos! He taught world history at a couple of colleges before settling into a private college prep high school in Central California. After he retired, Douglas began to write an urban fantasy series featuring hardboiled private eye Alexander Southerland as he cruises through the mean streets of Yerba City and interacts with trolls, femme fatales, shape-shifters, witches, and corrupt city officials. He is currently working on a new series featuring Shade the Collector.

Douglas is happily married to his co-editor, Rita. The two of them can be found most days pounding the pavement in their running shoes. Rita listens to all of Douglas' ideas and reads all of his work. Her advice is beyond value. In return, he makes her tea and coffee whenever she wants it. It's a pretty sweet deal. They have two cats named Cinderella and Prince who like to lay around the house and look pretty.

You can find Douglas' blog at douglaslumsden.substack.com

His works are available through amazon:
amazon.com/author/douglaslumsden

It Takes A Village

It Takes A Village

COUNTING

A Poem

By Joyce C Mandrake

Eyes are dim,
Legs are slow, unsteady in their march
sitting long, long days.
Counting threads, weaving
In and out. In and out.
Not seeing colors others have placed on a loom
So loved from years of sitting quietly.
Feet up and down here a steady march
Of up and down, up and down.
There are younger eyes, helping, learning.
There are mature eyes, encouraging, listening.
Eyes are dim,
Legs are slow, unsteady in their march
Weaving the past, the present and future among the living.

It Takes A Village

It Takes A Village

SWORDS TO PLOWSHARES

By Eric Klein

When asked what inspired this story, Eric responded:

> While finalizing this anthology I found another story bubbling up, one where the lowly medtech was forced to teach the members of the military team how to survive just so they would leave her alone to care for her patient.
>
> The things we have to do just to be allowed to get our own job done.

It Takes A Village

SWORDS TO PLOWSHARES — Eric Klein

And he shall judge among the nations, and shall rebuke many people: and they shall beat their swords into plowshares, and their spears into pruninghooks: nation shall not lift up sword against nation, neither shall they learn war anymore.
(Isaiah 2:4).

"That is all of them, extraction complete. Everyone strap in we are getting out of here hot, their artillery has us spotted. Once in orbit all troopers should be checked out before getting into their statis pods.... Holy guano that one was close."

> Personal log MedTech Poyern 'Tukher
> Mission day 12, Date 7BE.870F.83
>
> This last mission was declared a failure, the team had to be evaced out, the new lieutenant was badly injured, and I am working hard to nurse him back to health. He took a nasty shot to the head. Shouldn't leave any permanent damage, but I wish he would wake up, it would make treating him easier. They say that we are two days from the nearest base, so I need to keep him alive until then.

Entering the bridge I say, "Captain, I would like to report that all of the soldiers are in their statis pods. You were able to recover about half the squad. Only one serious injury, Lieutenant Shyzer 'Zzun is in the medpod for his head wound. I am not sure when he will wake, the readings show that he took a serious hit, and I am hoping that the internal swelling will go down over time."

"Well done, MedTech, that is better than I had hoped. Whoever planned that raid either had bad intel or was incompetent. It is as if they had never set foot groundside. They sent in a small team up against entrenched artillery and arial support. We were lucky to get any of them out."

"Captain, everyone should grab onto something or buckle in, they seem to have tracked our take off and have launched pursuit. I'm going to try to shake them by cutting through the debris field and then jumping."

~*~

> Personal log MedTech Poyern 'Tukher
> Mission day 13, Date 7BE.8861.03
>
> We have been a day in jump space and things are quiet. Getting off of the planet was difficult and they had to take us through the debris field. There were multiple bangs as things hit the ship, but we got away and were able to make the jump to safety. I was able to check on all the soldiers and get them into their statis pods before the jump.

General quarters sounds, followed by the pilot. "All hand strap in, we are dropping out of jump space in two minutes. We are losing jump cohesion and I want to leave under control and not have it dump us hard." The ship's AI starts a countdown from ninety seconds, and I rush to my station in the medbay. I get buckled in as I feel the jump field drop; I don't know if it was intentional or if it failed.

"We have entered normal space inside a stellar system. G class star, at least three planets that are in the scanner, one is in the goldilocks zone. Oh shit, where did that come from?" The ship lurches to the right (I think the marines call it starboard"?) and then quickly up. I can hear a few light bangs as something hits the hull. "Ok, we seem to have popped out of jump in the local asteroid field. We will be clear in another minute but came out much too close to a large one with two mini-moons."

It Takes A Village

Another, louder bang, and a scraping sound. "We are clear. Heading to that goldilocks planet. I will update as we get more information on it." The intercom clicks off.

After a half hour the bumps and bangs stop, and the pilot indicates that it is safe to get up. I head down to the mess to grab a meal. I find the pilot and we get to chatting about where we grew up. He comes from a subsurface colony on a moon around the fifth planet of the Zycma system as did the captain. His father handled the hydroponics in the atmosphere plant, while I grew up on a farm on Yrd.

~*~

> **Personal log MedTech Poyern 'Tukher**
> **Mission day 14, Date 7BE.89B2.83**
>
> It has been a full day since we took off, and we are slowly moving out of the asteroid field. Lieutenant Shyzer 'Zzun is still unconscious and the medpod display is off the scale for when he will be out. I really hope that we can get him to the station soon.

"All hands this is the captain speaking. We have analyzed planet two, it is in the goldilocks zone, has a breathable atmosphere and fresh water, but no signs of advanced life. We will set down there to repair the ship before resuming our flight to station Zex Eyner. For now, the soldiers can remain in statis to conserve resources, unless or until they are needed. This will let the engineering team work more efficiently without them getting in the way. We will reach orbit in an hour, we will orbit a few times to assess the planet, and then should be on the surface ten minutes later. Captain out."

~*~

It Takes A Village

"We have achieved orbital insertion and have scanned over two orbits. The planet has three continents, which are more or less equidistant from each other. One is mostly in the northern hemisphere, the other two are a bit further south. Our target is on the northern continent not too far from the sea along a nice wide river. On this one we can see vegetation and what looks like some herd animals. No sign of cities or even villages on any of the continents, nothing that looks like a port or other built sites, so we are presuming that either there are no higher life forms or that they are still too primitive to build cities. All hands strap in for landing."

I check the Lieutenant, there was no change, and strap in.

"We are starting our descent, our course and reentry window are confirmed. Ionization beginning. We have an alert, the AI is showing fault messages for a loss of pressure and an increase in temperature on the bridge. Adjust life support to compensate for the fluctuations."

"Roger, uh …" The broadcast from the bridge went silent, but I could hear something bouncing off the hull over my head followed by the sound of metal screaming and then silence.

I seem to recall being bounced once, but the next thing I knew I was hanging upside down, still strapped to my chair with a throbbing in my head. The medpod is next to me, and all lights are green. I try to carefully unstrap. This time I wake up on the ceiling looking up at my chair. A more detailed check of the medpod shows that it is functioning normally, even though it is upside down. The Lieutenant is still the same, with no new injuries from the crash. Oh shit, we crashed. I had better go check on the bridge crew and soldiers to see if anyone needs medical treatment.

I grab a medkit off the wall and work my way to the bridge. What little is left is scorched, with ripped metal and pieces of what looks like melted glass everywhere. I see no signs of the command crew or even their chairs, so I have to presume that they were all killed on reentry. I feel a breeze, and as I turn, I

It Takes A Village

can see that the windshield is gone, and I am feeling the outside air. Luckily it is breathable if a bit strange smelling.

I go outside to see where we are and what is left of the ship, it isn't much. The front of the ship is burned out, and while the core with medbay is mostly still there, the rest of the ship is gone, including the landing bay and the statis pods. I am all alone, with the Lieutenant on an unknown world. No time to freak out, take a deep breath and follow my training 'never become a second patient.' After the crisis I can have time to freak out. It's time to take stock and see how I survive to take care of my patient.

> Personal log MedTech Poyern 'Tukher
> Mission day 15, Date 7BE.8B04.03
>
> Stranded on a strange world, I have managed to find some water and some plants that register as safe and nutritious so I can use them in the medpod — if I can figure out how to get to the input hopper with the medpod upside down.

I have managed to start a fire and boil some water I collected from a nearby river. By watching some small animals I have identified a few potentially edible plants that I used the medbay to determine are not harmful and contain some nutrients. They were a bit tough to chew, so I am boiling them using a bent cabinet door as a pan. One of the plants tastes bitter and astringent so I put it aside rather than eat it. Starting a fire was harder than I remembered from when I was a kid. The ship came to rest in a small valley, with what looked like caves in the northern side. I have seen a few different kinds of animals. Mostly they resemble rodents or lizards, and at least one small flying type that is staying far from me and the ship.

I wasn't able to determine the day length yesterday, but today I was up soon after the sun rose over the horizon. My chronometer says that was about three in the morning, but I am going to see how things work out over the course of day and give a rough local time from there.

It Takes A Village

Just after midday I hear shouting. Looking back along the gouge made by the ship, I can see two people waving at me. Seeing me, they start to run down to the ship. It takes them almost twenty minutes to make it down. At first, they are excited to see me and start giving their report. It seems that their statis pods held together and opened when registered safe atmosphere. Stopping to catch their breath, they realize that I am not an officer or even a soldier, so they demand food pointing to my greens boiling over a fire. I explain that there aren't enough for me and the Lieutenant (mentioning him gets them to settle down), so I show them what the plants look like when raw and send one of them to collect the same greens and one kind of root (showing them leaves) so we can cook some food. The other I send for more water, both to consume and to use for cleaning. As I take one off the roots out of the water one of the privates reaches for it. I slap him away. "What are you an animal, go wash your paws first."

"Yes, ma'am."

Over the meal they loosen up a bit, and ask all sorts of questions about how I knew how to prepare the meal etc. I explain that I grew up on a farm on one of the colony planets. We would go out on wilderness survival exercises as part of our scout training. We learned how to start a fire, boil water, identify food plants (and animals), and other useful things.

A young man, Private Oeshalt 'Zzun, says that he was the son of a maintenance worker on PZ VGG. There were no habitual planets or moons in their system, just an asteroid belt full of useful metals that they remotely mined. When he came of age there was a call for recruits and his number came up for the draft. "This is my first time on dirt without someone shouting or shooting at me. It's kind of peaceful."

The other private, a young woman named Azrapitz 'Tukher, said that more or less the same happened to her on PZ DS. She had hoped to follow in her father's footsteps and do plumbing for the station and had been following

It Takes A Village

him around to learn by watching and helping, but she came up for the draft and that ended that.

After the meal we clean up as best we can and all get some sleep, crowding around the medpod.

> **Personal log MedTech Poyern 'Tukher**
> **Mission day 16, Date 7BE.8C55.83**
>
> At daybreak a few more soldiers arrived, cold and hungry. I got them searching for more of the edible plants and trying to track some of the animals. I need a few to see if they are safe to eat, and if they will provide the rest of the nutrients needed to replenish the medpod.

By mid-morning I have the six privates out trying to find more for us to eat. I now have one team looking for more of the leaves and roots that I already know are safe, a second team collecting other plants for me to test. And the third is trying to hunt or trap the local animals. That team has brought me several charred remains that were beyond the system's ability to test. They are having a hard time understanding that using their blasters on an animal less than a meter in size doesn't work for food. But all they have been taught is to kill without regard to what happens to their target. It seems I will have to teach them to trap and kill without using their blasters.

After lunch I got to chatting with Private Azrapitz 'Tukher to see what she knows about how to bring water closer to the medpod. I didn't care if it is piped or a channel, but that meant explaining what a channel is. I mention that I wanted to take her upstream to find a good point to bring the water to us, and almost as one the squad spoke up and said they wouldn't let us go alone. I agreed, it was an unknown world with unknown hazards. But while I agreed that we have an armed escort, I insisted on leaving two behind to watch over and protect the Lieutenant. They reluctantly acknowledged I was right, and that the Lieutenant needed guarding. Two agreed to stay behind.

It Takes A Village

Off we went, her with a meter-long pipe she found in the wreckage and her blaster. As we walked upstream, we discussed how running water to bathe, and cook would be helpful. We looked over the terrain and I pointed out that the stream came from higher in the hills, so if we could find a place that was high enough, then we could divert the water down towards our camp and then back out to the stream further down. Some of this took a little explaining; all her life water moved because of pumps and not gravity. But once the concept became clear, she started to expand on options. Bring the water down, and we could carve sequential pools to bathe in, for drinking and supplying the medpod, maybe even use it to help secure the area. It didn't take much encouragement to get her to really take off on these ideas, it was almost as if explaining what I wanted opened up a dam of creativity that was hiding inside of her.

We get to a point about six meters higher than the camp, and start to look at possible ways to get the water to come to us. She starts with the pipe she brought, but it is neither thick enough nor long enough to help. I use that pipe to draw in the dirt as I describe what a channel is, or as she finally understood, an artificially created stream bed. She was ready to start blasting at the stream and working her way down. But she understood when I suggested working the other way so the water wouldn't be in the way of the work. From that she actually came up with the concept of a sluice gate that could be opened or closed as needed to regulate the water flow. Next, I asked if they had ever used their blasters to dig trenches or any earthworks, and the very thought shocked her. Blasters were weapons to kill with, not tools.

I leave her with one of the guards watching over her as she tries to work out a way to dig the channel after being cautioned not to use the actual path until she knew how to make it. The other guard escorted me back to camp.

When we get back to camp, I sit with the three of them to see how to capture or kill animals without blasting them. We discuss their edged weapons

It Takes A Village

training; turns out each is carrying a knife and has some rough training in spearing. We then go into traps and snares. Seems that their combat training did include a (very) short section on capturing the enemy alive when required. I leave them discussing various pit traps and snares while I go check the medpod.

> **Personal log MedTech Poyern 'Tukher**
> **Mission day 17, Date 7BE.8DA7.03**
>
> **Lieutenant Shyzer 'Zzun is still unconscious and the medpod display still off the scale, but the system shows that it is functioning normally.**

Leaving two others to guard the medpod, I take the rest to see what Private Azrapitz 'Tukher has come up with as a concept for bring the water to our camp. She had practiced with shooting a short line of connected holes to bring the water. It could work, but the problem is that it is not even close to smooth bottom, so less easy to manage and control the depths. I ask them about the blasters, can they work as a laser rather than a pulse? It turns out that they can, but not for long. Describing the idea of a smooth path for the water, two of them try as Azrapitz and I watch. With a bit of practice they manage to carve out an inverted triangle that is close to smooth.

Walking back, we lay out a path explaining that it needs to go steadily lower as it progresses down towards camp. Azrapitz and I look where we can create a pool for drinking/cooking and pool for bathing lower downstream below our camp.

Over lunch I ask, "Didn't any of you have any wilderness survival in scouts or your military training? When I was young, I was taught in scouts there are several things to do in order to survive. First establish a base to work from. We have this area here where the medbay landed, there are hills right here to carve out some caves to use as a place to stay out of the rain. After we

It Takes A Village

get that, we'll need to find more food and arrange a good supply of water. Then we need to see what we have or can use from the ship. Once we are safe and fed, we can look at what comes next — can we find a way to send a message for rescue, can we build anything from the ship. But those will be a few weeks away so they can wait. Any questions?"

One of them asks, "How do you know this stuff? It wasn't in my basic training."

"Well, when I was little, I was trying to help work on the family farm. So, I learned a lot about plants and animals. Both how to grow them and how to heal them. Before I was drafted, I expected to study to become a veterinarian, but the military had other ideas — and even though I was strong enough for combat I was assigned to become a medic. Beyond that, each summer from when I was five, I was sent off to scouts to learn more. As we got older, it became more about survival and planning than about fun activities. How to find food, shelter, water, and everything you need to survive was emphasized to us. Now, this was on Ibnh Zex and that is nothing like here. But the same lessons apply. First, I tested that the water was not contaminated by strange metals or other poisons, then I checked that it didn't contain any harmful biologicals. But I still boil it to be sure, you never know what our inoculations will or won't protect us from. Then I checked the plants around the crash site to see what was safe and nutritious to eat. Both of these I then used to enhance the supply in the medpod as it can take almost any safe biomatter to create what is needed by the patient. There are some elements, like calcium, as well as proteins that are needed. This is why I had you out hunting so we could see what we could use. Identification of safe versus hazardous are just the extremes I am testing for now. Later I will test for optimal nutritional content, not just poisons, and we can use to enhance our diet."

I take a drink of water. "The channel I asked Private Azrapitz 'Tukher to make is to bring water closer both for convenience and safety. If planned right, it can be used both for consumption and bathing. This way no one has to go far after dark and we can set up a proper security perimeter." They all start nodding at the acknowledgment of security concerns. "I don't know about the rest of you, but I could use a real bath. Even in cold water."

> Personal log MedTech Poyern 'Tukher
> Mission day 18, Date 7BE.8EF8.83
>
> Lieutenant Shyzer 'Zzun is still unconscious and the medpod display has just come on to scale, no clear indication of when he will be released but his bones are knitted and other repairs are progressing.

 While I am tending to the Lieutenant, Private Azrapitz 'Tukher comes up bouncing with excitement. Like a little kid rushing for mommy, she grabs my had and pulls me from the medpod. After a minute of my almost being dragged while protesting she stops and announces, "here you go" as if she is announcing a major achievement. Looking down, I see the completed water channel. We have stopped a little upstream of the cave where there is a pool for collecting water for eating and drinking. About three meters downstream of there is an almost two-meter pool where we can bathe. She points to a spot just upstream of this where there is a smaller pool. "Here we can put hot rocks to warm the bathing water."

 As I look back at her she is eagerly looks up at me. I can tell she is awaiting a response. "I am impressed, and the idea of a hot, or at least warm, bath is amazing. Nice initiative."

 "Wait, there is more. I have set up the sluice gate at the top with a variable opening to let us control how much water flows. This way we can keep a regular amount and open it up to flush it out if needed."

 "Now, that is good thinking. It will keep the water from fouling up and allow us to keep fresh even after bathing. Very good work." I can see her

It Takes A Village

standing taller from my reaction. "So, let's warm up some rocks and the two of us get a warm bath."

"I wonder what we have that can be used as soap."

"Well, let's see, we have wood ash from the fire, and you brought us the water. If we can find an animal that has some fat, we could render that down and make soap. There is even a plant that smells fairly nice that we can use to make it smell better. We can make our own soap with that."

Getting back to the medbay we find Private Oeshalt 'Zzun holding a collection of small animal carcasses. "Look at what we found in the traps. Are they safe to eat?"

A check with the medpod scanner shows that one is probably poisonous to eat in any quantity, but the others should be safe. We take one of these and put it in the medpod nutrient processing unit and go to roast the rest. The poisonous one is quite fatty, so we try to render the fat for use in soap. I have them save the skins and bones for use around the camp. We gather some of that bitter and astringent-tasting plant and boil them down and smear the resulting gunk on the skins. I explain that "I am hoping that they have enough tannic acid to cure the skins a bit as we don't have extra salt and this is a test."

> Personal log MedTech Poyern 'Tukher
> Mission day 20, Date 7BE.919B.83
>
> Lieutenant Shyzer 'Zzun is still unconscious and the medpod display shows that his fever is down. The indicators are still not showing a countdown for his release, but all look promising. The nutrient levels, especially calcium, are way down. I need to get the team to collect more plants and animals for processing.

Just before sunset Sergent Inzhenr 'Tukher PZ G and Private Azrapitz 'Tukher ask if I can accompany them for an inspection of the camp. The various soldiers are all busy at different tasks. When did we get so many? I count eighteen of them doing different tasks. One is cooking an evening meal,

It Takes A Village

two are bathing, one is banging some metal part of the ship, but I don't recognize what they are making.

We loop back behind the medpod towards the hills, and they show me a large dark hole in the side of the closest hill. Walking into the cave shelter, they show me what they have done. The first room is a common area with a raised cooking platform (no more bending down to cook). Private Azrapitz points out that above it there are ventilation holes to let out the smoke that are cut diagonal to prevent rain from getting in.

Off of the main room are four small entries. We enter one and see sleep shelves around the walls. "Male barracks," Sergent Inzhenr announces. The next room is identical, "female barracks." The next room is smaller with a bigger door. "We can get the medpod in here until the Lieutenant is healed. There are holes to run the wires up top for solar panels. You may have noticed Private Oeshalt 'Tukher out there is making the stand for the solar panels to get optimum light." That explain what she is building. Stepping back to the common room, "This last room is for you as you aren't one of the soldiers. I figured you would prefer not to sleep in the barracks. We have carved out a few shelves in each room for storage and will make tables and chairs next. After we move the medpod inside, more spaces or rooms can be carved as needed. Next, I was thinking of a mess hall."

As we are leaving, Azrapitz points out a section of the wall that is carved out as if for a desk with a hole above it. "Tomorrow, I will be bringing running water into that basin for use while cooking. We will still have to go out for the bathroom, but you will have running water like civilized people. Sergent Inzhenr and I were discussing an actual constant flow bathroom, but that will wait until we get everything else done."

The two of them are practically bursting as they stare at me. "First a hot bath and now a house with room for everyone and even running water. I didn't think you could get so much done so fast. Great work!"

It Takes A Village

Inzhenr stops at the opening and points to some notches in the wall. "I have Private Leryr 'Zzun working on a door to secure this space. Air ventilation at the top and sealed against small creatures at the bottom. He should have it ready by tomorrow night."

> Personal log MedTech Poyern 'Tukher
> Mission day 25, Date 7BE.9833.03
>
> Lieutenant Shyzer 'Zzun is still unconscious and the medpod display shows that his fever is down. The indicators are still not showing a countdown for his release, but all look promising. It has taken a few days to lower the medpod and prepare it for the move. Today I checked that the nutrient levels are all topped up and it is ready for moving.

At midday we get the medpod in place and hooked up to the solar panels. Its room has pipes to allow it running water, and even a pipe to let it drain out downstream of the camp.

After that I am led on an inspection of the cave. Everyone has moved in, each with their personal sleep shelf, some bunk-bed style, all with their own shelf for personal things inside the bed nook and shelves carved into the wall next to their bed for clothing and anything else that they need. Each has their own cured animal-hide water skin. The kitchen has a proper cooking fire and several pots and pans. A late addition is a fully stacked wood rack, so no one has to go out for wood at night. As promised, after a few mishaps with the drain that resulted in flooding the floor (it helped clean it, so no problem there), the kitchen has running water that along with the medpod feeds out well below the bathing pool. The old cooking fire outside has been enhanced to be a smoker, so there is even a small larder of smoked meat and plants. We now have enough soap for both the kitchen and bathing area.

I am really impressed by their progress. This band of soldiers collected from across the federation have banded together and built us a real home.

It Takes A Village

Personal log MedTech Poyern 'Tukher
Mission day 32, Date 7BE.A16D.83

Lieutenant Shyzer 'Zzun is still unconscious and the medpod display shows that he should be released any day now.

Last night Sergent Inzhenr came knocking on my chamber door (mine is the only one with a door so far) and asked if we can speak in the morning. I am curious what she wants as he was acting a big nervous and didn't want to talk before bed.

Just after breakfast Inzhenr comes to speak with me alone. After a bit of small talk about things around the camp he seems to be hesitant to go on staring down at his feet.

"Alright, Inzhenr, what is it that you are having trouble telling me?"

"Well, I want to leave the camp for several days, and, well, I don't want to abandon you."

"Why do you want to leave?"

"Well, um, I was chatting with Private Skartigaf 'Zzun, and we think we can backtrack to the lost pods to see what can be used here in camp. But that would mean most if not all of us leaving you for at least a week to backtrack to the furthest pod and work our way back with what we can find. I am not even sure that we will find anything useful, but we need more metal and parts to keep building things here. Private Khyrurg 'Tukher thinks she passed some parts that may have been from the bridge and might have been from the communications consol."

"I see. You want to take everyone to see what you can bring back. That is actually a great idea. If you can get us even one statis pod, we can use it to store food longer than smoking will do. But those pods are really big and heavy, how will you bring anything back?"

It Takes A Village

"Private Rir 'Tukher has been working with some of the pipes and tubes, and has made a sort of chassis that can be attached to a statis pod to give it wheels for transporting back. The closet one that is still in good condition will be sent back, while the rest of us go on to see what else we can find. I can use every back we have for carrying, but don't want to leave you and the Lieutenant unprotected. So, with your permission I will leave Privates Azrapitz 'Tukher and Zelner 'Zzun to guard and help you while we are away."

"That is fine, but I want you to spend a day getting enough food and water for your trip. I don't know how far you will be from the river or what you will find along the way. You can take the team tomorrow."

He looks relieved, and goes to talk to the troops. We all gather to see what supplies they need and what we can do without (or quickly replace while they are gone). There is an air of excitement in them as they get ready for their first "away mission" since we crashed.

> **Personal log MedTech Poyern 'Tukher**
> **Mission day 39, Date 7BE.AAA8.03**
>
> **Lieutenant Shyzer 'Zzun is still unconscious and the medpod display shows that he should be released any day now. But it has been unchanged for the past two days.**
>
> **Sergent Inzhenr and the troops have been gone a week now. Late yesterday two privates arrived with a statis pod filled with the salvage they could find.**

We start unpacking the statis pod and Private Oeshalt 'Tukher is working on running additional wiring from the solar panels to the main room to power the pod. Azrapitz has measured it and is carving a nook in the wall that is shared with the room where the medpod is running.

Once the pod is in place Private Rir removes the wheels and packs them into a bag. He turns and salutes me. "I had best go catch up with Sergent Inzhenr, so he can bring more back using these wheels."

It Takes A Village

Private Oeshalt responds, "I can't leave yet, I need another day to hook this up."

"Zelner, grab your things and go with Rir. Oeshalt and Azrapitz can stay with me as I have need of both of their skills."

"Yes'm!" He runs into the barracks to grab his gear. They are on their way in no time.

"Ok, Oeshalt and Azrapitz, I have a challenge for the two of you. I saw some lights in the stuff that came out of the statis pod. It got me thinking. I need some light in the med room. Preferably, both one for the room and one I can move around as needed. This way, I can check on the Lieutenant and anyone that comes in needing treatment. A table for people to lay down while I treat them would be good, and maybe a space for another statis pod if they bring one back. Think you can handle that while they are away?"

They look at each other and in unison snap to attention, "Yes, ma'am."

"Well, don't just stand there looking smug, get to work." I smile at them.

> Personal log MedTech Poyern 'Tukher
> Mission day 46, Date 7BE.B3E2.83
>
> Lieutenant Shyzer 'Zzun is still unconscious and the medpod display shows that he should be released any time now, I wish the display would show something new it has been two weeks with the same indicator.
> Something big knocked over the smoker last night. We could hear it, but didn't dare go out to check.

The smoker was smashed and there are large prints in the ash around the remains. Strangely, none of the meat appears to be gone, just knocked around. Oeshalt and Azrapitz have gone back to carrying their larger guns while discussing adding lights outside of our home.

It Takes A Village

While we are cleaning up the mess and rinsing off the smoked meat Sergent Inzhenr and the troops return pulling not one or two, but five statis pods open and full of salvage. He takes one look at the mess and sends a few soldiers out to see if they can track whatever it was that knocked over the smoker.

The rest of the troop starts unloading the pods, they have quite a haul of parts and pieces of the ship. He reports that they failed to find anything that looked like radio equipment but have a number of light panels and other parts that should be useful. Among it are several more solar panels. I send Oeshalt and Azrapitz in to carve two more statis pod nooks in the medbay.

After a few hours, the troops return with what appears to be a large lizard, almost three meters in length. They are carrying it slung from a longer stick than I have seen around the camp. Zelner salutes the Sargent. "We found it downstream sunning on a rock. There were these tall, thin plants growing so we cut one to use to carry it. Turns out that they are mostly hollow." Looking over at me, "As you can see, they are quite strong. We think that they may be useful to build chairs and other things that we discussed you wanted around camp, ma'am. Things like utensils, shelves, etc."

Personal log MedTech Poyern 'Tukher
Mission day 53, Date 7BE.BD1D.03

Lieutenant Shyzer 'Zzun is still unconscious and the medpod display is finally counting down with less than an hour until release.

I tell the troops, and they rush to get cleaned up and ready for an inspection. Personally, I doubt that Lieutenant Shyzer will be up to much right out of the pod. After all, he hasn't walked in almost two months and was knocked out during the combat.

It Takes A Village

While they are getting ready, I clean up the medbay and check the rest of our home to make sure that it is neat and tidy. Other than the pile of salvage, our den and camp are spotless. The pool has been flushed with clean water and there are rocks warming so I can send Lieutenant Shyzer for a warm bath. Two months in the medpod after battle, and he will need to be washed off.

As predicted by the medpod, the Lieutenant wakes. He starts to scream out battle orders and seems disoriented to be in a medpod. He tries to get up and out of the machine, but he is weak and collapses back into it. He finally acknowledges my existence and reluctantly accepts a water skin and takes a drink. He then accepts my help getting out of the pod. He brushes off my attempt to report and shouts for the senior trooper to report.

Inzhenr was behind me and shouts out, "Sergent Inzhenr 'Tukher PZ G reporting sir." I turn and see him standing at rigid attention.

"Sergent, prepare the troops for another charge, we have to …"

"But, sir."

"No buts, Sergent. We have orders to take this planet and I won't let a little bump on my head stop our following orders. Now, get the troops ready for inspection."

"Now, you just hold it right there."

"Who are you to be ordering me around? You are just a medtech."

"Yes, and you are still a patient. So, until I discharge you, you will lay back down and get checked while we bring you up to speed."

"But…"

"That was no 'little bump' on your head that you received fifty-three days ago. That was a near fatal shot and the medpod has been putting you back together ever since. You took a nasty shot to the head, lost more than half of your squad and had to be evaced off the planet."

"Wait, we are not on Shtern Akht?"

It Takes A Village

"No, so you were about to go off and start a war with no one to fight. If you will let me finish, I will try to bring you up to date."

"Well, um, alright. Where are we and what is our situation? Where is the ship's captain?"

"See, now you are starting to think. After we were evaced they hit our ship as we went into orbit. In short, the ship was damaged, and we dropped out in this system. They tried to land for repairs. There was a crack in the windscreen, none of the crew made it. Before they attempted to land, I heard them say that we were in an uncharted stellar system, and this was the only habitable world. Over the past months we have been building a place to live while we collect what we can salvage. So far, nothing related to drive or communications has been found."

"We are on a non-federation world, with no communications and no transportation?"

"And no enemies or large life forms to fight. Our supplies are limited as we learn to use the native plants and animals for food and survival materials." I point to the water skin he is holding. "I think you will be quite surprised with what we have managed in just two months, especially when you consider most of the troops have never been on the ground without being shot at before."

I am not sure if it is the shock of everything I told him, or he wasn't fully recovered enough but he seems to black out. I lay him back in the medpod and close the lid. The indicator shows he is sleeping normally.

Personal log MedTech Poyern 'Tukher
Mission day 55, Date 7BE.CF92.03

Lieutenant Shyzer 'Zzun is did not wake up yesterday. The medpod display shows his systems recovering and he should be at full strength — just a bit weak when he wakens. I took the opportunity to read his medical file from his medichip. I never realized he was even younger than I am. If the data is up to date,

It Takes A Village

he must have just gotten out of the academy right before our mission.

I am eating breakfast when I hear Lieutenant Shyzer start to move. "That smells good. Do you think I could get something to eat?" His tone and demeanor are nothing like when he first woke two days ago.

"Sure. We were trying to smoke some of the native animal meat to preserve it before we recovered a statis pod. We now have something that passes as a decent bacon. We still haven't found a good supply of eggs. But there are roots that work well with the bacon. Let me get you a plate."

After he has eaten a proper meal (he kept wanting more bacon and less vegetables — but I insisted, so he would get stronger) I took him to wash up before a tour of our camp.

He was impressed with the solar power setup and how many modern comforts we had. And as he relaxed in the hot pool, he said, "I could never have organized this. I grew up on PZ QWV, running in the corridors was all I knew. Plants grew in hydroponic liquids, food came from a slot in the wall. When you were telling me about using the animals for survival materials and I saw that I had drank from an animal skin, it was too much for me. I panicked and passed out. When I woke, I took some time to think before the smells made me realize I was ravenous. Nothing in my background or training prepared me for living off the land. I guess that we are better off under civilian leadership as the military didn't prepare any of us for this." Standing up, he raises a paw in salute. "What are your orders, Madam Mayor?"

> *The wolf will live with the lamb, the leopard will lie down with the goat, the calf and the lion and the yearling together; and a little child will lead them.*
> *(Isaiah 11:6-9).*

It Takes A Village

ON HER MAJESTY'S MISSION

By Ulff Lehmann

When asked what inspired this story, Ulff responded:

> I wanted to write another Thyrn story but I didn't know what... I had all these disparate pieces about the history of the continent, the structure of Kalduuhn, Ma'tallon, the gods, and then I thought "how would one exploit the Rule of Consequence?"

It Takes A Village

ON HER MAJESTY'S MISSION — Ulff Lehmann

Good day. No, you have the right suite; this is your place, in her Majesty's palace, but your place all the same. Do come in, please. The name is Thyrn, I'm an exterminator, of sorts. Drink? Right, why the Scales am I offering you a drink in your own place. Do you mind if I? Cheers. My, my, you got a well stocked liquor cabinet here. Nice craftsmanship too. Breiamhbéan? Must have been a pain to get such a beaut, right? I mean, it's a long trip to Breiamhbéo, isn't it? Months.

What?

Oh, right. What am I doing here?

As I said, the name's Thyrn.

You don't remember me? Interesting, and you're telling the truth. I do remember you.

How do I know you're truthful?

You see, I'm a Knight of... yes, of course "of Kalduuhn," what else did you expect? Knight of the Soup Kitchen? We're in the bloody Royal Palace in the capital, in your bloody apartment suite, the lock wasn't tampered with. Of course I'm a Knight of Kalduuhn! No, please, don't be alarmed, if I wanted you dead, you would be. By your pallor, you have heard of us.

Right, the Cullings, good, some folks in this place remember. What? Yes, of course the court remembers. Well, mostly. We don't usually enter the Palace, unless it's on special invitation. No, of course you didn't invite me, I know that. Then... yes, now the wheels are turning, good. Yes, her Majesty, Queen Luertha Kassor herself invited me. And her steward opened the door to your apartment whilst you were dancing the night away.

Justice never sleeps, and that's why I'm here. Sleepless, just like you, only I didn't drink wine, until now. Oh damnation, that's a fucking good

It Takes A Village

vintage. That's old Gathranean grapes; you rarely find that stuff here anymore. Too much was lost during the slow decline of the Empire, you know. We gained some stuff too, our laws here in Kalduuhn, but what are laws compared to these grapes, eh?

Please, sit. Sorry, it's your place. I am your guest. Interesting conundrum, don't you think? You're a guest in the Queen's Palace, I mean, you rent this suite in the Palace, I work for the throne. Am I technically your guest, or am I merely her Majesty's Knight doing his duty, thus technically, you'd be my guest, by extension.

You're right, it's late, I best get to the point.

Now, you see, I know you. We met a few months ago, on the road to Breiamhbéo. Oh! See? You should have sat down. Please, let me help you. My, my, you're shaking.

Back then I was on my way back to Ma'tallon from the Eastern Empire, and you were on your way to East Gathran. You don't remember? And you're telling the truth. This is getting more and more interesting.

Now, you're in importing and exporting goods, yes? You sell the occasional steeloak trunk and pottery from here to there; and wine, silk, spices, and the cabinet, again, beautiful craftsmanship, from there to here, right?

You told me that you wanted to negotiate with an embassy of a far eastern realm which was at the Imperial Court. Can't recall the name of the country. Can you? You can't either? Interesting.

Now, we both know it's a bloody long trip to Breiamhbéo, a few months, one way. So naturally I was curious. How could you, a wealthy merchant, with good standing at court, personally make the trip east, whilst obeying the Rule of Consequence?

I shall remind you what the Rule of Consequence is? Seriously? It slipped your mind? It really did! Or you must have danced too much this night. All right...

It Takes A Village

When Gathran contracted, shrunk, we were the last province to declare independence. That was some fourteen hundred years ago. Long before your shit stained the world, human. I wasn't born then either, but we study history.

You do too? Then tell me, what is the responsibility of the wealthy, the powerful?

Oh, so you think you have no responsibility? Why then do you live in the Palace, eternally shrouded in shadows because the majority of the city is above our heads?

Ever wondered why the nobility and wealthy live down here where the air stinks of shit the instant a pipe bursts? It's to remind you, the wealthy and the powerful, that you must take care of the people less fortunate than you. Or should I say more honest than you? Let's face it; many of you rich folk would love to keep slaves instead of paying workers, yes? It would help the bottom line. And that's where humans and elves differ. You see, my ancestors were slaves, once upon a time.

No, it's not a Fiery Tale, there once were beings stalking the continents, vastly more powerful than anything you can imagine. And they kept my ancestors as slaves, for generations. We rebelled, butchered them, burned and buried their cities, and then, because we weren't that smart either, we allowed a few to claim dominion. Tribes, kingdoms, and one kingdom that conquered pretty much the entire fucking continent: Gathran. But greed and lust for power got those idiots too, and Gathran began to shrink as they lost more and more influence.

When Kalduuhn split, we were the first to be conquered and the last to break away, we looked to the past, and we sent learned people to all surviving Libraries in the former provinces. The changes that were happening throughout the lands were astonishing. The younger a province the quicker it reverted to the ways they had lived before Gathran; where only a few hundred years before there had been temples to the gods, there now were only shrines.

It Takes A Village

Tribes didn't need much recordkeeping, a Librarian became a Lorekeeper, no less blessed by Traghnalach, but instead of writing down all that happened to the tribe, they kept it in their minds. Like our ancestors must have done all those millennia ago, before Gathran. From those tribal regions, the sages gathered all surviving histories, all the scrolls the Librarians had written and stored. That's why ours is the Grand Library. Gathran didn't care; they were preoccupied with their intrigues. Older provinces kept many of the structures, and there the sages made copies, thousands of scrolls.

And then the sages compiled that knowledge, they had already read those scrolls they had copied, and soon a picture emerged. Gathran was built on the backs of workers, who carried the Empire. When the nobles paid attention, everything was well. When the mages began to hog power, the people suffered. And the more the mages fought for supremacy, the more the people suffered. Leghans went rogue, or deserted, or simply disbanded when the pay stopped. The Leghans guarded everything, they were the Empire, but if you don't feed your guard dogs, they will grow weak. Not that the mages cared.

Oh? What? Right, the nobles bred with mages, hoping to gain more control by controlling magic. Nobles became mages, until the noble houses were mage houses.

House Kassor, one of the few noble, not mage, houses that had survived from the very beginnings of the Empire, who had claimed dominion over Ma'tallon, and all of the former province of Kalduuhn, had commissioned the sages. And now, from all that gathered knowledge, House Kassor cooperated with the realm's Lawspeakers, with the other priests in an advisory position, created a book of laws that would govern this new kingdom.

Hey! Don't roll your eyes! You fucking asked for a history lesson!

One of the most important things they decreed was that the wealthy and powerful must always live in the shadow of the common people. You see,

It Takes A Village

if you aren't reminded of the fact that the common people could overwhelm and easily destroy you, if they only wanted, you will behave like an arrogant, entitled cunt. If you live above the commoners, or apart from them, you will be unaware of their wants and needs. The rich and powerful are so only at the sufferance of the people, and to prevent the rich and powerful from becoming the ignorant and intolerant, the first law was the Rule of Consequence. If the powerful and wealthy did not live in the shadow of the people for three quarters of the year, they would be destroyed by, you guessed it, us Knights.

We're the bastards you hear whispers about. We're the ones who butcher the families of those who think themselves above the law. You break the law; we fucking well make sure the law breaks you. Completely.

Now, why am I here?

Remember when I said we met?

Well, yes, we did meet, on the Old Road east to Breiamhbéo. And therein lies the problem. You see, the Eastern Empire is really heavy on traditions, on doing things the proper way, and they want to profit from every grain of pepper that crosses their border. So when a trader from, say, Ma'tallon meets with an embassy to the Imperial Court, the Emperor wants his share. So any contract, to be fully valid, has to be signed in person.

Now, a far eastern embassy to the Imperial Court has with them the slew of Lawspeakers, and hangers on, merchants whose only goal is to profit from a contract, hopefully exclusive, sanctioned by the Emperor. With so many priests of Lliania involved, any lie would be detected several dozen times over, from every Lawspeaker and Upholder anywhere near the Court.

This is where it gets interesting. You told me how much you're looking forward to signing new contracts with one of the silk merchants. And I sensed absolutely no lie.

What? Oh yes, I used to be a Lawspeaker, can't become a Knight without having been part of Lliania's clergy. We retain her gift of truth-seeing.

It Takes A Village

We can always tell if someone is speaking the truth. So, how could a wealthy merchant, who has the clout to travel to Breiamhbéo with the goal to gain an Imperial sanctioned contract, make a trip of half a year or more when they were sworn to obey the Law? I mean, three months is the trip there, two, if you're lucky. Then you need to wait until the Emperor, and the embassy, will hear your case. That can take another few months. Then there's the whole thing of, you know, negotiating the shit out of everything so that all parties involved are at least not disappointed, can take another month or so. We're talking about something that might well take a year.

How can a person who knows about the Rule of Consequence do this? Sure, you might be part of the Queen's embassy to the East, that brings certain privileges, but you traveled by yourself. With your guards, of course, but still.

Now, I was on my way back when we met, and you still had a month's worth of travel before you. I returned to Ma'tallon a week ago.

Ah, now I see you understand what the problem is.

I sent my apprentices out to make inquiries. Brisen the Younger and Talfyn are very efficient and discrete. So they asked questions. Of your bookkeepers, clerks, drovers. All seemed to be in order. The two dug deeper. Your parents died a few years ago. I would offer my condolences, but judging by the few mementos you keep in these chambers, I figure you're rather happy they're gone.

No, I do not suspect you of murdering them. But now that you mention it, did you?

Yeah, didn't think so but you brought it up.

Now, Brisen and Talfyn did, however, find a wet nurse. Ah, now that got a reaction. You look pale. Some wine perhaps?

There you go. See, your color is back.

It Takes A Village

The wet nurse, Hafren, is old now, but she remembers you well. Or rather she remembers the both of you. Cingrib must have been bored when she blessed your mother with twins.

Oh, don't look so surprised, it worked well enough, for the time being. I actually had to look into your parents' death, again, just to make sure.

Of what? Mate, no wonder you're the stand-in, I guess the Lady of Mischief decided to have some fun with your minds too.

Oh, now you get it. Yeah, twins are a big no-no for the gods, usually, so they could have punished your parents for not offing one of you at birth. No, they died a normal death. If you can call poison a normal death.

Did you ever look into who did that? Poison is a coward's weapon, a cut throat is much more satisfying, or impaling a bastard with spears. No, not hunting ones, although they're fun too. I'm talking about these babies. No, don't worry, I just want you to look at them. Yeah, these babies kept the late Lord Cynnor's children and wife upright as they flailed about. Quite the spectacle. Ever seen fish drown. I mean, not in water, no, but in air. We can't breathe under water; fish can't breathe out of the water. A fish on land will gasp for water to fill whatever passes for lungs. Well, the Lady and brats Cynnor pretty much did the same thing.

You see, they're screwed together, they're not really spears, more like giant-sized toothpicks, if you will, but that's quite a mouthful. So we call them spears. Not the same, I know, much like twins aren't really the same person. I bet even now Cingrib is laughing her ass off at this splendid jest. Did your parents come up with the idea? Hafren wasn't clear on that part, then again, she's old.

Who's Cingrib? Seriously? You humans can't think farther than you can spit, can you? Maybe it's our fault, not teaching you properly. Cingrib is the princess of the Bailey Majestic; she makes everyone look like a fool, if she feels like it. Whenever you see someone step in dog shit, or stumble, looking like an idiot, and you catch yourself laughing, that's Cingrib laughing through you. She delights in this sort of thing. If you have some bad luck, it's usually because you've done something to displease her. Ever kicked a beggar? Oh, you did! I can see it in your eyes. Had a string of bad luck afterwards? Stumbled into manure, your shoelaces tearing for no apparent reason, cut your hand while cutting bread? That's either her, or you're clumsy. Usually it's the former though. Beggars and vagabonds and hobos are her favored.

I don't know why, it's just the way she is.

Whimsical.

I mean look at you and your sibling, you're bloody twins. That rarely happens, and when it does, it's usually because she wants to see what the parents will do. Murdering the spare, giving it away. Who knows? The gods look down on us, and aside from their priests they rarely interfere. It's like watching a play for them, we're the actors, without a script, without a clue, other than the rules they give us through their clergy.

And Cingrib is the one who tosses oil onto the stage just to see who will stumble. She reminds us not to take things too seriously, to laugh at ourselves. And to be kind to those in need.

As I said, twins are rare. I've been around a while, and you're the first ones I've met. And that's the thing… when House Kassor and the Lawspeakers and sages cobbled together the Kalduuhnean Book of Laws, they didn't think of twins. You don't think of three-legged cows either, because they usually end up dead, so why bother?

The thing is, you two managed to pull this off for years now. Good, you have taken no spouse, and have no children; that shit would have complicated matters. Can you imagine having to share your bed with a stranger? Playing with children that are not your own? I mean, that's a recipe for disaster, and it would have revealed your game much earlier, and made things that much more messy.

It Takes A Village

Stop looking at the spears. I'm not here to impale you.

There, I put them away. Feeling better?

Good.

Queen Luertha knows, the Justiciar knows. How the Librarians didn't know, let's chalk it up to Cingrib, all right? Well, now they know too. And her Majesty wants to solve this without causing a scandal. Not only does she want this to go away with the least amount of chaos, no, she also wants to amend the law. You didn't abuse your unfair advantage, you didn't spit on the Rule of Consequence to flout your wealth. You're fair to your employees; don't cheat on your taxes. In short, you're a model citizen. Well, two model citizens. No, you're great at each being half of a good model citizen.

This is confusing, and the Law shouldn't be confusing. Nor should its keepers be confused either.

Now, we need help to amend the Law.

Don't get me wrong, had you acted like the late, unlamented Lord Cynnor, we'd have strung up the both of you by your ankles.

Oh, don't look so shocked, now. You followed the spirit of the Law, if not the letter, and we need your unique insight to adjust the letter. As I've already failed to explain, the Laws don't exist to terrorize the wealthy and powerful, much. I mean, where's the fun in not having a bunch of pansy-assed nobles pissing the breeches every once in a while? But ultimately the Laws are meant to encourage the wealthy and powerful to live more considerately, which you and your twin do, don't get me wrong. The Laws were based off the experiences of the past, but didn't take into account people like you. You pay your taxes without fuss, because you see the value in public works and education being funded properly. You pay your employees a living wage, because you know that when they don't have to worry about whether they make enough to pay the rent and such they will be better at their jobs. The Laws as they are written hinder your business which in turn hinders you. We want people like you to be the ideal, the shining example which others should follow. If they don't want to be on the receiving end of a Culling, that is. I mean, many people are selfish cunts, especially many "nobles" and "rich," otherwise they wouldn't be nobles.

What? Does that mean the Queen is also selfish? Are you shitting me? Luertha of House Kassor has never left the capital, she rarely wanders outside the thrice-cursed shadow that hangs over the entire fucking enclosure. She's like you and your twin, she leads by example. Four hundred years in this twilight. Sure, she has a garden, the racetrack, but it's all underneath the platforms that make up our glorious city.

"Thyrn," she said to me, "Thyrn, a ruler, a leader, must always lead by example. Our parents drilled that into us and our siblings, and we've drilled it into our children. We have to be the epitome of lawfulness, we serve the people, and if we forget that, the people will come crashing down on us."

My reply? "Yes, Majesty." What else could I have said?

So, the Queen wants you and your twin to help us improve the laws. Together with the Justiciar, of course. Believe me, she'll know if you try to pull a fast one with us. Not that I think you two will, but in our line of business trust is never as good as verification.

Needless to say, I'll feed you your sibling's entrails if you try to betray us. And vice versa.

Interested?

Well, it's either that or we'll put one of you in an iron mask, wall you into a cell, and let you age ungracefully.

You in?

It Takes A Village

About Ulff Lehmann

German born but English writing author, Ulff Lehmann, was raised reading, almost any and everything, from the classic Greek to Roman to Germanic myths to more appropriate fiction for children his age. Initially devouring books in his native language, he switched to reading English books during a yearlong stay in the USA as a foreign exchange student.

In the years since, he has lost count of the books he has read, unwilling to dig into the depths of his collection. An avid fantasy reader, he grew dissatisfied with the constant lack of technological evolution in many a fantasy world, and finally, when push came to shove, he began to realize not only his potential as a storyteller but also his vision of a mythical yet realistic world in which to settle the tale in he had been developing for 20 years.

You can find Ulff's works at
amazon.com/author/ulfflehmann

It Takes A Village

QUANTUM MONKEYS

By Assaph Mehr

When asked what inspired this story, Assaph responded:

> I grew up on stories by Asimov, Heinlein, Clarke, and others. At university, I studied computer science, played with neural networks and other emerging AI technologies. My day job involves developing and marketing software products, which for the past few years have had Machine Learning components (well before the current generative AI hype cycle). You could say I have been following the social-philosophical and professional-practical aspects of AI for most of my life.
>
> With both AI and the anthology on my mind, it's no wonder the idea of the care relationships between humans and machines popped into my head. But when sitting to write the story, it turned out quite different to what I originally envisaged. Is it utopian or dystopian? Or somewhere in between? You decide.

It Takes A Village

QUANTUM MONKEYS — Assaph Mehr

"Come on, Mark. Time for school! Did you get your lunch from the counter? Well, go get it and put it in your backpack, already! Hurry up and get in the car. You'd forget your head if it wasn't attached."

Thea sat in the driver's seat, and as soon as she heard her son buckle his seat belt she pressed the start button. "The usual route."

"Very well, Thea. We should be in Thrumpton College in fifteen minutes, but there are roadworks on the way to your office. I have put the suggested optimal route on the display for you."

Thea waved her hand at the dashboard to acknowledge the car as she played with the display to get her daily news feed up. The car pulled out of the garage and joined the busy street, while Thea read the highlights. Behind her she could hear Mark explaining something to the car, which obliged him by searching for the specific episode of his show to play on his display.

"And how is Mark doing today?" asked the attendant at school. As a brightly-decorated robot took Mark's bag and led him to the classroom, Thea thought not for the first time how lucky they were to get a placement here, and how well-worth the atrocious fees were. While Mark was happy with his robotic teachers looking like the latest popular cartoons and making his day one long, fun-filled episode, Thea reflected how finding a school that still had a human present — even if a single one, but throughout the day — was nearly impossible.

"He's fine," she replied to the man. "Do you have any special program for today?"

"Today we'll be continuing our focus on visual arts and creativity, helping the children practice the use of a digital stylus to imitate oil painting in the style of the masters. You should be able to follow his progress through the live feed."

Thea sipped her coffee at the office pod. She had a mandatory in-person meeting later — the only reason to come to the office — but she preferred coming in early and bagging the pod at the far end. No need to be amongst people more than necessary, might as well enjoy a quiet corner. She put on her display. With the advent of natural language spoken interfaces noise-cancelling headphones became a hard requirement, and the addition of augmented reality display goggles made for a whole-head contraption that was jokingly referred to as the 'facehugger.'

"Bring up the latest product adoption numbers, and cross-reference them with the categories established during market research."

The computer obliged her by presenting a graph on the holographic display of her AR goggles.

"Filter to the eighteen-to-twenty-five bracket. Rotate. Overlay trend data from social network scraping. Hm. Suggest three theories about the anomaly there."

The pod didn't even pause noticeably before starting to list possibilities in her ears. Her morning was spent chatting with the AI, exploring the world of numbers and translating it into a visual presentation that made sense. Once she was happy with the graphics it generated and the flow of information, she sent it to the company's board. She knew the humans would take time to read her report, but the AI sitting on the board would be able to give critique by the time she got back from her bathroom break. Productivity has increased to the speed in which humans were able to catch up.

~*~

It Takes A Village

The unkempt man mumbling to himself picked up a charred stick and began drawing on the concrete wall of the overpass. From a discreet distance away, a police robot with social-care module watched silently. The care module, machine-trained on zettabytes of human observational data, allowed the police robot to instantly correctly diagnose conditions in people from minuscule signs — from early onset of liver diseases to psychological makeup, the robot had tools to give each human in the community the best of care.

The old man, meanwhile, drew signs of gangs that have been disbanded fifty years prior and interlaced them with cartoon penises.

The robot silently filed a report with central before approaching the man. "Can I offer you a sandwich, sir?"

"Feck off, ya soulless tin can." The man didn't even turn, but continued to doodle.

"Do you have place to stay?" The police robot persisted. "Nights are getting cold."

"And what would you know about it, ya rusty train wreck?"

"Please, sir, we are programmed to care for you. I can take you to a shelter, where you'll be fed and kept warm and secure."

"Fuck you and your care, you rancid shit-stain fuck-muppet! I grew up on Terminator and Bladerunner. I even read Asimov's books, ya clogged-up public toilet, real books made from real paper, not that sanitised, censored, electronic stuff the government can edit even as you're looking at it. I know all about the rise of the machines!"

The robot didn't respond to the insults. It could display any emotion needed to build empathy, but it didn't feel them. That was the point of the social-care module, preventing the burn-out human agents felt at the constant abuse received from society's less fortunate. It proceeded according to protocol, offering help for the third time before leaving the human to its wishes. "Please, sir, we only mean to help — "

It Takes A Village

"You know where good intentions lead to? Eh, ya leaky bucket of shit? Skynet is hell on wheels! It's Dante's tenth circle, reserved for well-meaning politicians and tech bros!"

The old man picked up a tree branch and hit the police robot. While in no physical danger, the protocol was clear that aggression towards machines should not be tolerated as it could lead to aggression towards self or other humans. The robot let out a puff of sedative gas, caught the unconscious man before he hit the pavement, and gently arranged him in the recovery position. Within minutes the man was whisked to a shelter, and cleaning drones wiped the graffiti from the overpass wall, leaving a fresh canvas. The robot positioned itself back in the shadows, ready to catch the next petty delinquent and provide state-sanctioned care.

~*~

When Thea was done with the in-person meeting, which she thought could just as easily have been a video call, her phone was flashing a long list of missed calls. Frantically listening to messages, she pieced together that Mark had absconded from school at lunch time, only to be caught by a police robot defacing public infrastructure with spray-paint graffiti. She was instructed to make her way to the local police station to pick him up.

She was besides herself with worry, trying to get her car to break speed limits on the way, arguing with it and trying manual override. The car was well versed with identifying diminished capacity in humans, and no amount or cajoling or fiddling with the setting would ever cause it to let a person drive outside of designated safe spaces.

By the time Thea burst through the police station doors, face-recognition had already matched her to her case. She was half-way to the automated desk sergeant when a man in a black suit and narrow black tie came out of a side door marked "no public entry" and called her name.

"Is Mark OK? Has he been arrested? He's only twelve, surely you can't hold him, there are extenuating circumstances, his father isn't really in the picture —"

"Ms. Hordad, Mark's alright," the man put on his practiced calming voice. "Please, just come inside with me and I'll take you to him."

The man introduced himself as Ralph Waub. He didn't specify a police rank, but before Thea could ask he opened a door and said, "This way. I need to speak with you first."

The room had a desk with an office chair, a dated model of an augmented-reality facehugger lay on the desk, and a physical filing cabinet was positioned behind it. Ralph indicated the visitors' chairs.

"But you said you're taking me to Mark! You can't arrest him, surely, it only a juvenile misdemeanour at best. Can't we just make it go away? I promise I'll keep a closer rein on him —"

"Ms. Hordad, please. I think we started on the wrong foot. Mark isn't in trouble, quite the opposite. I'll take you to him in a minute and you can go home, but I just need to speak with you in private first."

Thea sat down in a visitor chair, unsettled but unsure.

"As I said, my name's Ralph Waub, and I'm with the department of children services, creative intelligence branch. Your son Mark was caught spray-painting images under the highway overpass, but the drawings were quite unique."

"Well, twelve-year-old boys. I've seen the drones keep repainting that patch. Surely there was nothing overly offensive for any length of time."

"No, no, you misunderstand. His drawings were original. Here, let me try to explain. Do you use one of these at work or home?" He lifted the augmented reality 'face helmet.' When Thea nodded, he continued. "Then you've seen how easy it is to generate content. New images, text, even movie clips you can direct by giving the AI behind it instructions and corrections. But in order to generate your content, the machine has first to be trained on existing materials. It learns from them, imitates them, and utilises them in content generation."

"Yeah, I create my presentations at work that way," Thea said.

"You generate the presentation assets. Creation is something else. The AI can only generate variations of what it has learnt and deconstructed. It can't create something new. You've heard about Borel's Infinite Monkey Theorem? No? It's an old idea, how if a million monkeys bashed a million typewriters for an infinite amount of time, one of them would eventually type the complete works of William Shakespeare. Well, with quantum computing we could make a decent approximation of this. Turns out the problem isn't in generating, in writing out, the complete works of Shakespeare. We can even automatically identify stretches of coherent content, whether text or imagery, but without a human we can't assign meaning, and thus value, to the generated content. The machine only generates, and can only identify, variations of previous work."

"Um, OK. But what does any of that have to do with my Mark?"

"See, his work is original. His paintings and style have a spark of something new. Art doesn't exist in a vacuum. It comes in response to previous works, true, but it combines them in new ways and adds something to make it meaningful to others. And this is a talent that we must nurture. We want him to concentrate on his artistic abilities, to grow them. We want to enlist him in a special program for creatives."

"So, he's not in trouble, and you're offering some kind of scholarship?"

"Indeed. See, our best definition of art is that, which when looked upon, people proclaim as art. He'll need human guidance, as research shows only emotional, human connection leads to it. Besides tutoring by our qualified teachers, he'll need to spend more time with you and others. Face-to-face, in-real-life time. Whatever you have been doing with him is great, but we need you to take some time off work. Only a couple of afternoons a week," Ralph hastily added when Thea seemed to speak, "but it has to be consistent and you have to spend the time interacting with him, taking him places, meeting other people."

"But my work…"

"Oh, don't worry about that. Not only will this be fully funded, but most companies value having creatives, including parents of creatives, on staff. I'd say your career will accelerate once they know you are nurturing talent during those afternoons. There's enough research that gifted employees with time to explore their innovative and inventive talents are good for a company's bottom line. Since it runs in families, they'll give you leeway — both for your own sake and to attract others."

"That's… great." Thea was still unsure about this sudden turn.

Ralph continued. "And as for your son's financial future, AI training companies pay huge sums for the rights to train on new works. We may have mastered artificial intelligence as a tool, but we haven't cracked consciousness, which seeds creativity. As each new application for AI is made available, it's quickly a race to the bottom where everyone generates such similar content that it no longer impresses. You must have seen it, generating presentations? It's really easy to get flash, but hard to stand out. It all just looks the same after a while. Those companies are starved to train their AIs on new material. I dare say, yours and your son's futures look rosy."

THE TRIAL OF THE TYPIST — ALTERNATIVE ENDING

By Meir Michael Fogel

"Not guilty," finished the speaker.

The Typist said to himself under his breath, "It works every time," with a chuckle. The Typist then turned around to his attorney and asked for the attorney's phone to wire the funds, to which the attorney agreed.

The prosecutor sighed and muttered under her breath, "Knew it. As soon as they called the medical simulators a 'private hobby,' they made the whole court case look like the prosecution was fishing. It is the start of slippery slope that is not good for the future."

The attorney smiled and shouted to the prosecutor, "Hey, the court case is already over."

"We shall see many more of this sort of case in the coming years."

"You are just being a pessimist." But, by then, the prosecutor could no longer hear them over the crowd.

The judge was already almost outside the courtroom, as he was late to his wedding anniversary date and did not want to get slowed down by reporters. The crowd and jury disappeared while reporters rushed in to ask the jury questions about which side of the argument they were on.

It Takes A Village

It Takes A Village

HER FINAL WISH

By Kody Boye

When asked what inspired this story, Kody responded:

My story, Her Final Wish, was built upon a single idea: what would hospice care look like in the future? And how would a young girl deal with the loss of someone dear to her? Cassie's grief is familiar to many of us, and in that sense, I imagined a fantastical future in which humanity has built skyscrapers to the stars, hospice care is mandated for the elderly, and where family is offered the chance to give their final goodbyes. Her Final Wish is about those familial bonds — and tells the story of one girl's emotional quest to make peace with the end of life.

It Takes A Village

HER FINAL WISH — Kody Boye

The wind blows in from the Gulf of Mexico on this crisp August afternoon. Ruffling my hair, and causing my heart to flutter, the gale brings with it memories of a time long past — of a simpler age during which I could look out at the setting sun and not have to pray.

At this late hour of the day, during which I feel as though I've cried all my tears, I struggle not to cry even more.

My grandmother's final wish is for us to let her go.

But letting go, they say, is always the hardest part.

I try not to allow my emotions to get the best of me, here, on this sun-kissed pier. But no matter how hard I try, I can't seem to fight back the wave of emotions that threaten to assault me.

For so long I thought she would live forever.

But now, she says, is the time to let go.

I lift my head to look out into the Gulf — at not only the beautiful sea, whose surface is swept along by the wind, but at the tower that stretches into the sky from the water's depths. Past the clouds the tower rises, and into the atmosphere it ultimately reaches, until, finally, it breaks that stunning barrier that separates us from the rest of the world, the universe.

The heavens, I think.

Grandma Hernandez, who is referred to by most as Grandma Star, was one of the first to pioneer the design of the space elevator, as well as to step foot within its surface.

Though so many had been afraid, she had looked the stars in the face, and said, This fear will not last.

And now, I think, she wants to return there, to the Tower Paradisíaca, otherwise known as the Tower to Paradise, to live out her final days.

It Takes A Village

As one of the pioneering engineers, and as someone who helped ferry the world into the modern space age, she, and members of her immediate family, are meant to be granted this final wish.

So many people are willing to see her off.

So many… except me.

~*~

I do not want to be a selfish girl. A spoiled brat. A terrible child. But the truth is that no one who loves another person wants to see them go, which is why I spend most of my time at the beach alongside my best friend.

"Do you not feel guilty?" she asks.

"What?" I reply.

She blows a bubble and then pops her gum with a loud smack. "I said: do you not feel guilty? About not spending more time with her, I mean?"

"I… I don't —"

It is a question I find impossible to answer. On one hand, guilt festers in me like a rat gnawing on day-old pizza. On another, I feel as if being there, with her, in her presence, while the National Space Committee and the Final Wishes Organization prepare her case, would do little more than upset me.

You can't be upset around her, my father had told me. You don't want her to see you suffering.

But how can I remain strong when I am so close to crumbling?

My best friend, Jamie, frowns as she considers me. Gone is her jovial tone, in which she had been singing, laughing, playing. In its place has emerged a seriousness that I feel would have been better spent elsewhere, all things considered.

"I'm sorry," she says.

"Don't be," I reply.

It Takes A Village

"I shouldn't have said what I said."

"But you're not wrong," I then reply. "Because, honestly?" I kick a rock that happens to be in my path, and watch it skip off the concrete until it goes bouncing off the pier and into the water. "Honestly, the truth is that I don't think I could bear being there. I'd just… crumble."

"Not all walls are meant to last forever, Cassie."

I allow this thought to weigh heavily upon me. Its gravity is like that of a moon, pulling the tide in one direction and then pushing it in another; and while standing here, upon these shores of endless suffering, I find myself wondering if I could allow those walls to fall, and if I could do so without leaving my grandmother in an emotional state.

"Jamie?" I say.

"Yeah?" my friend asks.

"What do you think I should do?"

"I think you should do what makes you comfortable. But you have to remember: you're going to have to bear whatever emotions that come after your grandmother is gone. Don't let one of them be regret."

Regret, I think.

With a short, honest nod, I turn my head to consider not just the ocean, but the Tower to Paradise, then say, "You're right, Jamie. You're absolutely right."

"Are you going to go home now?" my best friend asks.

"Yeah. I am."

"I'll see you later, then," Jamie says.

Before I can go, she reaches out and takes hold of my hand.

"Be safe," she says.

"I will," I reply.

But the truth of the matter is that there is no safety in matters of the heart. One either feels, or does not feel at all.

It Takes A Village

~*~

Normally, my walk home would leave me feeling invigorated, as under the sun-kissed sky my skin would be warm. However, on this day, I feel little more than cold.

Cold, I then think, because of what I know will soon follow.

My father is in the kitchen, kneading bread for the afternoon meal. My younger brother, meanwhile, plays virtual reality video games in the living room. My mother, thankfully, is not here, since I know she would dole out only handfuls of questions. The only other person in the house is my grandmother, and she's resting in an old, dark back room.

Like a badly-kept secret, I think, almost bitterly at that.

My father lifts his head to face me. "Hello, miha," he says. "How was your afternoon at the beach?"

"It was… fine," I say.

"Just fine?"

I offer a somber nod.

Sighing, my father lowers his eyes back to his bread, and continues to knead with the skill of someone who's learned to offer love through cooking. He could easily be letting a machine do it, but I don't think my father would be caught dead cutting corners with his cooking.

"Papa?" I ask. "Can I go see grandma?"

"Your grandmother is sleeping right now, Cassie."

"Luh… Later, then?"

"When the nurse comes," he says.

I turn my head to regard the study near the door. "Where is Mama?"

"She's at the market, picking up some meat. She should be home at any —"

It Takes A Village

Moment, he wants to say.

But the door opens behind me, nearly catching me in the small of the back.

"I'm sorry, Cassie," my mother says. "I didn't know you were there."

"It's fine," I say.

Maybe it's the sound of my voice, or its tone, or my inflection. Either way, my father frowns as he considers me, but doesn't press me for further answers. Rather, he rounds the island and approaches my mother, kissing her cheek. My mother presses a hand between his shoulders before saying, "I brought the steak you wanted."

"Good. I'll start tenderizing the meat."

"Do you need help?" I ask, in a voice that I find is small, even for me.

"No, miha," my mother says. "You can go to your room."

"The nurse will be here by six o'clock," my father then adds, in a voice that is weary, but considerate.

"Oh… Okay," I say.

I turn; and with hesitation I know is born from insecurity, with quiet and unsure doubt, cross the kitchen and begin to make my way down the hallway.

There is little I can do but sigh the moment I am far enough away for no one to hear.

I should be used to this routine by now, these acts of insecurity. They are, in many ways, branded into my mind, tattooed into my flesh. Regardless, I cannot help but reflect upon the series of events that have been occurring since my grandmother's health began its downward spiral almost a week-and-a-half ago.

The early mornings —

The laborious afternoons —

The dark evenings, and the long nights —

It Takes A Village

The Modern Medical Act has ensured that my grandmother has not gone without professional home health care throughout her illness. Though both my mother and father have been granted paid leave to take care of my grandmother as a result of the MMA, a nurse arrives twice a day — once at noon, and once at six PM — to determine my grandmother's needs, and to offer the emotional support necessary for us to continue forward as a family.

Hospice care, one of the nurses had said, is a trying time; and comfort, they had added, isn't just reserved for the one who is ill.

The transitional period a family goes through when one of their own is near death is, in many ways, astronomical. Worlds often change. Lives are altered. One's sense of purpose normally dangles precariously by a thread. Ultimately, the nurses had said, the end of life is always challenging.

My grandmother has been fighting her illness for quite some time. Now, it could be said, her time is drawing near.

I try not to think about this as I wander down the hall — as I attempt to direct my gaze to the floor — but find that my eyes wander, and my chin rises in kind.

The lone, cracked door at the end of the L-shaped hall calls me to look upon it. Inside, my grandmother rests; though even from this distance, I can hear the oxygen tank running, her breath wheezing.

I think, Would it be so wrong to peek in?

Perhaps not. But my father had told me not to; and for that reason, I will respect his wishes.

Sighing, I take a few steps forward.

I am just about to pass the room when a voice asks, "Cassandra? Is that you?"

"It's… it's me," I say.

"Can you come here?"

It Takes A Village

I turn my head to the cracked door — to the dark interior within. I frown. Sink my teeth into my lower lip. Cast a glance down the hall.

She asked for you, a small part of me says. *They can't get mad if she called.*

With a nod, I step forward, and push the door open as carefully as possible.

Then, I enter the room.

The sound of the oxygen machine buzzes in my ears upon entry, drawing my attention from the far side of the room, where the curtains allow only dappled light inside, to my grandmother's bedside. A heartrate monitor casts a low, ominous glow; and while it is almost impossible to see my grandmother in the dark, she lifts a hand and twists it palm up to wave me forward with her fingers.

I ask, "How are you feeling?"

She laughs — a low, quiet sound — and says, "Same as ever, dear. Same as ever."

I am careful to reach forward — to extend my hand and take hold of hers. Beneath my touch, her skin feels thin, almost like paper. It adds a sense of fragility that reminds me of how delicate she is.

"Did you need something?" I ask. "Maybe some water?"

"I just wanted to talk," she says.

Unsure what to say, I remain silent, and wait for her to speak. Now that I have drawn closer, I can see the light reflecting off her blue eyes, which sparkle brightly even though she has seen better days, better years.

"Grandma?" I ask.

"I'm sorry," she says. "I'm just… thinking."

"About what?"

"About how everything is going to play out from this point forward."

I open my mouth to speak, but stop before I can do so.

It Takes A Village

"I know you're scared," Grandma Star says.

"I'm… I — "

"It's okay to fear what you do not know, Cassandra."

"I know," I say.

"In many ways, I, too, am scared. But it isn't of dying. No." She shakes her head carefully. "If anything, I feel comfortable, knowing that this damned illness will soon be over. But… I am… in many ways… scared of what comes after."

"After?"

She nods. "Yes, my dear. After."

I want to say something — anything — to offer some words of comfort, some kind of consolation. But how is a girl of just fifteen supposed to comfort someone who is afraid of dying?

My grandmother sighs as she turns her head to look toward the windows, through which the evening's final rays of light attempt to pierce through. I watch her eyes falter, her lips purse. Then she says: "I am most concerned for you, however."

"Me?"

She nods. "Yes, Cassandra. I am concerned for you."

"You don't have to be afraid for me," I say, in as careful, yet weighted a voice as possible. "I'll… I'll be okay."

"You say that, my dear, but you and I both know the truth."

I cannot keep myself from frowning.

Thankfully, my grandmother either can't see the look on my face, or is sparing me the indignity of speaking of it. Soon, she is tightening her hand in mine, and saying, "I am looking forward to riding the tower."

"You did such an amazing thing," I say. "I still can't believe that you helped build it."

It Takes A Village

"Build it?" she asks, and laughs. "Oh no, dear. I didn't build the thing — at least, I didn't by myself. No." She shakes her head. "I designed the space elevator — and not only that: I was instrumental in explaining how the pieces fit together, from those at the bottom of the Gulf all the way up into the stars above."

I remember those days like they were yesterday — when, as a child, I would stare into the Gulf of Mexico and see the boats moving, the men working. During those few times my parents had brought me to the build site, I had watched as my grandmother stood in the distance, a radio in her hand, a schematic spread out on a table before her, people all around. My father had told me that she was doing something astronomical, something that was almost beyond the scale of human imagination; and at the time, I had been too young to understand, too innocent to comprehend. But as the years went on, and as the tower continued to grow, and I along with it, I'd realized that it truly was a feat of human engineering.

My grandmother — my Grandma Star, as they had been so fit to call her — was heralding us into a new age of human experience.

"It's just... so amazing," I say, when I come back from the memory. "To think that you did something so incredible, something that everyone in the world knows about, something everyone can see, will always see."

"You'll do great things too one day, Cassandra. I believe in you."

"Thank you, Grandma."

"Cassie!" my mother calls. "Dinner is ready!"

"You should go," my grandmother then says.

"Okay," I reply.

I slip my hand out of hers and turn toward the doorway.

"Cassandra?" my grandmother asks.

I turn my head to face her.

"Please, don't fear for me. In the end... all will be as it should."

It Takes A Village

"Okay," I say.

I slip out of the room without looking back.

~*~

I struggle not to feel small in the moments after I seat myself at the dinner table. Somewhat hungry, but not wanting to eat, I pick at the fresh bread and tender meat and seasoned vegetables with the knowledge that I carry an incredible burden — one that even my grandmother can see.

Across from me, my parents eat in silence, listening kindly to my younger brother as he regales them with stories about his virtual reality adventures in a fantasy land. We — and he in particular — are still not used to my parents being home so often.

"And then," my brother continues in a dramatic voice, "there was a dragon! It was huge. So huge that everyone went scrambling! All the villagers! All the cows! All the chickens! So I drew my sword, and cast a fireball, and I was just about to kill the dragon when — "

A knock comes at the door, silencing him mid-sentence.

"That'll be the nurse," my mother says.

My father wipes his mouth with a napkin, and says, "I'll get it."

"Are you sure — " my mother starts.

But my father has already risen, and is making his way toward the door before she can finish.

Sighing, my mother slides a piece of steak between her lips, and says, "Keep eating, Cassie, Andrew."

"But — " my little brother says.

My mother shakes her head, and lowers her eyes as the sound of the front door opening enters our ears.

"Hello," I hear my father say.

It Takes A Village

"Hello, Mister Hernandez," the nurse replies. "My name is Tiffany Rodriguez. I'm here to see Missus Hernandez."

"Yes. Please, come in."

The door yawns open with a creak. Closes with a dull thud. In walks my father, and behind him, a kind nurse in green scrubs.

"Hello," she says.

"Hello," my mother replies.

Me and my little brother have been trained to keep silent during these visits, so we merely nod and continue eating.

"She's this way," my father says.

The two of them make their way down the hall a short moment later, leaving me, my brother, and our mother in silence.

"Mama," Andrew says.

"Yes, Andrew?"

"When is grandma going up the elevator to see the stars?"

"I believe they're still working on it, dear. Now please, be quiet and eat. We don't want to upset your father."

Those words — upset your father — are haunting, in a way that makes me feel small, in a way that makes me feel insignificant. For weeks I have watched my father go from a kind, easygoing man to a shell of that. He is mostly quiet now. Often reserved. Almost constantly anxious. I know he is anxious about his work at the solar plant, and that, without the routine, he is often nervous, but I also understand that he often spends his days anguishing over my grandmother's health, over her untimely wellbeing.

I want, so desperately, to be able to do something — anything — to comfort him. But I understand, more than anything, that grief is a storm one must weather personally. So, I do as I always do, and keep to myself.

It Takes A Village

Frowning, I push the asparagus around the plate. Gone is the semblance of an appetite I once had. In its place has emerged a void that I feel can never be truly satisfied.

"May I be excused?" I ask.

"You've hardly eaten," my mother says.

"I know. It's just..." I lower my gaze. "I'm not hungry anymore."

"Go ahead and go to your room, Casandra. I'll put it away for you."

Thankfully, my mother has always been attuned to our emotions; and as a result, has not often questioned us during stages of grief. For this I am more than grateful.

Because otherwise, I think, I do not know what I would do.

Halfway to my room, I come to a halt. Curiosity, some more morbid than not, prompts me to walk further down the hall, and come to a halt outside my grandmother's door.

"I don't understand what's taking so long," my father says. "She was one of their head scientists. Why did it take them so long to do anything?"

"The Modern Medical Act deals with cases of all types," I hear Nurse Rodriguez reply, "as do the Final Wishes Organization. To be honest: the fact that she was a government employee has worked to her advantage. Many die before the Organization can do anything."

"But can't they do anything more? Or go any faster?"

"Your mother's case is an incredible one, Mister Hernandez. The world — and the United States in particular — is honoring her contribution to humankind, for heralding us into the space age once more. We should be thankful that they are working so swiftly."

My father sighs — a long, drawn out sound. Then he says: "Thank you for letting us know, Miss Rodriguez."

"It's my pleasure," the nurse replies. "I'm happy to have been of some help."

It Takes A Village

I skirt away from the room and dart inside my own before anyone can slip into the hall.

Inside, I lean against the wall, take several long, deep breaths, and try my hardest to consider everything I have just heard.

It's almost impossible to believe.

My grandmother — one of the leading scientists on the space elevator — could've lost her life without getting her final wish.

I swallow a breath. Try my hardest not to cry.

Then, I try to be thankful.

Thankful.

For her position in life. For what it has afforded her.

Then, soon after, I allow the tears to fall.

~*~

"Your grandmother's request has been accepted," my father says. "The Final Wishes Organization has agreed to pay for hospice care in Tower of Paradise."

My mother sighs. My little brother looks on with wide eyes. I, meanwhile, can only stare.

The moment of gratitude is disturbed only when my little brother asks: "What does… hospice mean?"

"It means a home for the terminally ill," my father then says. "It's… what doctors do for people during the end of their lives."

"You mean… grandma's going to die?" my brother asks.

Neither my mother, nor father, immediately respond.

With tears in his eyes, and a soft sob forming on his lips, my little brother turns and starts toward the doorway.

"Where are you going?" I ask.

"To see grandma," my little brother replies. "To tell her not to die."

"Andrew — " I start.

But my little brother is already starting toward the hallway.

Thankfully, my mother moves to intervene — first standing, then darting into the hall.

"Andrew," she says, taking hold of my little brother's shoulders. "You need to leave Grandma be."

"But why?" he asks, lip trembling, eyes weeping. "Why does she have to die?"

My mother looks from my little brother, then to my father — who, with his eyes lost, his lips curled into a frown, gazes toward them as if they are something horrible to behold.

When my father finally does speak, it's to say: "Everyone dies eventually, Andrew."

"But why?"

"Because that's the way the world works."

My little brother lets loose a long, drawn-out sob, prompting slivers of emotions from not only my father, but me as well.

Try as I might to contain myself, I cannot help but sob.

Why, I wonder, does life have to be so cruel?

~*~

There is no easy way to deal with these emotions. Filled with tragedy, with grief, I return to my room after dinner has unceremoniously ended and draw the curtains across my windows. Then, I crawl into bed, and try and will myself to sleep.

Fortunately for me, my bed is comfortable, and offers respite from a cruel world.

It Takes A Village

Unfortunately, I find myself drifting off to sleep not long after.

The dreams that follow play out in a blur.

Me, standing in a field of flowers —

A figure, looming in the distance —

An everlasting ocean, extending as far as the eye can see —

A tower, rising as high as the heavens.

I gaze upon the Tower Paradisíaca that rises from the Gulf of Mexico with uncertainty I know is born of dread. My heart feels hollow, my mind uneasy. Worst yet: I now realize that the figure standing in the field in front of me is a semblance of my grandmother during kinder, healthier days.

"Grandma?" I ask. "Is that you?"

She turns to face me, Grandma Star — and though there is a smile on her face, there is a remoteness in her gaze that mirrors that which I see now, in the present, in the real and unfortunate world.

"It's me, dear," Grandma Star says.

I ask, "Where are we?"

And she says, "Paradisíaca."

A kaleidoscope of butterflies bursts from the field of wildflowers at our feet. Fluttering about — wings flared, colors alarming — they lift into the air as if they are a cloud of smog, not only filling me with wonder, but fear.

Is this some kind of sign? a part of me wonders. A sign that things will be fine in the future? A warning of what I may feel in the present?

Ahead, my grandmother lifts a hand, and allows a single butterfly to alight on her outstretched fingers.

"I think," my grandmother says, "that I will call this one Peace."

Peace, I think.

While a part of me feels small — and wonders, deep down, if I can truly endure the storm that will follow — another realizes that her time is drawing to an end.

It Takes A Village

It is the cruelest feeling of all.

~*~

I am gently awoken by hands at my shoulders, and my father saying, "Wake up, Cassandra. Wake up."

I open my eyes to find my father looking down at me, his kind, gentle blue eyes somber in this dark, early hour of the morning.

A moment of fear rushes through me.

I ask, "Is Grandma — "

"She is fine," my father says. "But we must get ready. They are preparing to take us to the tower."

The tower, I think.

Paradisíaca.

With a small, gentle nod, I push myself upright and consider the world around me for several moments before finally asking, "How long will we be there?"

"They've said to pack clothes for two weeks."

"Okay."

"Shower, brush your teeth, and get dressed. The shuttle is coming to take us there within an hour."

An hour, I think.

In many respects, it seems like such a long time, during which so many things, so many wonders, could occur. In others, however, it feels like such a fleeting moment.

As my father slips out of the room, leaving me to consider not just my feelings on the matter, but my emotions as well, I take a moment to compose myself. Then I rise, gather fresh clothes, and make my way into the bathroom in the hall.

It Takes A Village

Knowing the boundaries of time that have been set in place, I do not take my time while showering, nor do I do so while brushing my teeth, or dressing in a fine summer dress. The Texas summer is still warm, and though fall is just around the corner, the weather continues to be warm, which I am more than thankful for.

Not just for me, I think, but her.

My grandmother, who would undoubtedly suffer in the cruel and unfortunate cold.

By the time I exit the restroom, I turn to face the kitchen, only to find that the dining table has been pushed back, and my parents are standing by, seemingly awaiting our departure.

"What's going on?" I ask. "Why are we just standing here?"

My mother turns from where she stands with a plate, and extends it to me a moment later. "We'll eat in a bit," she says, "once we enter the tower. Until then, eat this."

The peanut-buttered toast will nourish me on this hard day, and keep me full until necessary.

"They're about to arrive to transport your grandmother now," my mother says.

I turn my eyes to my brother, who stands at my father's side, his eyes lowered, his lips pursed. Then I lift my gaze to face my father, and find that he is not unlike my brother in this moment, during which our worlds are finally starting to change.

This is the falling action, a part of me says, in her monumental story.

Soon, we will be joining members of the Final Wishes Organization, and riding the elevator to the stars.

While a part of me feels a certain sense of awe in knowing that, another can only feel grief.

Outside, an ambulance pulls backward into our drive.

It Takes A Village

"Well," my father says in a low and somber voice. "I guess this is it."

My mother's only response is to reach out, set a hand on his arm, and wait for the medics to arrive.

~*~

The ride to the hospital is filled with lingering uncertainties, with ominous dread. Cold, even though it is bright and summery, I wrap a shawl around my shoulders, and try my hardest not to tremble as my brother gazes out the window.

"It's so big!" he says, allowing his gaze to rise to the sky alongside the tower.

"It is," my mother says.

"Your grandmother was in charge of its construction, you know?" my father asks, as if it is a crowning achievement in his own life, his personal pride and joy.

"I know, Dad," my brother says.

I, meanwhile, remain silent; because even as we pull up to the hospital, and make our way into a spot especially designated for Final Wishes recipients and their families, I find my heart pounding, my mind racing.

I think, Do not be afraid.

But heights, it can be said, are not meant to be braved. Never were people meant to scale mountains, or brave the skies in planes. Knowing that we will first be taking a helicopter, then riding an elevator to space, leaves me in a position of utmost doubt, in callous dread.

My father turns to face me as my little brother and mother climb out of the car, and asks, "Are you all right?"

"I'm — fine," I say. "Don't worry about me."

It Takes A Village

He watches me for a moment, as if expecting me to say something further. When I do not, however, he sighs, and says, "Come on. Let's go."

Making our way into the hospital, and then navigating the bureaucratic systems set in place, makes me thankful that I am so young. At the same time, I can sense the apprehension in the air, the unbridled tension that radiates from my father's body.

He asks, "Is everything ready?"

To which a receptionist replies by saying, "Almost, sir."

"Almost?"

"Yes. We are working on preparing your transport and finalizing your accommodations as we speak."

As a result, we are made to sit in the waiting room alongside other people — who, with their heads bowed to screens and even paper books, appear ignorant as can be to the plights of others, the dread they might be facing.

My little brother says, "Cassie?"

I say, "Yes?"

He asks, "Are you scared to go up into space?"

And I reply by saying: "Somewhat."

My father frowns, but doesn't say anything. He is obviously lost in his own thoughts, his own feelings, his own memories, good or bad or in-between as they happen to be.

My mother says, "Let's hush now. The people here want quiet."

Whether or not that is true I cannot be for certain. However, I tell myself not to think on this, and instead, remain silent as my mother asks.

It is only when a very official-looking man in a striped suit steps forward and asks, "The Hernandez family?" that I lift my eyes from my lap to consider the world around me.

"That's us," my father says.

It Takes A Village

"Please, come this way. We're ready to take you to Tower Paradisíaca."

People around us look up. Wonder. Stare.

In their eyes there is a certain hesitation, an awestruck question, that leaves me feeling small.

I do not have long to consider it, however.

Instead, I turn and follow the gentleman through the halls.

~*~

Boarding the helicopter and securing our seatbelts into place should leave me reeling with panic. Instead, I feel a certain hollowness that I know comes from a sense of dread.

Over what will come, a part of me says. Over what is meant to come.

My brother looks out at the Tower Paradisíaca as the overhead rotors begin to spin. He says, "Wow! I can't believe we're going there!"

My father says, "Neither can I."

Even though we have headsets on and can hear what one another is saying, my mother cautions us to remain silent — and for good reason. A wind from a coming storm buffets the Gulf, and causes the helicopter to tremble as we rise into the air.

I think, God, and pray for safety for not just us, but my grandmother, who is already in the air, and making her way toward Tower Paradisíaca as we speak.

As the helicopter rises, slowly but effortlessly coasting the currents, I find my stomach churning, my gut constricting.

I tell myself to remain calm. That everything will be all right. That this will be the easiest part of our journey.

Then, slowly, I turn my head, and watch the distance between us become less.

It Takes A Village

In mere minutes, we will be climbing into the Tower Paradisíaca, and leaving everything we have known and loved behind.

~*~

A port opens for our helicopter as we draw close, and upon it we land before it is drawn into the elevator's superstructure. Cold, from exposure to the storm, but warming now that we are inside the tower, I rub my hands along my arms and lift my eyes as the helicopter's door opens, revealing another man in a striped suit.

He says, "Welcome, Hernandez family, to Tower Paradisíaca. We are honored to be part of Missus Hernandez' legacy, as well as her final wish."

"Thank you," my father says, though in a way that makes me think he isn't fully processing the words as he should.

"We have prepared your lodgings," the gentleman says. "Please, come with us."

We disembark from the helicopter — and after taking hold of our suitcases, our meager belongings that will carry us through the next few days, we make our way toward a doorway, through which I know the Tower Paradisíaca truly lies. Stepping forward feels like a dream. Actually feeling the ground beneath my feet? That makes it all the more real.

And all the scarier, I think, to know what is about to come.

I take a moment to compose myself as we approach the doorway — as toward our future we walk.

The moment the threshold opens is the moment I feel my anxieties slip away, and wonder replace them tenfold.

Though I have known the tower to be huge, the structure is beyond massive, and inside there exists a plethora of activity. There are people all about — some wandering, others milling about. The scent of food is carried upon air-conditioned currents, and businesses, which feature everything from clothing stores to entertainment boutiques, stand side-to-side, back-to-back. Lights line this platform, and rise along the walls to heights greater than I could have ever imagined.

It is, in a word, stunning.

"Wow," my brother says.

"I... I can't believe it," I reply.

"Neither can I," my father replies. "Neither can I."

My mother crosses herself, and whispers what I believe to be a silent prayer.

The gentleman accompanying us says, "Come. We will rise to the medical bay at Space Level."

Space Level, I think.

We follow him to an elevator at the far end of the platform. Wait for him to swipe a keycard to access it. Step inside, hauling our luggage, both emotional and not, along with us.

As the elevator door closes, I turn to regard the glass window that looks out at the ocean, and find my eyes trailing skyward.

Then, the elevator begins to rise, at a brisk but comfortable pace.

"You have no need to be afraid," the gentleman says. "The tower is pressurized to withstand the tests of space."

"Where is my mother?" my father asks.

"Missus Hernandez is being medically cleared on Earth Level to transport to Space Level. You will see her soon enough."

I close my eyes as we pass through a massive, cottony mass of clouds, then open them a moment later, only to look down at the world below is.

To know that we are so high up is beyond amazing. To know that we will soon see the stars? That is another thing entirely.

It Takes A Village

I lift my eyes. Watch the cloud cover begin to fade. See darkness take its place.

Then, I see lights. Millions of lights. Maybe even billions of them. All stretching endlessly across the horizon, across space and time.

I feel a tender part of my heart swell with pride over what my grandmother was able to accomplish. Then, I feel a tendril of sorrow take its place.

It won't be long, I think, until this is all over.

But what will happen once we have endured such an experience? Will we go on to live ordinary lives, touched as they happened to be by the marvels of technology? Or will we be forever altered by the cosmic nature that is the world beyond our planet Earth?

Unable to know, I take a long, deep breath, then expel it accordingly.

I know I cannot be afraid.

Now, I must be strong.

~*~

The lodgings provided for us are beyond immaculate, and I look out at the gravity of space as if I am a child looking at the stars for the first time. Captivated, both by the sight and the experience, I press a hand to the glass that separates us from the world beyond, and find a swell of emotion surging through me.

My mother says, "You two must be hungry."

"Can we order room service?" my brother asks. "Can we get whatever we want?"

"We've been offered room and board while we're here," she replies. "But, please, remember: we are here thanks to the organization's kindness. We do not want to overindulge if we can help it."

It Takes A Village

Andrew nods, cautiously, as if he has suddenly become aware of the implications of this trip, grand in scope as it happens to be.

Frowning, I turn to face the doorway leading out of our shared room. I ask, "Mom?"

She replies, "Yes, Cassie?"

"Where is Dad?"

"He's with your grandmother," she replies, but that is all she says. She, too, has grown distant, but I know it is only because she is worried about my father, about how he might be feeling, thankful or grief-stricken as he happens to be.

I approach the touchscreen device that is embedded into the far wall, near where the dining table rests, and say, "Come here, Andrew. Let's order us something to eat."

"But shouldn't we wait for Dad?" Andrew asks.

"Mom'll know what he'll like," I say, turning my head to face her. "Won't you, Mom?"

"I — " she starts, then says, "Yes. I… I suppose I will."

Andrew takes mere moments to step forward and cycle through the menu with me.

~*~

We are eating a nice meal about a half-an-hour later, which is fine but not opulent. Though my father has yet to return, his food still resting on a covered, heated plate, the rest of us eat in silence. My mother picks at her food much like a finch — only casually, as if she fears it will leap up and bite her. It's enough to set me on edge, because the longer my father is gone, the more convinced I am that something has happened.

"Mama?" I ask after what seems like an eternity of silence.

It Takes A Village

"Yes, Cassie?" she replies.

"Do you know what's taking Dad so long?"

"He's with your grandmother," my mother says. "He'll be back when he needs to be."

I open my mouth to speak, but stop not long afterward.

You can't force information out of them, a part of me offers. You know you can't.

Still, being in the dark, pitch-black as it happens to be, is doing nothing for my conscience. Rather, it is causing me to feel panic, paranoia, and most of all, pain.

I frown not long after, and resume picking at my food in silence.

That is when the door opens, and my father steps inside.

"Can I talk to you?" he asks, lifting his eyes to face my mother.

She offers a slow, hesitant nod, and stands a moment later. "Stay here," she says, more to Andrew than she does to me.

"But — " my little brother says.

She shakes her head, then, and makes her way to the doorway.

They have no sooner left the room when I rise.

"Cassie?" my brother asks. "Where are you — "

"Shh," I whisper, and press a finger to my lips. "I want to hear what they're saying."

"But Mom said — "

I shake my head, and turn to make my way toward the doorway.

When I press my ear against it, I can just make out the sounds of them talking.

"Joseph," my mother says. "What's going on? Why were you gone for so long?"

"Because I needed to be there," my father replies. "Because she wanted my blessing."

It Takes A Village

"For what?"

"To let go."

I blink. Heart pounding, blood rushing to my ears, my fingers curl into fists, and a moment of disbelief assaults me.

To let go? I think.

Has it really come to that? Has my grandmother deteriorated so much that we will only be here for a few more hours? That her journey will finally be almost over?

I lift my hand to my mouth, and try my hardest to stifle a cry.

"Cassie?" my brother asks. "What's wrong?"

"I — " I start. "I don't — "

My brother takes hold of my hand.

I jump, startled, and spin to face him.

"What's going on?" my little brother asks. "Why do you look so scared?"

I swallow the growing lump in my throat, careful to choose my words. Then I say: "It's… it's because Grandma — "

My little brother can only stare.

"It's because Grandma doesn't have much time left," I say.

"You mean — " my brother starts to say.

But I nod before he can finish.

My brother lowers his eyes. Sniffles.

I say, "Don't cry, Andy. You can't. They'll know we heard if you do."

"I… I know," he says, and sniffles once more. "I just… I didn't… didn't know — "

"That she was so sick," I reply. "I… I know."

I step forward, then; and though Andrew has seemed a continent away since he entered puberty a year ago, I take him into my arms, and wrap him in the tightest hug possible.

It Takes A Village

"It's going to be okay," I whisper. "If she's saying it's time to go… it means she's ready to let go."

"But are we?" he says.

Though as much as I want to speak, I know I cannot.

So, I do the only thing I think possible.

I tighten my hold on my brother, and hold him tight.

~*~

My mother and father return not long after they have departed. In their eyes there is a certain hesitation — a world of grief not yet born. However, there is also a determination, one I understand is meant to do right by us.

I am not surprised when my father speaks, nor when he says, "We need to say goodbye to your grandmother tonight."

"Tonight?" I ask.

My father offers a hesitant nod. "Yes. Tonight."

"When?" my little brother asks.

"As soon as possible."

A quiet disturbs the room — and for a moment, it seems as if the whole world has ceased to exist: that we, so high in the sky, in a place beyond the Earth, are simply players in a cruel and unfortunate game. My mother sighs. My little brother closes his eyes. And I — I think of what my best friend had said, about how I could not go into this without telling her how much I loved my grandmother.

You're going to have to bear whatever emotions that come after your grandmother is gone, my best friend had said. *Don't let one of them be regret.*

It Takes A Village

I want to cry. To swim in oceans warm and shallow. To feel, like any child should, alive and well. But I know, here and now, that I must brave these trenches, these horrible landmines of hurt. Because if I don't…

I will never be able to forgive myself.

It is for that reason, and for so many more, that I say, "Okay. I'm… I'm ready."

My father turns to face me. Gone is the hesitation in his eyes. In its place has emerged a certain determination — a determination I know only comes when someone is willing to face the hardest of things.

"All right," he then says. "Let's… let's go."

~*~

We are taken to the one of the highest rooms in the upper medical bay, within which my grandmother rests kindly — her hospital bed to a broad window, out which we can see eternity and everything it encompasses. The sight alone is enough to leave me feeling small, reeling in every sense of the word. But knowing that it is finally time to let go?

My father steps toward my grandmother's bedside, and knowingly nods at the doctor who stands nearby, and says, "We're here, Mom."

"Joseph," my mother says. "Cassie. Andrew. Marsha. You came."

"We wouldn't miss this for the world," my mother says.

We step forward, then — slowly, carefully, with intent I know is born of a family who has suffered, and who will only continue to suffer after she has gone. My mother's hand is the first to grace my grandmother's arm, and mine — it touches her right hand, beneath which I can feel soft skin, so pliable that I feel trenches and mountains could be formed within it.

My grandmother turns her head to look at Andrew, and says, "Come here, Andy."

It Takes A Village

She offers her left hand, which my brother takes carefully.

"I know I've told you both so many times before," she says, "but I want you to know that... even though I am going to be gone... that I will always watch over you."

"Thank you," I whisper.

My grandmother turns to face the doctor standing nearby. "Doctor Garland?" she asks.

"Yes, Missus Hernandez?"

"Please... give me something to help me feel better."

"Yes, Missus Hernandez."

The doctor steps forward, then; and with a nurse at his side, considers a long needle upon a metal table. He nods. She lifts it gently. Considers it carefully. Looks from my mother, my father, then to my grandmother. The doctor tells my grandmother, "This will make you drowsy. You may fall asleep."

"That's okay," she says. "I'm ready."

The nurse primes the needle at the intravenous drip running into her arm, and nods before injecting the medication into the port.

"Look, Grandma," my younger brother says, extending a hand to point out the window. "A shooting star!"

"Make a wish," I then whisper, as I try my hardest not to cry. "Make a wish, Grandma."

It takes a moment for her to process our words. But when she does, my grandmother opens her eyes, so wide that she might as well have seen the face of God. Then she opens her mouth in awe — for though I cannot understand what she knows, or feels, or even what she sees, I know that life is beautiful, that this world and even those beyond are just the same.

For a moment, I feel she will not speak.

Then, she says a single word.

"Star."

It Takes A Village

And though her hands have trembled for so long — and though her eyes have been open for more than ninety years — she looks on at the world as she sees it is, and allows a single tear to fall from her face.

I think of those days when me and Andy were young — when Grandma, with her kind eyes and wide-open arms, would take us on walks along the Gulf, along the pier that I spent that previous day with my best friend on. I remember her telling me about my father's importance at the solar plant, and my mother's as a psychologist. She'd told each of us, in a way that only she could, that everyone has a place in this world — and that, even though we do not know what that might be at first, we ultimately find it in time.

There will come a day, she then said, as she tightened her hands around each of ours, that you will find purpose in your life. I found mine when I designed the tower.

I think of those days quite clearly — of her taking care of me and my brother while my mother and father were gone to work, or off on errands, or even when they were just off together, when she had her days off — and I think, God. How could life have been so simple, so innocent, that we could have never dreamed of these days, this untimely end.

As I gaze into my grandmother's eyes — and as I see a lifetime of her presence flash before my eyes — I find myself wondering if she, too, is thinking the same.

But when she closes her eyes —

And when I know she takes her final breath —

It takes only a moment for the doctor to declare what we already know. "She is gone," he says.

And though I told myself I would be strong, I cannot help but crumble.

It Takes A Village

As we stand here — together, as a family, looking on at the shooting star as it falls across the distance — I find myself yearning for all those days, those memories, her kindness, and her loving arms.

Her final wish was to see the stars.

Now, I know, she is a part of them.

About Kody Boye

Kody Boye is a young adult horror, fantasy, and science-fiction writer currently residing in the Rio Grande Valley of South Texas. First published in the Yellow Mama Webzine, he has gone on to write works such as The Beautiful Ones and When They Came trilogies, as well as The Red Wolf Saga.

Find out more about Kody on his blog: kodyboye.com

And his works on Amazon at:
amazon.com/author/kodyboye

It Takes A Village

It Takes A Village

CARING CREDITS

by Marie-Hélène Lebeault

When asked what inspired this story, Marie-Hélène responded:

> The inspiration for "Caring Credits" came from witnessing the disconnect in our technology-driven world and a fascination with traditional bartering systems. I wondered, what if we could reinvent the concept of value, trading time and care instead of money? Personal experiences with caregiving and the healthcare system's shortcomings further fueled this idea, pushing me to imagine a place where community and mutual support redefine success. Harmony Haven was born from a desire to explore these alternatives, blending my interest in bartering's simplicity and equity with a narrative that challenges our notions of connection and worth.

It Takes A Village

CARING CREDITS — Marie-Hélène Lebeault

In Harmony Haven, time is the currency of care, weaving a community where every hour shared transforms lives.

Maya sat hunched over her sleek, holographic workstation, the soft hum of her computer the only sound in the darkened room. The glow from the screen cast an ethereal light across her focused face as she parsed through lines of code, her fingers dancing over the virtual keyboard with practiced ease. The abrupt, jarring ring of her SmartSlate broke the silence.

She hesitated as she gazed at the small device used for everything from communication to taking a person's temperature. Her deadline was looming, and she already knew she wouldn't have enough time to finish the project her boss assigned that day. The caller ID displayed her mother's image, compelling her to answer.

"Hey, Mom," Maya said, trying to mask her worry with a cheerful tone.

"Hi, honey," her mother's voice crackled through, breathy and tired, though she tried to sound upbeat. "I didn't want to bother you, but..."

The words trailed off, but Maya knew the sentence's end all too well. It was the same every time: her mother's health was declining; the treatments were exhausting, and the distance between them felt like an ever-expanding void.

"It's okay, Mom," Maya said. "You're not bothering me."

"I know you're busy, but I got a call from the doctor. He wants me to go in for more tests. Your aunt will come stay with me for a few days."

Maya listened, her heart sinking with each word, feeling the weight of her mother's solitude and pain. They talked, time slipping away until the project deadline came and went. Maya turned from her station as her boss sent

It Takes A Village

messages demanding what was delaying her. Time with her mother was just too precious.

The call ended with promises of a visit soon, words that felt hollow even as she said them. Work kept her tethered to her workstation, far from her mother. She stared at the silent SmartSlate, a lifeline that felt inadequate to bridge the gap of miles and silence.

The room felt colder now, and the technological marvels around her were stark reminders of her isolation. Maya's gaze drifted to the window, where the shiny chrome-colored city reflected a night of faux stars.

Turning back to her workstation, Maya's eyes caught a pamphlet she had picked up on her way home from work—home, to where more work was noted. "Come to Harmony Haven and join a community of unity."

The pamphlet contained information about the village, specifically their Time Bank concept, a barter system based on services instead of goods.

She had dismissed it before, a quaint community initiative that seemed too idealistic, too communal for her taste. But now, it whispered a promise of connection, of support, something she yearned for her mother and herself.

With a deep sigh, Maya typed a message back to her boss. She needed a change. One that perhaps she would find in Harmony Haven. At that moment, she decided. She would explore this Time Bank system, skeptical but driven by a burgeoning hope. Perhaps this was what she needed so that she would have some more time with her mother.

~*~

Maya's DrivePod hummed to a stop in the main parking lot at Harmony Haven. The self-driving car's door slid open with a gentle hiss, and Maya stepped out into the warm, fragrant air. As she stretched, her gaze drifted over the houses that, though modern in appearance, seemed to whisper tales of an ancient past.

The village was alive with children's laughter, chasing each other around the perfectly manicured gardens. Birds chirped in the trees, mingling with the distant hum of drones. Seeing the village just as depicted in the promotional hologram surprised her. Here, time wasn't just a commodity; it was the currency of care, the backbone of an economy that valued human connection above all else.

Maya remained skeptical. How could such an ideological system be practical? Life in the metropolis had been too busy to contemplate anything but the briefest stints of volunteering. Time was money and time spent needed to yield returns. It was a guiding principle in her job as a software engineer. Yet, the seamless blend of nature and technology and the happy villagers beckoned.

She pulled her SmartSlate from her purse and called her mother. As expected, there was no answer; her mother would be at the hospital for treatment.

"I've arrived safely," Maya said, recording a message. "I'll call you after I'm settled in."

With a sigh, she slipped the SmartSlate back into her purse.

As she dragged her suitcase towards her new home, the sound of her wheels against the cobblestone path seemed to announce an outsider, an observer from a world where efficiency was king and personal gain was the goal. She still didn't understand how anything here could work, but if it did, maybe she could finally help her mother.

Harmony Haven was an experiment in living differently, challenging the foundations of her beliefs. It boasted a blend of advanced technology, the latest, with a grassroots approach to community. Human connection was all-important here, and the concept of communal caregiving was at the heart of this place.

It Takes A Village

Maya paused at her doorstep, the keycard heavy in her hand, not just a tool to unlock a door but a symbol of her choice to step into this unknown. The decision to move wasn't just about a new job or the allure of innovation; it was a desperate measure, a hope to find a solution for her mother's care that the cold efficiency of her previous world could not offer. It was a venture into the depths of a question she had never dared to ask: What if there was more to life than the relentless pursuit of success? What if, in this village, she could find the answer?

Taking a deep breath, Maya stepped inside. The door closed behind her with a soft click that seemed to seal her fate.

As the first light of day spilled into her new living room, Maya felt the weight of her skepticism lift, replaced by the faintest sense of hope. Perhaps, in this place where time flowed differently, she could find a new way to define what it meant to live, care, and belong.

~*~

The following day found Maya walking towards the heart of the community, a digital copy of the Time Bank brochure open on her SmartSlate. Nerves tightened her stomach as she approached the Community Center. It was a modern, glass-paneled building that buzzed with activity, different from the cold, sterile environments she had known in her old life.

It was so different that she wasn't sure this was her best idea. What if all this was a mistake? She had to give up her well-paid job to move to Harmony Haven. She still had work, but it didn't pay nearly as much. Money was practically useless here, so people didn't care as much about wages.

But even with that high-paying job, she reminded herself that she didn't have enough time or money to help her mother.

It Takes A Village

Squaring her shoulders, she stepped inside. A vibrant mosaic of community life greeted her. Children's laughter echoed from a play area, while groups of adults engaged in lively discussions around tables laden with plans and projects. Several stations were set up throughout the room, looking for volunteers. She passed displays for a community garden, teachers for the nature school, and a coach for a volleyball team.

Maya approached the reception desk, catching the attention of a woman whose warm smile shone through the translucent glow of her holoscreen. As the woman glanced up, her eyes, bright with genuine interest, connected with Maya's. With a graceful gesture, she swiped the holoscreen aside, clearing the space between them, and stood to greet Maya.

"Good morning! How can we assist you today?" the woman asked, her tone inviting.

Maya cleared her throat as she shifted from foot to foot. "I'm Maya. I just moved to Harmony."

"Welcome, Maya," the woman said. "I'm Carol. What can I do for you today?"

"I'm interested in learning about the Time Bank," Maya admitted, almost sheepishly.

The woman's smile broadened. "Wonderful! You're in the right place. I help coordinate the Time Bank program here. Let me show you how it works."

Carol led Maya to a comfortable seating area, gesturing for her to take a seat as she pulled up a presentation on a large screen.

"The Time Bank is a community-driven system where members can exchange services, measured in hours rather than monetary value," she began. "From gardening and grocery shopping to tutoring and tech support, every task is equal in value, one hour for another, regardless of the service's market value."

It Takes A Village

Maya laced her fingers over her knees. "So, an hour of flipping burgers equals an hour of a life-saving surgery?"

Carol smiled gently. "Yes. An hour is equal to an hour. Imagine, instead of working a hundred hours to pay for that surgery, you can share a talent or read stories to children for a few hours. In our community, a lack of wealth doesn't mean that you go without life's necessities." She paused, displaying a graph on the holoscreen.

"As you contribute your time to help others, you earn hours you can spend on services you need. It's based on the principle that everyone has something valuable to offer, and it strengthens community bonds," Carol continued, her enthusiasm infectious.

Maya listened, a mix of skepticism and curiosity churning inside her. "But how do you ensure people contribute equally? What if someone takes more than they give? It sounds like a logistical nightmare."

Carol nodded, anticipating the question. "We have a system in place for tracking contributions and needs. It's rare, but if someone takes without giving, we reach out to understand why. Sometimes it's a matter of finding the right opportunities for them to contribute. It's about building a culture of mutual support, not strict accounting. We all have times when we can't give as much as we would like. Humans were made for connection, not the isolation modern society has become."

The concept was simple, yet revolutionary to Maya. That every individual's time could have the same value was humbling and empowering. She thought about her skills, what she could offer, and the possibilities she might receive. Being part of a community where giving and receiving care was the norm chipped away at her skepticism.

It didn't seem possible that it could work, but if an hour of her time paid for an hour of treatment for her mother? She could barely take care of herself anymore, let alone work. Right now, she was relying on a faceless

It Takes A Village

government to take care of her, and those benefits were being whittled down every year.

Maya took a deep breath, her determination growing firmer. "And anyone can join? Even if they're new to the community, or not in it at all?"

"Absolutely," Carol beamed. "The Time Bank is open to everyone. It's a great way to get to know your neighbors and feel connected."

"What if I'm not trying to feel connected?" Maya pressed. "What if I just want the benefits?"

Carol's smile grew shrewd. "Then I would say you need us the most. What do you say? You'll start with ten hours of time credits as a sign of good faith."

Maya chewed her lip, considering the leap of faith this represented. The thought of her mother, alone and in need, flashed through her mind. Ten hours. If her mother and aunt could have someone come to their home and help for ten hours, it would significantly improve their lives. Here was a chance to help her redefine her place within this new community.

"I'll try it," Maya said, a tentative smile breaking through her usual reserve.

As she left the Community Center with her head filled with ideas and the Time Bank app on her SmartSlate, Maya felt a subtle shift within her. Carol's enthusiastic response and the promise of a new, interconnected way of living sparked a flicker of hope in Maya's heart, a feeling she hadn't experienced in a long time. She was still a skeptic, but now, she was a skeptic willing to explore the possibilities of what could be achieved with the simple yet profound exchange of time.

A lovely café stood across from the Community Center, so Maya approached it. She ordered a cup of coffee and found a spot at a table for one. It buzzed with the energy of the morning rush, yet Maya felt a bubble of calm around her as she contemplated her next steps.

It Takes A Village

She opened her SmartSlate, navigating to the Time Bank's digital platform. This well-designed app seemed to pulse with the life of the community it served. The first thing she found was her credits. Sure enough, there were ten hours logged for her use already. She hovered over it, hesitating.

What could her mother and aunt use the most? Her aunt worked all the time, and with her mother's health problems, she couldn't do much around the house. A cleaning, then. Once Maya banked fresh hours, she could get some home-cooked meals.

She tapped on a request feature and typed in what she needed, as well as where her mother was located. Using the EcoSwift Rail Network would only take an hour to get there. If Maya had found remote work, she would have already moved in with her mother and aunt.

Once I know this will work, I'll send for them, she promised herself.

After making her request, she received a message asking to attend a welcome meeting at the Community Hall that night. She accepted the invitation and then moved on to the other requests, looking for things that she might help with.

A single parent needed tutoring for their child in mathematics, an elderly couple needed help with their garden, and a tech-challenged artist sought help setting up a website for their work. Each request was a window into the lives of her neighbors, reflecting needs that were as diverse as they were personal.

Maya typed up an offer to help with the artist's website. It fit perfectly with her coding experience. Then she closed the SmartSlate and drank her coffee, enjoying the sunlight through the window.

~*~

It Takes A Village

That night, Maya's stomach swam with apprehension and excitement as she returned to the Community Center. With booths tucked away on the sides, the vast circle of chairs was in prominent view. Carol greeted Maya warmly and introduced her to a few others. As she glanced around, Maya relaxed. It was clear she was far from the only nervous newcomer. People of all ages and backgrounds had gathered together. The hall was alive with many greetings and hugs.

"Let's all take our seats," Carol said.

Maya found an empty chair. Carol welcomed everyone and gave a rundown of the Time Bank as she had told Maya that morning.

"The exchange of time and skills isn't just transactional," Carol continued. "It's relational, building connections that transcend the simple act of giving and receiving help."

As the meeting progressed, members took turns speaking, some offering their skills and others voicing their needs. A retired carpenter offered woodworking workshops. Seeking help to learn new software, a young graphic designer offered help in teaching some techniques. A busy parent requested help with meal preparation during a hectic week.

When it came Maya's turn to speak, she hesitated, feeling the weight of her outsider status. But the encouraging nods and smiles from those around her spurred her on.

"Hi, I'm Maya. I'm new here," she began, her voice steadier than she felt. "As a software engineer, I can provide tech support, assist with coding, or teach basic computer skills. My mother lives across the country, and her needs are many. I'm looking for people to commute and help around the house, make meals, run errands, or even visit her when I can't."

The response was immediate and warm, with several members asking about her skills and offering in return skills of their own that Maya hadn't even realized she might need.

It Takes A Village

One was a gardening enthusiast who could help Maya start her own vegetable garden, something she had always wanted to do but never had the time or knowledge for. Fresh vegetables she could send to her mother would help her maintain a more balanced diet.

As the meeting drew to a close, Maya felt an unexpected sense of belonging. She had come seeking a way to help her mother. Still, she opened up to the potential of becoming an integral part of this community.

Walking home under the starlit sky, Maya had a spring in her step. The Time Bank, with its simple premise of mutual aid, had shown her a path to assist her mother from afar and weave herself into the fabric of her new community. For the first time since her arrival, Maya looked forward to the days ahead, eager to explore the depth of connections that the Time Bank promised.

~*~

The sun had just dipped below the horizon, painting the sky in shades of orange and pink. Maya stood outside a quaint house on the edge of the community. Her hands trembled slightly as she double-checked her SmartSlate to ensure she was in the right place. This was the address of her first official task through the Time Bank—a babysitting request from a single mother needing a few hours to attend a night class.

With a deep breath to calm her nerves, Maya rang the doorbell. Moments later, the door swung open, revealing a woman with a harried but grateful smile and a lively toddler peeking from behind her legs.

"Maya? Oh, thank you for coming on such short notice. I'm Sara, and this tornado here is Eli," the woman said. Her relief was evident as she ushered Maya inside.

"It's good to meet you," Maya answered.

It Takes A Village

Eli stuck his tongue out at her and ran off, giggling.

The initial awkwardness dissipated as Sara explained Eli's bedtime routine, his favorite bedtime story ("Captain Spacebear's Galactic Adventure"), and his aversion to broccoli. Eli kept interrupting, showing Maya his toys and telling her about the features of their home—for instance, the blue wall. Maya was taken aback by how friendly the child was.

She had minimal experience with children, which she had warned Sara about when she offered help. Now, she listened intently to Sara's explanations, nodding and asking occasional questions to ensure she got everything right.

"If he won't settle, take him for a walk to the park," Sara told her. "Sometimes he has a hard time getting to sleep."

"I'll do my best," Maya promised.

After Sara left, Maya found herself alone with Eli, who regarded her while sucking his thumb. His friendly demeanor seemed to dampen suspicion with his mother's departure.

"So, Eli, what do you say we find Captain Spacebear's book?" she suggested, hoping to win him over.

To her surprise, Eli warmed up to her quickly, guiding her to his treasure trove of toys and books. Reading the story to Eli with animated voices and exaggerated expressions, Maya felt a warmth she hadn't expected. She watched Eli fight against the pull of sleep, his eyes fluttering shut, only to snap open as if resisting the end of the day was heroic.

It took several times to read the same story. Still, eventually, Eli succumbed to sleep, his breathing deep and his face peaceful. Maya tucked the sleeping child into bed, feeling a profound sense of accomplishment. It wasn't a complex coding challenge or a software launch, but it felt just as significant at that moment.

The house was quiet, save for the occasional creak and sigh of settling wood. Maya moved to the living room. She sent a message to her mother—

undoubtedly asleep at this hour—telling her she would receive several frozen meals the next day. Sara ran a meal delivery service for Harmony residents. She had a few extras that she promised in exchange for Maya babysitting.

Sara returned home to find Eli sleeping soundly. The gratitude in her eyes was unmistakable. She hugged Maya tightly.

"Thank you."

"No, thank you," Maya said. "You don't understand how much this means to me."

Sara laughed. "I think I do. I was once a newcomer in Harmony, too."

Maya felt an unexpected lightness as she walked home under the starry night. She had stepped into this house as a stranger, and now she felt a part of something deeply human—care, trust, connection. For the first time, she felt like she belonged to a community. She was part of a web of care that extended beyond the confines of her own needs and interests, a realization that both humbled and inspired her.

She looked up at the night sky. The stars shone a little brighter and reflected the newfound spark within her.

~*~

In the weeks that followed her successful evening with Eli, Maya threw herself into the Time Bank with a newfound zeal. She balanced her work with tasks that supported the community. But though she was busy, she never felt like she was burning out as she had in her previous job. On the contrary, she felt invigorated as she became more tightly woven into the fabric of the community.

One sunny afternoon, Maya sat at a picnic table in the local park, surrounded by eager teenagers. She was there to fulfill a request for a coding workshop, something she had proposed in a burst of confidence. The teens participated in a community youth program, many of whom had never considered coding a potential skill or career path.

As Maya walked them through the basics of the program, using analogies from cooking to explain concepts like variables and functions, she watched their faces light up with understanding and excitement. Maya encouraged the teens to think of coding as a tool for solving problems and bringing their ideas to life.

They created a simple program that animated their names on the screen. High-fives and excited chatter spread through the room as they wondered what they might make next. Maya, watching the scene, felt a surge of pride and satisfaction. She had not only imparted knowledge but had also sparked curiosity and ambition.

Another task took her to the home of Mr. Jenkins, an elderly widower known in the community for his love of gardening but who had broken his leg. Her job was to help him with household chores, but she discovered Mr. Jenkins had much more to offer than a task list. As Maya did her work, Mr. Jenkins shared stories from his youth, tales of the community's early days, and wisdom on everything from gardening to life's unpredictable nature. In return, Maya shared her experiences with her mother and her fears about health and quality of life.

"As soon as I have enough saved up, I'm going to hire people to help me move her to Harmony," she told Mr. Jenkins.

Mr. Jenkins chuckled as he laced his fingers over his lap. "Why, when can you ask the people here to help you?"

Maya had never considered that before. Her heart swelled as she realized she could move her mother to Harmony much sooner. She just needed to be healthy enough to make the journey.

"Thank you," she said to Mr. Jenkins when the evening was done.

It Takes A Village

"Oh, thank you," Mr. Jenkins answered. "Come back anytime—not just as a helper but as a friend. Oh, and you should check out the community garden project. It'll be a great way to build your time credits."

~*~

Maya was at her workstation, lost in a sea of code, when her SmartSlate pinged with a message that instantly drew her out of her digital world. It was from her aunt, succinct and unsettling: "Your mom needs more care. We need to figure this out."

Her heart sank. Her mother's health had been a simmering concern. Maya had managed through the Time Bank, arranging for local volunteers to check in and help. But her mother's condition was worsening, demanding more than what occasional visits could provide.

Sitting back, Maya felt the weight of her situation. She was hundreds of miles away, with a job she couldn't leave at a moment's notice, and her time credits were running low. The miles between her and her mother now felt like an emotional chasm.

Her mind turned to Mr. Jenkins' suggestion of asking the community to help her move her mother. But she had no credits to pay for such a massive work.

She remembered what Carol had said that day when she joined the Time Bank: "The exchange of time and skills isn't just transactional. It's relational, building connections that transcend the simple act of giving and receiving help."

With a deep, steadying breath, Maya composed a message to the Time Bank community. She explained her mother's situation: the need for increased care and her current inability to meet those needs with her available time credits. She hesitated before sending the message, aware she was exposing her vulnerability to near strangers.

But this was why she had come to Harmony. It wasn't just about giving; it was also about being able to accept. She chewed her lip as she sent the message.

The response was immediate and overwhelming. Offers of help poured in, not just as time credits but also advice, support, and shared experiences. The community she knew through individual tasks and brief encounters rallied around her, a testament to the bonds formed in shared service.

Tears formed in her eyes as she called her mother. "Guess what, Mom? You're coming to Harmony."

~*~

Her mother waved as Maya stepped out of the HoverLoad. She rushed over to where her mother sat in a wheelchair and threw her arms around her. It had been so long since they had last seen one another—it felt like forever.

"Who are all these people?" her mother asked her as she viewed the people who came to help.

Maya beamed. "Friends."

Her aunt, who stood just behind her mother, folded her arms. "Friends? But you've barely been at this Harmony place for three months."

"Harmony is a friendly place," Maya answered.

Her aunt fretted as the crew loaded up her mom's belongings. "It just seems too good to be true."

Maya hugged her. "You can come visit and see for yourself. It's a wonderful place."

Her aunt shrugged. "Maybe I will if I ever get the time."

It Takes A Village

"Maybe we'll be able to give you some," Carol said as she came over, a grin spreading over her face. "Have you heard of the Time Bank?"

~*~

When her mother moved to Harmony, Maya became extra determined to help others who needed generosity. That is how she found herself in the bustling atmosphere of the community kitchen, an initiative designed to provide meals for those in need. The air was thick with the aroma of spices and the warmth of ovens working overtime.

"Welcome, Maya! We're thrilled to have you help us today," Anna, the kitchen's coordinator, said. She wore a smile, and an apron adorned with flour.

"Thank you. I'm more accustomed to ordering takeout than cooking, but I hope I can be useful," Maya said.

Anna gave Maya an apron and a quick rundown of the kitchen's operation. "Today, you'll help prepare the meal, package it, and distribute it."

As Maya chopped vegetables, stirred pots, and helped line up the prepared meals for distribution, she found a rhythm in the shared activity. The kitchen was a hive of activity, with volunteers of all ages working side by side, their chatter and laughter creating a melody of camaraderie.

Maya opened up, sharing stories of her own life and listening to others. There was Mark, a retired teacher who found joy in cooking for others; Lily, a high school student passionate about food justice; and George, who loved to cook and saw the kitchen as his way of giving back. She found it amazing how many stories brought the volunteers here.

"Now that we're cooking tomorrow's meals, you and Mark are going to deliver the food we packed today," Anna told her. "We have many people who depend on us."

Maya nodded seriously. She helped load up the van and set off with Mark to deliver the food. He told her about his years of teaching.

"I never thought I would be a good teacher, but I helped some of the local teenagers start to code," Maya said as they drove. "It was very gratifying. I'm realizing that teaching isn't just about telling people what to do and think, but also about teaching them how to figure things out on their own."

Mark laughed. "That's the spirit of it. Oh, I hope you don't mind that I will visit your mother tomorrow. She's going to teach me how to knit."

Tears pricked Maya's eyes. That was what Harmony was all about. Her mother may be too ill to do much, but she could still knit.

The food deliveries went well. At each stop, she met members of her community she would have never crossed paths with otherwise: a young mother juggling two jobs, an elderly man living alone, and a family new to the area and struggling to settle in. Each thank you and smile of gratitude struck a chord in Maya. She realized that the community kitchen was more than just about providing meals; it was about nourishing souls, about letting people know they were not alone, that their community stood with them.

As the day wound down and Maya hung up her apron, she felt a profound sense of fulfillment. She had gone in worried about her lack of culinary skills, but she left with a heart full of warmth and realized that it wasn't about being the best cook in the kitchen. It was about showing up, contributing what she could, and being part of something greater than herself.

As she headed home, she checked her Time Bank credits. To her surprise, she found she had gained enough to cover the rest of her mother's move, plus extras. A radiant smile spread over her face as she donated half of them back to the Time Bank, to be used for anyone who needed just a little extra help.

Maya had come to the community looking for a way to support her mother, but she had found a second family. She realized that while she might not change the world alone, she could change the world around her, one hour at a time.

~*~

The community garden was a beautiful space, reclaimed from an abandoned lot. The greenhouses were bio-adaptive, with smart glass that dimmed to balance temperature and light, optimizing conditions for each plant species. Robotic bees flitted between blooms, ensuring pollination where natural bees were scarce.

Raised flower beds had moisture sensors and nutrient injectors, which meticulously calibrated soil conditions using real-time data analytics. Hydroponic towers soared skyward, their roots suspended in nutrient-rich mist, conserving space and water. Along the pathways, interactive plant identifiers displayed holographic information about each species, from medicinal uses to historical facts, more information than Maya ever thought she'd ever need about plant life. Maya was happy that the paths were wheelchair accessible, and she pushed her mom to the center of the garden.

At the heart of the garden, a centralized AI hub nicknamed "Gaia" monitored the entire ecosystem's health, deploying drones for aerial seeding and maintenance tasks. It was also a gathering place, so Maya had selected it for this special celebration.

She beamed at Sara, who had been vital to helping her figure out the food. Then there was Carol, who helped connect her to the people to set up the event.

"You have so many friends now," Maya's mother said, reaching to pat Maya's hand. "I'm so proud of you."

Maya's aunt nodded. "This place really seems to be as good as you said."

It Takes A Village

"Oh, none of that," Maya's mother said. "That's my sister, always the skeptic. Look, Maya, there's that handsome young Mark."

"And there's Mr. Jenkins, eager for a wheelchair race," Maya laughed. She pushed her mother to be next to her friend, and they started instantly comparing the features of their new wheelchairs, purchased by a community fundraising project.

As Maya checked to ensure everything was ready, she glanced back at her mother. She had a new vibrancy, recounting her days filled with visits, activities, and the surprising joy of meeting so many kind-hearted people. She had joined the Time Bank, too. She had built her own credits by teaching knitting, making video calls to children in the hospital, and even recording herself reading books for people who wanted to hear the stories while they worked.

Motivated by the community's generosity, Maya organized this event at the gardens as a thank-you. Despite her lack of culinary skills, it was a modest affair, with homemade decorations and a spread of dishes Maya herself helped to prepare. She wanted to give back a tangible expression of her gratitude.

After everyone had gathered, Maya took her place on a small stage in front of the crowd. Her confidence shone from her, starkly contrasting to the woman who had first arrived in the community, skeptical and reserved.

"Thank you all so much for everything you have done for me and my family," she started. Her voice wavered, heavy with emotion, but grew stronger as she continued. "I came to Harmony with little hope. I felt as though the world was a heavy, lonely place. Harmony and all it stood for seemed to be an impossible dream."

She paused, remembering how hollow she had been when she first bought a house here. "I was desperate for any new shred of hope that I could improve my mother's life. I came, thinking that I would only give because of what I could get back. I came here thinking that at the heart of humanity was selfishness.

"But I was wrong," she continued, her eyes burning with fresh tears. She beamed at the gathered crowd. "I learned I love to give. I love to be part of something larger than myself. That the selfishness I'd felt was born of loneliness and fear. Now I stand here and want to give to everyone so that no one will ever feel alone again."

Her mother clasped her hands over her heart, beaming with pride at her daughter. Beside her, her aunt gave a small smile. Harmony was winning her over, too.

Maya smiled as she lifted her arms to the friends and neighbors who had formed a community and an extended family.

"Through giving, I've received so much more. A sense of belonging, purpose, and a community that stands together through challenges and celebrations. This experience, born out of crisis, illuminates the Time Bank's true essence: a testament to the strength of community ties and the transformative power of collective care and compassion.

"I've seen firsthand the incredible impact the Time Bank has on our lives," Maya said, her gaze sweeping across the crowd, meeting the eyes of those who had stood by her and her mother. "Time used to be a resource I measured in deadlines and deliverables. Now, it's a currency of care, of possibility."

She smiled and thought about the web of relationships forged by exchanging time, how those connections had nurtured her and her mother through challenging times, and how they had enriched her life beyond measure.

The crowd smiled at one another. She wasn't the only one thinking about how this transformative idea had taken root. So many people had already benefited from the project. Their little community had transformed, blossoming like the flowers all around them.

It Takes A Village

"The Time Bank taught me it's not about how much time we have," she continued, her gaze lifting to the sky, "but how we choose to spend it. In this community, we spend it on each other, building something greater than ourselves. But I believe we can do even more. We support each other and reach out to the wider community, to share what we've built here."

She proposed several initiatives: a mentorship program linking experienced members with newcomers to guide them through their first exchanges, a community outreach program to bring more residents into the fold, and a digital platform upgrade to better match needs and offerings.

The response was electric, her ideas sparking discussions and further suggestions. Everyone was excited about the prospect of building something even more beautiful. Maya returned to her mother, who beamed at her.

"This place is good for you," her mother said.

Maya smiled. "It's good for us all."

Together, they participated in the festivities, from the communal meal to the storytelling circle, where tales of the community's history and hopes for the future were woven together. The event was a beautiful blend of celebration and gratitude, acknowledging individual contributions that created a collective bounty.

As the day passed to a starlit night, Maya found a quiet moment to reflect on her journey. The garden, with its lush greenery and the soft laughter and music weaving through the air, stood as a testament to what people achieved when they came together, bound by a shared commitment to nurture and support one another.

Maya's journey reflected a broader transformation from isolation to integration, skepticism to advocacy. It was a story of how, by opening our hearts and calendars to others, we could change our lives and create a ripple effect, strengthening the fabric of our communities.

It Takes A Village

As Maya rejoined the festivities, her heart full, she knew this was just the beginning. The Time Bank and the community it symbolized were living, evolving entities, with every member's contribution adding to its strength and vitality. In giving their time, they were all weaving a tapestry of care, support, and belonging that would endure, a legacy of time well spent.

It Takes A Village

About Marie-Hélène Lebeault

Marie-Hélène Lebeault is a celebrated Canadian author renowned for her extensive contributions to the speculative fiction genre. Specializing in young adult novels, her works are imbued with themes of magic, fantasy, and time-travel, paired with vital coming-of-age narratives. Beyond her passion for crafting captivating stories, Marie-Hélène enjoys outdoor activities like hiking and cycling, as well as unwinding on the beach with a book. A retired educator, she has enriched the literary landscape with over 30 young adult books, including the acclaimed The Evers Series, Blood Magick Trilogy, Defenders of the Realm, and the Chronicles of the Starborne Cadets, alongside a charming series of picture books aimed at younger readers. Residing in Quebec with her adult children, Marie-Hélène continues to inspire readers with tales of adventure and the magic of discovery, leaving a lasting impact on the world of young adult and children's literature.

You can find Marie-Hélène works at mhlebeault.com
Her newsletter on landing.mailerlite.com/webforms/landing/c4j9g7

And her other works on Amazon:

amazon.com/stores/author/B086JFWCDT

It Takes A Village

SUGGESTED READING

Following are articles and books — both fiction and non-fiction — that match the theme of the anthology. If you found these stories insightful, you may wish to read further on the subject.

All entries are listed alphabetically by author name.

Fiction

- Bradbury, Ray — Farenheir 451
- Heinlein, Robert — Stranger In A Strange Land
- Le Guin, Ursula K. — Left hand of Darkness
- Le Guin, Ursula K. — The Telling
- Shelly, Mary — Frankenstein

Related TV episodes

- Korean TV show "Diary of a Prosecutor" depicts gender differences in episode 8.
- In the TV show "Girls5eva" season 2, episode 1, has a great scene where one of the protagonists (Dawn, played by Sara Bareilles) confronts another mom at her kid's school (Cara, played by Heidi Gardner) about the inclusion

of fathers in planning after-school activities. That scene ends with a male gay couple expressing relief that their kid will finally be included.

Non-Fiction

Books

- Archer, Selma, and Demopoulos Zack - Working Caregivers: The Invisible Employees Kindle Edition
- Boeri, Tito, Patacchini, Eleonora and Peri, Giovanni (eds). Unexplored Dimensions of Discrimination.
- Bol, Jasmijn C. and Fogel-Yaari, Hila - Death by a Thousand Cuts: The Impact of Gender Bias on Career Progression
- Goldsmith, Marshall and Helgesen, Sally - How Women Rise
- Washington, Keith - Caregiving Full-Time and Working Full-Time: Managing Dual Roles and Responsibilities Paperback
- Whitty-Collins, Gill - Why Men Win at Work

Articles

- Bol, J. C., and Fogel-Yaari, H. 2023. Death by a thousand cuts: The impact of gender bias on career progression. In Why Diversity, Equity, and Inclusion Matter: Challenges and Solutions (Chapter 4). Singapore: World Scientific Publishing Co. Pte. Ltd. https://worldscientific.com/doi/abs/10.1142/9789811278419_0004
- Bryant, K. 2024. Redefining motherhood and careers in today's work arena. Forbes, January 29, 2024. https://www.forbes.com/sites/kalinabryant/2024/01/29/redefining-motherhood-and-careers-in-todays-work-arena/?sh=6e4bd6861a7e

- Durante, K. M., Griskevicius, V., Simpson, J. A., Cantú, S. M., and Tybur, J. M. 2012. Sex ratio and women's career choice: Does a scarcity of men lead women to choose briefcase over baby? Journal of Personality and Social Psychology, 103(1), 121–134.

- Eagly, A. H., Carli, L. L., and Carli, L. L. 2007. Through the labyrinth: The truth about how women become leaders (Vol. 11). Boston, MA: Harvard Business School Press.

- Goldin, C. 2014. A grand gender convergence: Its last chapter. American Economic Review, 104(4), 1091-1119.

- Mikolajczak, M., and Roskam, I. 2018. A theoretical and clinical framework for parental burnout: The balance between risks and resources (BR2). Frontiers in psychology, 9, 361705.

- Parker, K. 2015. Women more than men adjust their careers for family life. Pew Research Center. https://www.pewresearch.org/short-reads/2015/10/01/women-more-than-men-adjust-their-careers-for-family-life/

- Shpancer, N. 2023. Parental burnout: When parenting becomes too much. Psychology Today, August 1, 2023. https://www.psychologytoday.com/us/blog/insight-therapy/202307/parental-burnout-when-parenting-becomes-too-much

- Smith, D. G., and Johnson, W. B. 2020. Gender equity starts in the home. Harvard Business Review. May 4, 2020.

- Stone, P. 2007. Opting out?: Why women really quit careers and head home. University of California Press.